Modern EXTRA!

Modern Romance™ is proud to bring
Modern EXTRA!, a unique collection of stories,
some revisited and others new, by our
best loved authors.

In this special edition, we offer you the chance to
enjoy again the classic story, THE BELLINI
BRIDE by bestselling author Michelle Reid.

Plus – we've also got a *brand new* Christmas short
story, A MARRIAGE PROPOSAL FOR
CHRISTMAS, by top author Carole Mortimer,
all in one bigger volume!

Mistress to a Millionaire:
she's his in the bedroom but he can't buy her love

More passion for your money!

Michelle Reid grew up on the southern edges of Manchester, the youngest in a family of five lively children. But now she lives in the beautiful county of Cheshire with her busy executive husband and two grown-up daughters. She loves reading, the ballet, and playing tennis when she gets the chance. She hates cooking, cleaning, and despises ironing! Sleep she can do without and produces some of her best written work during the early hours of the morning.

Carole Mortimer was born in England, the youngest of three children. She began writing in 1978, and has now written over ninety books for Harlequin Mills & Boon. Carole has four sons, Matthew, Joshua, Timothy and Peter, and a bearded collie called Merlyn. She says, 'I'm happily married to Peter senior; we're best friends as well as lovers, which is probably the best recipe for a successful relationship. We live on the Isle of Man.'

You can find out more about Michelle and Carole at www.millsandboon.co.uk

Look out for more titles from these authors coming soon in Modern Romance™

THE VENGEANCE AFFAIR by Carole Mortimer

On sale Februay 2005

THE PURCHASED WIFE by Michelle Reid

On sale May 2005

MISTRESS TO A MILLIONAIRE

THE BELLINI BRIDE
by
Michelle Reid

A MARRIAGE PROPOSAL
by
Carole Mortimer

MILLS & BOON®

*MILLS & BOON and MILLS & BOON with the Rose Device
are registered trademarks of the publisher.*

*First published in Great Britain 2004
by Harlequin Mills & Boon Limited, Eton House, 18-24 Paradise Road,
Richmond, Surrey TW9 1SR*

MISTRESS TO A MILLIONAIRE © Harlequin Enterprises II B.V., 2004

The Bellini Bride was first published in Great Britain by
Harlequin Mills & Boon Limited in a separate, single volume.
The Bellini Bride © Michelle Reid 2001

A Marriage Proposal for Christmas first published by
Harlequin Mills & Boon Limited 2004
A Marriage Proposal for Christmas © Carole Mortimer 2004

ISBN 0 263 84525 7

154-1104

*Printed and bound in Spain
by Litografia Rosés S.A., Barcelona*

THE BELLINI
BRIDE

BY
MICHELLE REID

CHAPTER ONE

THE BED was a sea of rumpled white linen. Tangled amongst it Marco Bellini could see a long golden leg bent at the knee and the smooth silken-curve of a hip and thigh. The rest was covered by fine white sheeting but for a slender arm and the rippling swathe of strawberry-blonde hair flowing away from the kind of profile that would have launched ships in times gone by.

Only her name was not Helen, it was Antonia, and, although her beauty might have launched many metaphorical ships in her time, there was no disputing to whom she now belonged.

Leaning back against the balcony rail, Marco allowed himself a smile as he brought his coffee cup to his lips. It was still very early, but the sun was already hot against his naked back. He had come out onto the terrace directly from his shower, and the white towel draped low around his narrow hips was his only concession to modesty, here, in his summer villa perched high on the hill above Portofino, where the only eyes to see him belonged to the seagulls soaring on the early morning currents of air.

And Antonia, of course, if she bothered to wake up. But, unlike him, she didn't have to be back in Milan by nine o'clock, so she had no reason to rise this early. Although…he then added ruefully to that, if she did happen to awaken now, it would be the simplest thing in the world for him to linger long enough to drop the towel and join her back in the bed.

But not yet, Marco told himself as he took another sip from his cup. The coffee was hot, black and strong and was just another pleasure he enjoyed lingering over while he leant here watching his woman sleep.

In the year they had been together he had never seen Antonia look anything but beautiful. Dressed to slay or stripped bare to the exquisite skin nature had given her, she exuded a beauty that by far outclassed any other woman he had known. He was proud to be her lover, proud that only he held the right to place a possessive hand upon any part of her anatomy. Proud that she only had eyes for him.

But did he love her? he asked himself.

No, he admitted heavily. He didn't love her. He loved how she looked, and how she always made him feel. And he would willingly have laid down his own life if it meant him saving hers. But true love had to go deeper than that. He had to love *what* she was, and he didn't.

A sigh caught in the depth of his chest. A cloud blotted out the sun. A seagull shrieked in protest. The coffee suddenly tasted bitter. Putting the cup aside he turned to stare at the misted-blue waters of the Mediterranean shimmering in the distance—and wished to hell he knew what he was going to do about her.

Letting her go was out of the question. Letting her stay meant trouble in more ways than one. Out there, across hills and lush valleys that made up his beautiful Italy, trouble was brewing. It came in the form of an autocratic mother and an ailing father with an urgent desire to see his son safely married and settled before he died.

Marrying Antonia, even without the true-love bit, would be the easiest thing in the world for him to do. She was young, she was beautiful and she loved him totally.

But what parent would condone their only son, and the heir to the great Bellini fortune, marrying himself to a woman like Antonia?

A woman with the kind of past that was destined to dog her for ever. A woman with the kind of past that would reflect poorly on him *and* his family name.

A woman who made the perfect mistress—but could never be the perfect wife for him.

Another sigh whispered from him. Maybe Antonia heard it, because she began to stir. Recovering his coffee-cup, Marco turned to watch her slide lazily onto her back then, even before she bothered to open her eyes, send an arm out to search the empty space beside her in the bed. It was a gesture so familiar to him that he actually felt the hairs on his chest prickle as if she had reached out and touched him. The sensation placed the smile back on his lips, because it pleased him to know that the first thing she always thought about on waking was him.

When she found no warm male body lying beside her, her next move was to open her lovely eyes, pause for a moment to allow the remnants of sleep to disperse, then, in a single smooth graceful movement, she sat up and began to search for him.

She found him almost instantly. A warm lover's smile touched her lovely mouth. '*Ciao*,' she greeted him softly.

His response was a lazy masculine gleam over the rim of his cup, while inside he became aware of the chemical responses already beginning to stir his blood. She moved him in so many ways he didn't dare count them.

Sliding out of the bed, she lifted her arms above her head and indulged in a long lazy stretch that highlighted every perfect contour of her very naked frame from slender toes to delicate fingertips. Her light golden skin shone like the finest silk ever created. Her wonderful hair tumbled in loosely spiralling threads down her arching spine. In all his life Marco had never known any woman quite so perfect as Antonia. Her face, her hair, her sensational body—the way she moved as she began to walk towards him.

Like the world's most dangerous siren, she roused the male senses without even having to try. Even the sun worshipped her by coming out from behind its cloud at the same moment she stepped onto the terrace, pooling her in soft golden light as she continued her slow graceful journey towards him.

It was no wonder Stefan Kranst had been so obsessed with her, Marco thought with a sudden grimness. No wonder he'd painted her every single way an artist could paint an obsession. Seeing her like this, he could easily understand why the man had felt so compelled to preserve her naked image. For years Antonia had appeared in all of his paintings, not always the main focal point but always the slender naked figure you looked for whenever you found yourself viewing a Kranst.

But in his desire to make Antonia immortal he had turned her into every man's titillating fantasy. Her naked form now adorned the walls of the rich and famous. When she walked into a room those in the know stopped and stared in intimate recognition.

Did she care? No. Did she blush with embarrassment or hide her eyes in shame? Not this woman, who was as comfortable with her body as she was comfortable with those wretched paintings.

As for him? Marco was very much aware that Antonia's notoriety as Stefan Kranst's famous nude model gave him a certain kudos amongst his envious peers. But it didn't mean he liked it, only that he had learnt to accept it because, like Kranst in a way, he was obsessed with the woman—though not the haunted creature held captive in oils.

Coming to a halt directly in front of him, Antonia said absolutely nothing but just held his gaze as she folded slender white fingers over the strong brown ones he had wrapped around his coffee cup. Her eyes gleamed like topaz in the sun, his darkened into humour as she guided the cup towards her own mouth and took a few delicate sips at the coffee before just as silently lifting the cup to his own mouth.

More than happy to play this little game the way she wanted him to play it, Marco obediently drank while their eyes remained locked in the beginnings of seduction. With both mouths moistened by warm black coffee, she then guided the cup away, lifted herself up on bare tiptoes, and replaced it with a kiss.

The aroma of coffee swirled all around them, its erotic taste flavoured their mouths, the points of her breasts hovered a soft-breath away from his chest and, beneath the towel, his body began to respond.

This was making love on a different level, this was intimacy so deep it touched parts of him never otherwise touched.

As she drew away again, her eyes held a promise. Maybe he would take her up on it in a minute, Marco idly considered. But for now he was content to enjoy the more simple pleasure of being the passive one while she did the seducing.

She began it by touching a finger to the satin tight hollow of his shoulder. 'You showered without me,' she complained.

He smiled a lazy smile. 'You were asleep,' he reminded her.

She was not in the least bit impressed by that answer, and her mouth took on a sulky pout. Taking the coffee-cup from his fingers she put it aside, took possession of both his hands and fed them round her slender waist, then lifted her own up to curve his nape. One small step and she was fitting her hips into the cradle of his hips and pressing her wonderful breasts against him. Then her head tilted back a little, her sulky mouth parted—and claimed his with another kiss designed to devour.

He would have to be made of stone not to respond to her. He would have to be half the man he actually was not to want what was being offered to him. It was special. *She* was special. He didn't want to lose it.

'What was that for?' She broke the kiss to demand when she felt him shiver.

'The sun has gone in again,' he said.

And it had, he noticed. Like a bad omen, it had slid behind another cloud the moment he'd begun thinking about the future.

'Big softy,' she chided, her fingers tangling lovingly into his hair. 'You want to try standing like this on an English balcony. You would die of frostbite, being such a thin-blooded Italian.'

He was supposed to laugh or come back with a light counter-charge, Marco was well aware of that. But he could do neither because he was suddenly seeing *her* standing naked on that English balcony.

Seeing her exactly as she had once been caught for posterity in a Kranst painting.

'You would know, of course,' was therefore the cynical taunt that slid from him.

Her sudden stillness was electric. If he'd slapped her he couldn't have achieved a better response. Kiss-warmed lips lost all of their softness. Warm topaz became cold grey glass. With a single step she completely separated herself from him and, without a single word, she turned and walked back into the bedroom.

Remorse played havoc with his conscience as he watched her sensual stride take her towards the bathroom. The urge to go after her and apologise came a couple of short seconds too late. The door closed, he heard the bolt slide home and knew he now had one hell of a task on his hands to put right the wrong he had just done.

'*Damn,*' he cursed as he spun away.

The sun crept out from behind its cloud again. He scowled at it. Scowled at the seagull soaring overhead. Then he scowled at himself because he knew that putting right a wrong would not solve the dilemma that was sitting right on his doorstep waiting to be addressed.

On the other side of the bathroom door, Antonia stood with her eyes closed, waiting for the hurt contracting the muscles around her heart to ease. It hadn't been the words but the way he had said them, with derision, deliberately aimed to cut.

Stefan, she thought wearily. It always came back to Stefan, and Marco's inability to accept the life she had led before she met him. For a man who prided himself on his fast-track modern sophistication, he harboured some truly archaic principles.

One of these days she would find the strength to stand firm and challenge those principles, and this right he felt he had to speak to her like that, she promised herself.

But not yet, she conceded heavily. She just didn't have

that kind of strength yet. Because to challenge him meant challenging their whole relationship, and the day she did that Antonia knew would be the same day she lost Marco for good.

Though that moment was coming closer, she recognised, as the hurt began to fade much sooner than it usually did after one of his well-aimed barbs. And she found she could open her eyes and actually look at herself in the mirror opposite without wincing at what she saw.

And what did she see?

She saw a scarlet woman, she grimly mocked that reflection. A woman who was a mistress to a man who wasn't even married but who still classed her as a mistress not a lover. In her view, there was a very important difference between the two titles. To be a man's lover carried a certain amount of moral equality. To be his mistress showed a distinct lack of moral value. And was there such thing as a master to level out the playing field? No, of course not. He remained simply the lover, with no stigma at all attached to the title. You could have a pair of lovers but you could not have a pair of mistresses—not in this context anyway. No, that unenviable title belonged exclusively to her own fair sex.

Sex being the operative word here. She lived in his home, she slept in his bed, and she relied on his financial generosity for her day-to-day survival. In return she gave him her absolute loyalty and her body—the true definition of a mistress, in other words.

Not a bad life for a girl who came from nothing, she supposed. In fact, it would be pretty much a perfect life— if she didn't love him as desperately as she did. Loving Marco made it a miserable life.

How had Stefan described Marco when he'd tried to

talk her out of coming to Italy to live with him? 'He's one of life's élite,' he'd said. 'He might want your body, but he will never want you the way you want him to want you. You're not of the fellowship, my darling. It is a simple fact of life that élite marries élite.'

Tough but wise words, as she'd found out the hard way. And if she had any sense at all she would get out, she told her reflection. She would gather up what little bit of pride she had left, and go, before he cleaned her out completely.

And maybe she would do—soon, she resolved.

But she turned away from the mirror as she thought it, knowing that it would take more than the occasional cruel remark on his part to make her leave him. She loved him too much and had stuck with him too long to give up so easily.

Which didn't mean she was going to forgive him, she determined as she stepped into the shower cubicle. Forgiveness came at a price, and Marco was going to have to pay that price with some serious grovelling.

A smile touched her mouth, the very idea of making the arrogant Marco Bellini grovel doing wonders for her mood.

He was gone from the bedroom by the time she reappeared. Gone from the villa too, she discovered when she came downstairs to find Nina, the maid, clearing away what looked like a hastily eaten breakfast.

'Signor Bellini left for Milan ten minutes ago, signorina,' she informed her. 'He said to remind you about the party tonight and to tell you to drive carefully, for the summer traffic between here and Milan is reputed to be very bad.'

Antonia thanked the maid for the message, and smiled

in recognition of the routine. Marco was making himself
scarce because he knew he had hurt her, but making sure
he kept the lines of communication open as he went.

Why? Because for a big tough corporate leader, with a
reputed heart of stone and a tongue of steel, when it came
to her, he hated dissension. He might not love her the way
she wanted to be loved, but he loved her enough to feel
uncomfortable when he had upset her. And, being a very
selfish man, Marco liked to be comfortable in his private
life.

Hence the message telling her to drive carefully, and
the reminder about the party tonight. This was Marco putting down the first stepping-stones back to his precious
comfort. Other stepping-stones would follow at timely in-
tervals, Antonia predicted as she sat down to eat breakfast,
alone for the first time in the week they had just spent
here doing very little but making love and sleeping.

A week he'd arranged as a surprise treat for her birthday—along with the natty red Lotus which now stood in
the courtyard waiting for her to drive it back to Milan.
Last year he had given her a sweet little Fiat to use to get
around in. But she had only been with him for a month
then, so the value of the gift had reflected that.

Like a bonus for time put in, she likened, and wondered
what he would think a fitting bonus for her next birthday.

If she was still around, she added, felt her heart give a
tug, and got up from the table to go back upstairs to pack,
refusing to answer that little sarcasm—or question why
her heart had given that singular tug.

An hour later, dressed in a pair of slender white Capri
pants and a skimpy red T-shirt, her hair stylishly contained on the top of her head, Antonia was sitting in the

creamy interior of the red Lotus, reading the note Marco had left for her on the dashboard.

'Respect the car's power and it will respect you,' it said. 'I prefer you to arrive home to me in one beautiful piece.'

Antonia's smile held a hint of softness this time—not at the message itself so much as the way that Marco had taken time to pause long enough to sit here and write this before climbing into his Ferrari and driving away.

It was another stepping-stone neatly laid, and she was still smiling when she put her new toy into gear, then began following his long journey back to Milan, idly pondering on what his next move would be.

He was nothing if not a brilliant tactician. He waited until she'd reached the outskirts of Milan before making contact again.

Then her mobile began to ring.

Glancing down to where it sat in its hands-free housing, Antonia pondered for a few rings whether to ignore it and just let him stew. But, in the end, irresistible temptation won over stubbornness and, with a flick of a button, she sanctioned the connection.

'Ciao, mi amore.' The deep dark tones of his voice filled the car-space, soft, warm and aimed to seduce, she felt tingles of excitement run down her spine. 'You were, of course, too busy concentrating on your driving to answer the phone straight away.'

Not a question exactly, but more a remark loaded with satire. He knew she had hesitated over whether to speak to him.

'What do you want?' she demanded curtly.

'That depends,' he murmured suggestively, 'on where you are right now…'

'Walking naked down Monte Napoleon, living up to expectations,' she promptly tossed back at him, naming a particularly classy area within Milan's famous Quadrilatero.

As a direct hit back at what he had said to her this morning, it should have caught him on the raw. Instead, it was the turn of his appreciative laughter to coil itself all around her. Antonia wriggled in her seat and wished she could hate him. But what she was experiencing was far from hate, and it took a couple of risky manoeuvres through the heavy traffic to help dispel the sensation.

'And to think,' he said eventually, 'I refused lunch at Dino's just to talk to you.'

'Bad move, *caro*,' Antonia responded. 'Dino's was by far your better option.'

'And you sulk like a prima donna,' he smoothly threw back.

He was right and she did. But then she felt justified. Still, the remark held a warning she would be a fool not to heed. 'You told me you had back-to-back meetings all day,' she murmured with less sarcasm. 'Lunch at Dino's is usually an all-afternoon thing.'

'I surprise myself sometimes with my own efficiency,' was his light reply.

'And your conceit,' she added.

'*Si*, that too,' he had the arrogance to agree.

Despite not wanting it to, Antonia felt her mouth twitch into a grin. In truth, his arrogance and conceit were major parts of what made Marco the charismatic person he was. Plus his sensational dark good looks, she then wryly added as she sped off the *autostrada* and headed for the city centre. Then there was his great body, and his prowess as lover, and the way he...

'In truth, lunch at Dino's was never an option.' The sound of his voice grabbed her attention back again. 'The morning meetings ran overtime. The first one of the afternoon begins in half an hour. So here I am, sitting at my desk, with a take-away sandwich to ease my hunger, a newspaper to feed my mind—and a desperate desire to hear you say something nice to me.'

'Huh,' was all she offered.

'You really want me to grovel, don't you?' his rueful voice drawled.

'Preferably on your knees,' Antonia confirmed.

'Mmm,' Marco murmured. 'Now this sounds interesting. There are so many—many ways I can beg your forgiveness from that position.'

Her impulsive burst of laughter refused to be held in check. Across the city haze, in his plush office, Marco leant back in his chair and smiled a satisfied smile. Then, with the charm of a master, he turned the conversation to more ordinary things, like the performance of the Lotus, what she intended to do with her afternoon, and what time they needed to leave the apartment this evening to attend the first wedding anniversary party being thrown by his best friend Franco and his lovely wife Nicola.

By the time he replaced the receiver, Marco was satisfyingly sure that this morning's stupidity on his part had been carefully soothed away and he could begin to relax again.

Reaching out, he picked up his sandwich and removed it from its wrapping, then collected up his newspaper, he lifted his feet onto the corner of the desk, and settled back to enjoy a half-hour of leisure before his next meeting began with a pair of young hopefuls who wanted his financial backing for their very good idea but fell short of his investment criteria by possessing the business skills of a pair of gnats!

Until five minutes ago he had been intending to send them away with the curt advice to learn how to run a business before attempting to start one. But now he felt much more amenable. Maybe he would even offer to oversee the project himself!

Then he opened the newspaper and any hint of amenability died a death in that moment. For there staring out at him was none other than—Stefan Kranst. He was standing inside one of Milan's most respected private art galleries. And the full-page article was really a plug for the Romano Gallery, where the artist was planning to exhibit next week.

But that wasn't the thing that was knotting up Marco. It was the unsavoury suspicion that if Kranst was in town then Antonia must know about it, but she hadn't mentioned a word to him!

Did she know?

Was she planning to meet up with him secretly? She had done it before at least once, to his knowledge.

Antonia might have left Kranst to come to live in Milan with him, but the ex-lovers had not parted enemies. During a trip to London earlier this year, he had discovered by pure accident that she had spent a whole day with Kranst.

'Don't tell me who I can and who I can't see!' she'd declared when he'd objected. 'Stefan will always be very special to me, and if you can't cope with that, then that's your problem, not mine, Marco.'

It had been one of a very few times when she'd actually looked ready to walk away from him if he tried to push the issue. He hadn't pushed it. But, for the first time in his life, he'd experienced the ugly burn of jealousy, when he'd realised that Kranst held a power over Antonia that was a challenge to his own.

He didn't like it. He didn't like the knowledge that he'd backed down from taking up that challenge. And he didn't like Kranst turning up in Milan just when Marco was having to do some serious thinking about his relationship with Antonia.

It was either immaculate timing on Kranst's part or yet another bad omen. Either way, the sandwich never got eaten and the two young hopefuls lost all chance of meeting an amiable Marco Bellini that day. If it hadn't been for the fact that Marco was still functioning clearly enough to recognise an unmissable opportunity in what they were proposing, he would have taken great delight in kicking them out!

Irritation alternated with disturbing bouts of skin-prickling restlessness throughout the rest of the afternoon. Sudden flashes of Antonia and Kranst holed-up somewhere secret played games with his head.

In the end he could stand it no longer and went back to the privacy of his office to pick up the phone. Her mobile was switched off. Irritation ripped through him, then he remembered her telling him she was going straight back to the apartment, so he rang there instead.

All he got was his own pre-recorded message telling him that no one was available to take his call.

Antonia was standing in a tiny backstreet in another, less fashionable part of the city, fitting a key into a door. Once inside, she walked the narrow hallway and began climbing bare-boarded flights of stairs, passing by small dingy offices belonging to the kinds of businesses Marco looked down upon from his lofty position at the top of the corporate tree. Some of the tenants knew her, some didn't, most looked curiously at her, smiled politely and left her alone. She liked it that way. For this place was her secret. A part of her life Marco didn't control.

On the very top landing, she went to the only door there and fitted another key into its lock. Stepping inside, she carefully closed the door again and then, turning round, she looked about her and quite simply smiled...

CHAPTER TWO

WALKING through the front door to the Milan apartment was always a pleasure. And the first thing Antonia did as she stepped into it some hours later was pause for a moment to reacquaint herself with surroundings that were a thousand times different from those she had just come from.

Occupying the entire top floor of a modern city block, Marco's home was an interior designer's idea of heaven. No detail had been skimped in an effort to achieve its harmonious ambience.

The hall was large and light and airy, the rooms leading off from it furnished with a clever mix of classical, old and new. Nothing offended the eye. There were formal rooms used only for entertaining, less grand rooms for when they did not. The kitchen was a cook's paradise, all four *en-suite* bedrooms designed to co-ordinate with the pastel colours applied to the walls. And everywhere you went you walked on the very best in Italian ceramic, passing between priceless works of art that adorned the walls.

Like his famous art-collecting ancestors, Marco had inherited an eye for what was just that bit special. Both he and his mother were generous patrons of the arts. What either of them bought, others took particular notice of. And, as with his taste in décor, he thought nothing of mixing the totally unknown with old respected masters— and of course it had worked beautifully.

But she didn't have time to stand here considering all

of this right now, Antonia told herself wryly. She was late and she knew it. Somehow, time seemed to have got away from her today, and she was aware that she'd only just made it back before Marco usually arrived home.

Live dangerously, why don't you? she scolded herself as she headed directly for the bedroom, meaning to make it look as if she had been in there for ages getting ready for the evening when he did eventually get in.

It turned out to be a wasted effort for, as fate would have it, Marco didn't appear until she was already dressed for the evening and beginning to wonder what had happened to him.

Then the bedroom door suddenly swung open and he came striding in.

'You're late,' she immediately chided.

'I have a watch,' he clipped back, and walked right past her without even sparing her a glance.

Frowning slightly, Antonia watched him begin pulling off his jacket in a way that spoke volumes about his mood.

'Bad day?' she quizzed.

'Bad everything,' he said grimly.

'Hence no welcoming smile for me, no kiss hello?' Teasing though her voice sounded, she was serious. After the efforts he'd put in, sweet-talking himself back into her favour, this new attitude was threatening to send him right back to square one if he wasn't careful.

Maybe he realised it because, after tossing the jacket onto the bed, he then stood for a moment flexing his wide shoulders as if he was trying to dislodge whatever it was that was bugging him. As she watched solid muscle move beneath pale blue shirting, Antonia felt the usual sprinkling of pleasure warm her insides, and would have gone to him and helped ease those tense muscles—if he hadn't released a sigh and turned to look at her.

The expression on his face held her stationary. His eyes were glinting with barely suppressed anger, his features hard and grim and unusually pale. In a single brief sweep he gave her appearance the once-over, then his mouth tightened and he turned away again.

Warning bells began to ring in her head. 'What's wrong?' she asked sharply.

'Nothing,' he clipped out. Then on another short sigh added, 'Give me ten minutes to make myself human and we will begin this conversation again, I think.'

'Fair enough,' she agreed. It wasn't often she'd witnessed the darker side of Marco, but on those few occasions she had done so, she'd learned very quickly to tread warily around him until he had calmed down. But she was still frowning as she let herself out of the bedroom, wondering what could have happened this afternoon to put him in that kind of mood.

Bad meeting? A fortune lost on the Stock Exchange? she mused as she walked into the small sitting room and straight over to the drinks bar to mix him his favourite whisky sour while she waited for him to join her.

The ten minutes he'd allocated himself had obviously not been long enough, was her first observation when he joined her. He came into the room with his hair still slightly damp from his quick shower and his fingers impatiently tugging the white cuffs to his shirt into line with the black silk edges of his dinner jacket—and it was clear, by the look on his face, that he was feeling no better.

'Here, try this. It might help,' she drily suggested, offering him the prepared drink.

But, 'No time,' he refused. 'And anyway, I'm driving.'

With that, he diverted over to the mirror and began messing with his bow-tie.

And the hand holding out the whisky sour sank slowly back to the drinks bar as it began to dawn on Antonia that his mood had nothing to do with a bad day at the office, but had something to do with her.

'All right,' she said, deciding to take him on so they could get whatever it was that was annoying him out of the way before the evening began. 'Tell me what it is I'm supposed to have done to make you so angry.'

'Who said you'd done anything?' Bow-tie perfect, shirt-cuffs straight, he turned his attention to checking his watch. 'If you're ready, we should get going...'

If she was ready... Dipping her eyes to look down at the slender red silk dress she was wearing—newly bought this afternoon with Marco in mind because he loved to see her in red—Antonia felt her own happy mood shatter. The dress, the way she'd done up her hair so only the odd fine silk tendril caressed her nape, and even the blush-red lipstick she was wearing, had all been chosen with his pleasure in mind.

And it hurt that he was deliberately ignoring that. That his voice might sound mellow but the message was cold. Cold like the silence he was now allowing to develop, even when he must know what she was thinking because he deciphered atmospheres in a room as easily as he deciphered a page full of figures.

The man was an accounting genius, it therefore went without saying that he wanted her to feel this hurt. But more painful was the knowledge that he had done this to her twice in one day.

What was the matter with him? What was he trying to tell her with these violent swings in his mood?

That he'd had enough? That she'd begun to irritate him so much that he couldn't seem to look at her without taking a verbal swipe at her?

The idea wasn't a new one. She had been suspecting it on and off for a while, though until this morning they had just enjoyed a whole week of near perfect harmony and she had begun to believe that she'd been imagining his growing irritation with her.

But now, as she stood here in this carefully orchestrated silence, the suspicion returned with a vengeance. Was she growing stale? Did he want out? Had the week away been arranged in an effort to recapture what he was no longer feeling for her?

Twice in one day, she repeated to herself. Twice he'd been deliberately hurtful.

'*Cara?*' he prompted her to answer.

The endearment made her insides wince. 'Yes,' she said quietly. 'I'm ready.'

But, as she turned away to retrieve her little red purse from where she had left it, she found herself wondering exactly what it was she was ready for. Losing him?

A sharp pain caught her breath for a moment, holding her still while she waited for it to ease in much the same way she had done this morning. By that example the sensation should have dispersed quickly. But it didn't. In fact, the more sure she became that he was tiring of her, the more it was beginning to hurt. Yet she had always known that this could only ever be a temporary affair, she tried to reason. And, as some people were always eager to tell her, she had lasted longer than most.

Those were usually the same people who were also quick to explain that when Marco Bellini married it would be to a woman of his own social standing. Someone with money, someone with class, someone with a lineage to match the superior weight of his. And, most importantly, someone his parents would welcome with open arms.

Certainly not a little English nobody who had never known her father. A woman who wasn't deemed fit to even be in the same room as any of his relatives. And, worse, a woman who didn't mind exposing her body to the world.

'What's this?' The questioning sound of Marco's voice impinged on her bleak summing up of herself. Having to blink a couple of times before she could face him, she found him standing there with a gold-wrapped flat package in his hands.

'Oh, it's a gift for Franco and Nicola.' Eyes still slightly glazed, she turned away again. 'I realised we hadn't got them anything, so I went shopping before coming on here…'

Shopping.

For several moments Marco couldn't move a single muscle. Remorse was cutting into him for the second time that day. While he'd been suspecting her of meeting secretly with Stefan Kranst she'd been trawling the shops, looking for an anniversary gift for his own two closest friends.

He didn't know what to do. He didn't know what to say to put right the wrong he'd done her—yet again. 'I'm sorry, *cara*,' seemed the only thing to offer. 'I should have thought about this myself.'

There was a double meaning to the last part, though he was relieved Antonia couldn't know it. She winced at the *cara*, though, he noticed. Shrugged at the rest. 'It doesn't matter. Your money paid for it.'

With that she walked stiffly away, leaving her very derisive offering hanging in the air behind her. With a silent curse aimed at his own nasty suspicions, Marco followed, grimly deciding to keep his mouth shut since he was well aware that he had successfully managed to wipe her clean of all hint of good humour by now.

And she looked gorgeous, delectable, good enough to eat—though he knew he had left it too late to tell her that. The dress was short, red and very sexy the way it clung to every slender curve she possessed. It made him want to run his hands all over her, but that was just another pleasure he had denied himself with his lousy mood.

Antonia lifted the latch on the front door and stepped through, leaving Marco to set the alarm and lock up, while she called the lift. It arrived as he did. They stepped inside it. The lift took them down towards the basement with Antonia occupying one corner, he another, and the atmosphere was so thick he could have cut it with a knife.

If the English were brilliant at only one thing, then it would have to be their ability to freeze people out, he mused as he viewed her glacial expression.

'Do you want me to apologise for taking my bad temper out on you?' he sighed eventually.

'What—again?' she drawled. Then, 'No, don't bother,' she advised, before he could answer. 'No doubt you'll be doing it again before too long, which renders your apologies pretty meaningless gestures.'

Perhaps he deserved that, Marco conceded. But irritation began to bite into him again. He didn't like being treated like a leper just because he'd made a natural mistake.

Natural? He quizzed himself.

Yes, damn natural, he insisted arrogantly. He might no longer suspect her of spending the afternoon with Kranst, but that didn't mean she didn't *know* the man was here in Milan!

Well, he was damned if he was going to bring the subject up first, he decided, grimly aware that he didn't really want to know the answer. For to know the answer meant dealing with it. And he didn't want to deal with anything that could risk his relationship with Antonia. Not until he had made up his own mind where it was going to go, anyway.

So, with that niggling little confession to chew on, he let the atmosphere remain thick for the next thirty seconds it took the lift to sink. They left it side by side, to walk between the rows of parked cars towards his Ferrari, passing by her neatly parked red Lotus without either of them sparing it a glance.

Three days old and she doesn't even see it. Which, in its own way, made the car just another wasted gesture on his part, he noted testily. She had been ecstatic when he took her away for a week as part of her birthday present, but the car had produced only the usual polite remarks people use when they're given something they're really not that impressed with.

With ingrained good manners that went back a lifetime, he opened the passenger door of the Ferrari and remained standing by it while Antonia slipped gracefully inside. For the briefest of moments only a few centimetres separated them. It was the closest they'd been since this morning on the balcony in Portofino, he realised, as her delicate perfume filled his nostrils and his senses reacted in their usual way.

Grimly, he ignored their message, when only yesterday he would have been freely indulging every sense he possessed.

With his lips pressed together in a steadily darkening mood of discontent, he placed the gift for Franco and Nicola on her lap, closed the door, then rounded the car bonnet to get in beside her. As he settled himself into his seat he caught a glimpse of her icy profile, clenched his teeth together, and turned his attention to getting them moving.

And the silence between them was still so bad it murdered normal body functions like breathing and swallowing. He couldn't stand it. 'Are you going to tell me what's in the parcel?' he asked as lightly as he could in the circumstances.

'A painting,' she answered briefly.

Having already worked that part out for himself, by the shape and the feel of the gift, Marco took a deep breath for patience. 'What kind of painting?' he prompted.

'Why?' she flicked back. 'Are you worried that I don't have the right credentials to choose something acceptable for your friends?'

At which point he gave up. In this kind of mood she was impossible. Sinking back into stiff silence, neither spoke again for the rest of the journey.

Franco and Nicola de Maggio lived in a large house in one of the select residential areas out on the edges of the city. Arriving so late meant it was difficult to find a parking space in the long driveway. Cursing beneath his breath, Marco had to do some pretty deft manoeuvring to slot the long car in between two others already parked. By the time he switched off the engine the atmosphere between them was so tight you could have played an overture on its taut threads.

It was no wonder Antonia was eager to escape from it.

Marco released a hard sigh as he watched her fumble

in her rush to unlock her seat belt. 'The filthy atmosphere remains here in the car,' he bit out warningly. They were about to go amongst *his* friends, after all. He had no wish for them to witness his less than harmonious love life.

The false smile she turned on him set a nerve ticking in his jaw—and had other parts of him rising to its provocative bait. He could soften her in seconds, right here, in these cramped confines. He knew a few simple moves that would remind her as to *why* she was even sitting here at all!

'Get out of the car,' he growled at her before he replaced the thought with a very satisfying action.

Antonia didn't need telling for she was already opening the door. Stepping out of air-conditioned coolness into the heat of an Italian summer evening, she stood there taking in a few deep breaths of that air in the vague hopes that it would help warm her up inside.

No chance. Now the suspicion that he was growing weary of her had set itself as cold hard fact in her head, the idea of feeling warm ever again was impossible to imagine.

In truth, she had almost refused to come tonight. For a few minutes, back there in the apartment, she had almost taken the mammoth step of taking the initiative and calling it a day. She had her pride after all. And *it* had no wish to cling on to something that was already dying, even if Marco was willing to hang on until the whole affair had finally strangled itself to death.

But then he'd brought her attention to the gift for Franco and Nicola and she'd changed her mind. The couple might be Marco's friends, but they had also become *her* friends over the last year—Nicola especially. Leaving Marco was one thing. Doing it on the night of Nicola's wedding anniversary party would cast a black cloud over her friend's special night, and she had no wish to do that.

And anyway, she admitted, as she waited for Marco to come and join her, she *wanted* to be here. She wanted to go out with a smile and her head held high, not slink off into the darkness like a pet dog that had lost favour with its master.

Tomorrow she would leave, she determined, as the master arrived at her side. His hand came to rest against her back. His jacket sleeve brushed her bare arm. Her flesh began to tingle as she absorbed the impact of a pure male magnetism that never ceased to excite her, no matter what the mood between them was like.

Her chin was level with his shoulder, her eyes with his mouth. If she turned her head just a fraction she would be able to see the perfectly honed contours that made up his handsome face. But she didn't even need to move her head to pick up the tangy scent of him, because she was inhaling it with every breath that she took as they walked together towards the house.

Inside was awash with music and laughter. The moment they walked through the door it was like stepping into a different world. It came as a shock—the kind of shock that made Antonia pause and blink a couple of times in an effort to make the transition from hostility and darkness to merriment and light.

Then a cry of delight went up, and she saw their hostess separate herself from the group of people she had been with. In tow behind her was the man she had been married to for a year today.

Tall and dark, handsome and sleek, Franco de Maggio was very much of Marco's ilk. It should have made the two men natural rivals—but the truth was the opposite.

They had known each other since kindergarten and been close friends ever since.

With her long black hair, stunningly beautiful dark brown eyes and dressed in slinky black crêpe that moulded her sensational figure, Nicola de Maggio was everything that Antonia was not. She was Italian, she had money in her own right, and her place beside Franco or another man like him had never been in any doubt from the day she had been born into her privileged life.

She belonged here. To Nicola, being a part of this society came as naturally to her as the inner warmth she exuded, which defied anyone not to instinctively like her simply for herself.

Antonia had liked her from the first moment they met, she as Marco's very new lover, Nicola as Franco's new bride. Liking had deepened into real affection since then. They were now good close friends—much like Marco and Franco. Yet Antonia had never ceased to be aware that she was the cuckoo in the nest.

Their smiles were genuine, their greetings were warm—and gave Antonia the excuse to move away from Marco's touch. On receiving their gift, their thanks were sincere. With a few teasing quizzes on what it might be, it was placed with all the other gifts waiting to be opened. 'It feels like our wedding day all over again,' Nicola sighed out happily. 'Wait until it's your turn, Antonia, and you will know just how blessed I feel.'

Marco stiffened, Antonia froze. Seeing their reaction, Nicola went quite pale. With a sharp glance at all three of them, Franco swiftly stepped into the breach. 'I think you should explain *how* blessed, *amore*,' he murmured softly, placing an arm around his wife's slender shoulders.

And it was a protective arm. An arm that said, It's okay.

Not your fault. I'm here to smooth this out for you. Antonia wanted to run away, because it was as clear as day that Marco wasn't here to smooth anything out for her.

'We are going to have a baby!' Nicola suddenly announced in an anxiously rushed hush. 'Only we weren't going to say anything until later...'

She should be smiling, bubbling over with delight, but she couldn't because she was feeling so uncomfortable after what she'd said. So, pulling herself together, Antonia did it for her. 'Oh, that's wonderful news!' she exclaimed, and smiled—my God, how she smiled. She smiled as she hugged Nicola, and smiled as she kissed Franco's rather grim cheek. She even smiled up at Marco, though she wanted to hit him rather than smile at him.

His arm found her waist and he drew her close again. It was such a brave gesture, considering Nicola had just turned him to stone in horror. He even found a light rejoinder. 'Dinner next week,' he insisted. 'Just the four of us to wet the baby's head.'

I won't be here next week, Antonia thought, and smiled through that little knowledge also.

'You do that *after* the baby is born!' Nicola protested.

'Then we will wet the waiting *mamma's* head,' Marco compromised, and kissed the waiting *mamma's* now smiling mouth.

Between them all a nasty moment had been neatly smoothed over. Nicola was happy again, as she should be. Franco on the other hand looked curious as to what was going on between Marco and Antonia but was willing to hold his tongue.

Thankfully, a new bunch of latecomers arrived, giving

the happy couple an excuse to escape. Once again, Antonia moved away from Marco's touch.

The worst of it was, he let her go.

So she threw herself headlong into the party to end all parties, as far she was concerned. For tomorrow I leave, was the chant playing over and over inside her head as she laughed and chatted happily away in Italian, the language being second nature to her, having spent the first five years of her life living here. And she danced, and ate very sparingly, and drank champagne by the glassful without knowing she was doing it.

Managing to corner her an hour later, Nicola demanded to know what was going on. 'If you two are avoiding each other like this because of what I said, then I am so sorry!' she cried. 'I can't tell you how awful I felt, setting you up in that dreadful way!'

'Don't be silly.' Antonia tried to smile it off—again. 'It really didn't matter.'

'If course it mattered,' Nicola insisted. 'I hurt you and infuriated Marco! He's barely speaking to anyone while you are partying as if this is your last night on this earth!'

Many a true word, Antonia thought bleakly. 'If Marco is still angry over an innocent remark, then shame on him and his overgrown ego,' she said. 'What did he think I was going to do? Jump in and ask him when I get to feel blessed?'

'You've lasted longer than any of his other lovers.' Nicola gently offered a phrase Antonia had grown very weary of hearing recently. Especially when it helped to mark that the end was most definitely nigh. 'That has to mean something, doesn't it?' Nicola pleaded.

Did it? 'It means I must be good at my job,' she provided, eyes hardening into cynicism. 'Do you think I'll be head-hunted when word gets around that I'm back on the market?'

Nicola's beautiful mouth dropped open. Across the room, standing by the drinks bar, Marco saw it happen and wondered what the hell Antonia had said to make Nicola gape like that.

Nothing nice, he concluded as he watched Nicola search the room until her eyes made contact with his. In a definite flurry, she looked quickly away again. And his senses were suddenly on full alert.

He didn't like this. He didn't like any of it. The whole damn day had gone from bad to worse, seemingly without him having any control whatsoever over it. Now something else was happening here that he didn't understand. Okay, Antonia was angry with him, he allowed. So he was a moody devil and probably deserved the way she was avoiding him like the plague. But whatever she'd just said to Nicola had been more than a complaint about his bad temper. His friend's wife had actually looked shocked and horrified.

Nicola was talking to her urgently—telling her that he was watching them, he realised, when Antonia turned so he could see the cold cast of defiance in her beautiful face. Their eyes made contact. If looks could kill, he'd be dead now, Marco acknowledged, and raised his glass to her in a silent toast meant to convey that he really didn't give a damn if she was hating him.

But it wasn't true. And that was his biggest problem where Antonia was concerned. Even now, while exchanging metaphorical knives across a crowded room, she lit him up so fiercely inside that if there was a polite way of doing it he would be getting her out of here and alone so he could demonstrate just how she affected him.

And that just about said it all as to why he was having these damned hard constant battles with himself. He wanted her. He *always* wanted her! Angry or not. Crowded room or not.

Why the hell should he give up something he still desired as much as this?

Almost as if on cue, the moment he planted that important point in his head, fate dealt him a lousy hand just to show to him that he wasn't the only person with a choice in this relationship.

A slight disturbance by the door caught Antonia's attention. She looked that way, Marco followed her gaze—then felt everything inside him close down completely when he found himself looking at none other than Stefan Kranst himself.

The moment Antonia saw him her beautiful face lit up, her gorgeous mouth broke into a sensational smile. And she struck out towards Kranst like a pigeon recognising home.

CHAPTER THREE

STANDING on the sidelines, Marco watched them meet, watched them smile, watched them murmur to each other. He watched Antonia lift her hand to his shoulders and Stefan Kranst slide his hands around her waist—then their mouths came together in a tender soft kiss.

He tried telling himself that it was just a greeting—that it was as natural as any other kiss exchanged tonight. But it wasn't true, and everyone knew it. Which was why conversations stopped, heads turned, and the whole room watched Marco Bellini's mistress embrace her ex-lover with brazen ease.

Strikingly tall and fair, Stefan Kranst might be ten years older than Marco, but he had as little trouble as Marco securing any woman of his choice. And *Dio*, he had secured a few during the year since Antonia had left him, Marco recalled deridingly.

But this woman was now *his* woman. She lived in his home, she slept in his bed, and she clothed herself with his money. Which made that lush red-painted mouth Kranst was kissing *his* exclusive property.

The primitive heat of an age-old burn of possessiveness began to form blisters inside the wall of his chest, the urge to go over there and drag them apart holding him absolutely still while he fought to contain such an utterly crass act. Everyone was watching, waiting—hoping, in their cruel little way, that he was going to do exactly that and cause the kind of nice juicy scene they could dine out on for the next month.

And her dress was too short, her legs too long, and her slender ankles too sexily elevated by the heels of her shiny-red backless shoes, Marco observed—refusing to remember that he had thought the exact opposite before he had witnessed her wrapped in that particular man's arms.

Had she done it for effect? Had she worn the dress because she'd known all along that Kranst would be here tonight and had wanted to please him? No bra, he remembered, dropping his eyes to the twin points of her breasts hovering a half centimetre away from Kranst's chest. He knew what that felt like. He knew what was happening to Kranst right now, because the bastard also knew what it felt like to hold Antonia that close.

No proper panties, either, knowing her. His eyes moved lower, checking for a tell-tale panty-line and finding none, which meant she was wearing one of those sexy little g-strings she liked to favour now and then.

Usually for his exclusive pleasure. So, when he saw Kranst's long artistic fingers splay over the slender curve of her hips, Marco took it as a personal insult to see her accept the intimacy as if the man still had every right to place his hands on her like that!

The sudden burst of soft laughter brought his hard gaze flicking upwards in time to catch that laughter animating just about every exquisite feature on her face. Then one of her hands curled around Kranst's nape, and they began talking to each other as if it was perfectly acceptable for them to behave like this in public.

But it was not acceptable, and she should know it. She should know that such behaviour with a man everyone here knew had been her lover before Marco only made her look cheap and made him look a fool!

Was she doing it deliberately? Was this her way of letting him know that he wasn't the only fish in her sea?

Sometimes he hated her. Sometimes he hated her so much he was bewildered as to how he could want her so badly, feeling the way he did. She wasn't his type. She had *never* been his type. She was too young, too uncultured and just too damn flighty! Or why else would she choose to stand out like an exotic flower in flimsy red silk while the rest of the room wore classy black chic?

Someone slid up beside him. 'Well, *caro*, she certainly knows how to make a man welcome,' a very mocking female voice drawled.

Gritting his teeth together behind the determinedly relaxed line of his mouth, Marco ignored Louisa Florenza's silken barb, and maintained his silence as the two of them stood watching Stefan Kranst begin edging Antonia backwards a few steps until he had put them both on the tiny dance floor.

Her hand remained curled around his nape. Both of his rested on her slender waist as he set them swaying to the music while they continued to talk. And their concentration on each other was so absolute that it was clear Antonia had completely forgotten all about the man she had actually come here with!

'You know, you cannot fail to be impressed by her complete lack of guile.' Louisa smoothly injected her next poisoned barb. 'Most women would be dying of embarrassment if they were confronted by their ex-lover in a room packed full of the friends of her present lover. But she doesn't seem to care at all!'

'You are standing next to me, *cara*,' Marco pointed out. 'Do you see me dying of embarrassment?'

As a reply, Louisa linked her arm through the crook of

his arm. 'We had some good times, Marco, hmm?' she murmured wistfully.

Good times? Watching Antonia swaying sensually to the music, he promised himself that if the gap between their bodies grew any smaller he would go over there and... 'You were a cat with claws, Louisa,' he drily reminded her. 'Which made the good times very few and far between.'

'I purred like a kitten in your bed, though,' she came back, with an example of that sensual purr.

It did nothing for him, which further annoyed him because it had used to do many things for him. But now all he could hear was another woman's soft sighs breathing tremulous pleas that could drive him out of his mind.

'And you liked to feel my claws now and again...'

'I still bear the scars,' he clipped.

'Good,' she said, but he sensed the knowledge getting through to her that his mind—and his body—was very much elsewhere right now. 'I hope you will always bear them. For what you are feeling now, as you watch her make love to him on the dance floor, is what I feel every time I see you with her. And those scars will last for ever, Marco, I can assure you.'

The bitterness in her tone finally caught his attention. Turning his head, he looked down into the face of one of Italy's most beautiful women—and smiled a very sardonic smile. 'Any scars you retain from me, *bella mia*,' he drawled, 'belong exclusively to the loss of that intravenous drip you had attached to my money.'

Unfazed by the accusation, Louisa held his very mocking gaze. 'Are you implying that *she* does not enjoy the same privilege?'

'No,' he conceded, and his smile began to tighten as he returned his attention to the two closely linked bodies on the dance floor. 'But she has yet to abuse that particular privilege.'

'Clever girl,' Louisa commended.

Not so clever, Marco countered silently as he watched her soft-blonde head give a small shake that set the paste diamonds decorating the clasp holding up her lovely hair shimmering in the lights. Then she put her hand across Kranst's mouth to stop whatever it was he was saying to her.

Was he asking her to go back to him? Was he asking to paint her again? Was he talking sex to her just as Louisa was talking sex to him?

Intimacy was the absolute devil, he decided. A forsaken intimacy was even worse. It gave people you no longer felt a thing for a power over you you could never take back.

'He still wants her.' Louisa's remark hit him dead centre, as if she could tap into his thoughts.

'His desires don't interest me,' he answered dismissively. The real point was—did Antonia still want Kranst?

Then another thought slid silk-like into his head, filling him with something disturbingly like dismay. Could it be that Antonia was becoming tired of *him*?

The very suggestion was so alien to him that he couldn't quite work out how to handle it. No woman in his memory had even considered walking away from him until he was ready to let them go!

Then—no. Marco dismissed that idea with a contempt even he recognised as arrogance. She adored him. She always had done. If he walked over there right now and took her in his arms she would become his loving siren again within seconds, and Kranst would be the one left forgotten on the sidelines.

'He has the looks, *caro*.' Once again Louisa tapped into

his thinking. 'He has the body and the reputation of a great lover. And although he may not have the social standing you possess, he can claim star quality, which cancels out the proud Bellini name. In fact,' she concluded tauntingly 'the only thing you seem to have that he doesn't are the financial resources you claim she doesn't abuse. But it is interesting how it always comes back to the money, hmm?'

Even to his own surprise, Marco released a burst of laughter. Because he was seeing the new red Lotus Antonia had walked past tonight as if it wasn't there. He was seeing a safe full of jewels she hardly ever asked to wear because she preferred to wear paste, like the clasp dressing her hair. And he was seeing an account in his own bank into which he paid a regular amount of money that she rarely spent.

So, no, avarice was not Antonia's besetting sin. But at least Louisa's peevish barb had put the humour back into his mood, so he repaid her by bending down to kiss her pouting mouth. She clung to him. He wasn't surprised— only indifferent—which was a shame, really, because Louisa would be his mother's idea of the perfect Bellini bride.

Shame—big shame—she wasn't his own.

'There,' Antonia declared. 'Didn't I tell you?'

Antonia was seeing that kiss Marco had just bestowed on Louisa Florenza as the final proof she needed to confirm that he was tiring of her.

'Men like Bellini do not replace old with older,' Stefan drawled sardonically. 'And you've just been kissing me,' he further pointed out. 'I would be flattered to think it was because you wanted me as your replacement lover, but we both know it wouldn't be true.'

'I love you more than anyone else on this earth, and I wish I'd never met him,' Antonia told him so tragically that Stefan had to sigh.

'My darling, the man is besotted with you. One only has to look at the too-cool way he is handling this little scene you're so carefully laying on for his benefit to know he's paying you back by doing the same to you.'

'If he loved me, he would be over here punching your lights out instead of laughing with her.'

'Well, thanks a lot,' Stefan drawled.

'It's all your fault, anyway,' she informed him churlishly. 'If you hadn't put my likeness into your stupid paintings, *he* wouldn't have bothered coming looking for me in the first place!'

'I didn't encourage you to fall for the rake.' It was Stefan's turn to laugh, and Marco's turn to listen to him doing it. 'You did that all on your own, Antonia. And I distinctly remember warning you off.'

It was such a painful little truth that she felt the tears suddenly flood into her eyes. Seeing them, Stefan released another sigh and pulled her just that little bit closer.

'You've been with him for over a year,' he gently reminded her. 'That's a whole lot longer than any other woman in his harem.'

'And the next person to tell me that will probably receive a slap,' she responded bitterly.

'But it still has to count for something, my darling,' he persisted. 'Can you honestly swear that he's actually said he no longer wants you?'

All Antonia did was smile cynically. For how many hints did she need tossed at her to know what was going on inside Marco's head? Even the week in Portofino was beginning to look like their swan-song to her. They'd had a row a few days before, over his intention to spend several days with his parents on their Tuscany estate. And she'd taken offence that even after a year together he was still refusing to let her meet them. 'Anyone would think you were ashamed of me,' she'd said.

'My father is ill,' he'd replied. 'Show a little consideration for the plight of others.'

But he hadn't denied the accusation that he was ashamed. And his face had closed up, just as it always did when they touched on the subject of his exalted family. So he'd gone alone to Tuscany. She hadn't heard from him once in the three days he'd been there. And when he'd come back he'd been so moody and irritable that the sudden decision to spend a week together in Portofino had come as a complete surprise.

'That depends on your definition of *want*,' she said to Stefan with a bleak little smile. 'He still *wants* me in his bed, but out of it I just irritate the hell out of him.'

'Hence the hungry vamp act here with me, designed to *irritate* him even more so,' Stefan heavily concluded. 'Do you have a death wish or something, Antonia? Because, love you or hate you, Marco Bellini is not the kind of man you embarrass in front of his friends,' he warned very seriously. 'He'll strike back so hard you won't know what's hit you.'

From the corner of her vision she saw Marco join them on the dance floor with Louisa clasped in his arms. As Stefan swung her around she caught sight of Nicola standing watching them with anxious eyes while, beside her, Franco simply looked angry. And as it suddenly occurred to her that there was a lot of watchful tension eddying around in the atmosphere, she finally realised what had made Stefan issue the warning.

A calamity was brewing in Nicola's drawing room and,

in her eagerness to score points off Marco's arrogant pride, she was unwittingly the cause of it.

'How did you manage to get an invite to this party?' she asked Stefan, suddenly realising that neither Franco or Nicola would be so insensitive as to invite him here, knowing his past relationship with their best friend's current mistress.

He smiled a brief smile. 'I came with Rosetta Romano,' he explained, naming the famous owner of the Romano Gallery in the Quadrilatero. 'I was good enough to step into the breach at short notice when her planned artist cancelled during a fit of temperament. So hawking me around Milan's most fashionable is her way of buying a bit of free advertising before the show opens.'

'Signora Romano obviously didn't know she would be causing one hell of a gaffe putting you, me and Marco in the same air-space,' Antonia said drily.

'Of course she knew.' Stefan grinned. 'How much free publicity do you estimate she'll get from setting up this potentially explosive scene?'

'And not just for the Romano Gallery,' she added, meaning that Stefan Kranst wasn't opposed to using notoriety to alert interest in his work.

His shrug was an arrogant acknowledgement of that. 'I'm a painter, not a diplomat. And anyway,' he added, looking into her eyes again, 'I wanted to see you, but trying to reach you through normal sources is virtually impossible. I've been leaving messages with your housekeeper all week, Antonia. Did you actually receive any of them?'

His meaning was clear. But Antonia shook her head at it. 'We've been away on a week's holiday,' she explained. 'And only arrived back late this afternoon. Today is the housekeeper's day off. I haven't seen Carlotta, had a

chance to check messages or do anything other than get
ready to come here.'

'So the guy hasn't resorted to censoring your messages
yet?' He smiled a trifle cynically. 'I did begin to wonder
when I couldn't get to speak to you personally,' he admitted. 'Because you can bet your sweet smile, my darling, that the moment I agreed to show in Milan, then Mr
Patron of the Arts knew about it.'

He was implying that Marco had known about him being here in Milan and had deliberately kept the information from her! It seemed an appropriate moment for the
music to stop. Stefan walked her to the edge of the floor
and said nothing while she came to terms with the ugly
possibility that he could well be right. For if anyone knew
exactly what was happening on the art scene, here in
Milan, then it was most definitely Marco!

The rat, she fumed. He might no longer want her for
himself, but his inflated ego wouldn't sanction him having
to witness her with a man who would *always* want her!

'Here.' Stefan offered her a glass of champagne. 'Drink
this. You might feel better.'

Stubbornly dismissing the knowledge that she'd probably had more than enough champagne for one wretched
night, she accepted the glass and drank the whole lot in
a couple of determined gulps.

Champagne bubbles began to mix with anger in her
blood. It was a dangerous combination. 'I think I hate
him,' she announced with a deep sense of satisfaction for
having said the words out loud.

'Well, in that case the next few minutes should be interesting,' Stefan murmured levelly. Dropping his eyes
from a point somewhere over her left shoulder, he mocked
her vehemence with a wry challenge. 'This may be a good
moment for you to decide how much you hate him,' he

suggested. 'Because war is about to be declared, my darling.'

He had to mean Marco, she realised, and felt the champagne bubbles start to pop. Her soft mouth parted, her eyes grew dark, and a helpless kind of indecision sent her hand out to swap her empty glass for his full one.

On a sigh, Stefan gave a shake of his head. 'You sweet idiot,' he murmured. 'Didn't it occur to you even once that *you* might not be ready for a showdown with him?'

An astute question, and a painful one, because she had considered and accepted only this morning that she wasn't ready for any kind of showdown with Marco. Now here she was, standing on the very threshold of one hell of a row—and in a room packed full of his loyal supporters.

Cuckoo in the nest didn't even cover what she suddenly began to feel like.

'Be brave, my friend,' Stefan softly encouraged. Then— 'Good evening, Marco.' He smiled. 'It's a pleasure to see you again…'

But it wasn't a pleasure for any of them. Standing close to Stefan still, Antonia was assailed by the familiar scent of Marco before she was assailed by the full impact of his physical presence. He arrived at her side, his shoulder level with her chin. As usual her skin began to shimmer at the near contact, her fingers curling tensely round the glass while she waited for him to say something totally unforgivable.

Yet all he did was offer Stefan his hand to shake and return the polite greeting without any obvious sign of animosity. 'You're showing at Romano's all next week, I believe.' As smoothly as that, Marco informed Antonia that he had known Stefan was here in Milan but had not bothered to tell her.

'The doors open on Saturday,' Stefan confirmed. 'I was

just asking Antonia if you were both coming to my private viewing on Friday evening,' he added, with lying ease.

'And of course she assured you that we wouldn't miss it,' Marco returned in the same lying vein.

'Of course,' Stefan smoothly confirmed. 'Especially when I told her I have something for her to collect from me while she's there.' The smile at her puzzled frown and the teasing brush of a finger to her jutting chin were done, she was sure, simply to annoy Marco. 'Let's call it a belated birthday surprise,' he suggested. 'If you still have my *Mirror Woman*, Marco, then it may have some interest to you too,' he added lightly.

It was a baited hook.

'Sounds intriguing.' Marco smiled, but Antonia stiffened at the mention of the painting that had given Stefan his fame—and herself her notoriety.

She had only seen it once since the first evening she had arrived in Marco's apartment a year ago. The painting had been hanging in his study. When he'd shown it to her she hadn't been able to hide her dismay, because she hadn't realised that Marco actually *owned* the painting.

Marco had since moved it to a secure room connected to the study where he kept his more—personal investments.

Now Stefan was implying that he had another one just like it. And though she knew he was quite capable of producing a hundred paintings exactly the same, without needing the live model to do it, it disturbed her deeply to hear Stefan taunting Marco with the suggestion that he had returned to putting her in his paintings. Which led her straight to another question that set her trembling a little as she looked into his lean smooth indolently smiling face.

Had Stefan gone back on his promise to her?

Her eyes begged the question but Stefan refused to notice. Beside her Marco was playing it so casual she wondered if he even cared. But then, if she was on her way out, why should he care? she then asked herself. And, like this morning, she simply turned and walked away, with no stomach to play this game.

Only this time Marco didn't let her get far before his hand was capturing one of hers. She tried to tug free.

'Stop it,' he said, turning her round until he could see her face. Her eyes were too dark, her cheeks too pale, and her soft mouth was trembling. Marco knew the look, he knew she was hurting, but the knowledge that it wasn't him who had done the hurting this time didn't help to lighten his mood one little bit.

One part of him wanted to beat the hell out of Kranst for being so insensitive as to mention the *Mirror Woman*, when Marco was sure he must know the way it could upset her. While another part wanted to blast *her* to smithereens for still being so vulnerable to something she had, after all, posed for in all her naked glory!

'You reap what you sow, *cara*,' he told her grimly, took the glass from her fingers and put it aside, then pulled her the few steps needed to bring them onto the dance floor and folded her into his arms. 'Now dance,' he commanded, holding her close even while she tried to strain away from him. 'Remember where you are and who you will be hurting if you cause a scene here.'

As if on cue, Franco and Nicola danced in close to them. '*Ciao*,' Nicola greeted awkwardly. 'You two enjoying yourselves?'

She had to know that enjoyment was the last thing either he or Antonia were experiencing. 'We're having a wonderful time,' Antonia answered smilingly, coiling an intimate hand around Marco's neck—and dug her nails in. 'I love it when Marco comes over all macho.'

Franco flashed him a sardonic look, Nicola avoided eye contact completely. 'So long as you're happy,' their poor hostess mumbled, and looked relieved when her husband manoeuvred them away again.

'She hates scenes,' Marco sighed. 'She always has done.'

'I hate you,' Antonia responded. 'Does that mean I get a sympathetic sigh too?'

One part of him wanted to grin, the other part was furious. 'No,' he retaliated. 'You get to go home with the guy you hate and receive your just reward in private.'

With that he reached up and unclipped her nails, held onto the hand and trapped it between their bodies. 'Now look at me and smile,' he gritted. 'Or I think I might just kiss you senseless.'

If he expected the threat to subdue her, he soon learned otherwise when she had the absolute audacity to pull out one of her secret weapons that she kept under wraps for most of the time. Her head tipped backwards, her eyes grew sultry, and, setting the pink tip of her tongue between her even white teeth, she snaked up on her toe-tips and licked the thin line of his angry mouth.

Fire engulfed his body at the speed of lightning. Erogenous zones came alive with an urgency that stung.

Had she kissed Kranst like this? Made *him* feel like this?

Madre di Dio, he couldn't deal with the green streak of furious jealousy that went rampaging through him. 'We're leaving,' he announced.

'I want to stay,' she pouted, playing the seductress for all she was worth now, with sensual eyes and promising mouth and the inviting sway of her beautiful body.

In one corner of his consciousness he was totally engrossed in her, loving it—loving her defiance, her willingness to take him on, her deliberate public seduction. But another part was wondering if Kranst had incited this. With the flat of an angry palm pressed to her lower body he felt the smoothness of naked flesh beneath the clinging red fabric, and remembered Kranst's hand grazing the same area.

She quivered for him. Had she quivered for Kranst? From the periphery of his vision he could see Kranst standing there watching them. He felt a bloody black fury begin to throb with his heartbeat, and he bit out silkily, 'I'm game if you are.'

Lips gone so dry they were fused together, Antonia felt the sheer heat of that challenge burn right down to her tingling toes. In any mood Marco was a breathtaking study of male beauty, but bad tempered and aroused he was awakening senses she hadn't known existed before she met him. Weak, sensual, female senses. The one which made man the aggressor and woman his more than willing slave.

She hated it—hated all of it.

'Okay,' she whispered unsteadily. 'We can leave…'

CHAPTER FOUR

THE drive back to the apartment was achieved in silence. Both tense, both angry for their own reasons. Both so sexually on edge that the atmosphere almost sizzled.

Antonia was out of the car even as Marco was still parking it. Making straight for the lift, she then committed the ultimate sin of not waiting for him before sending it up to the top floor. Having to kick his heels in the basement waiting for the lift to come back for him did nothing to improve his temper.

He arrived in the bedroom to discover that she had already locked herself into the bathroom. He could hear the shower running, and her red dress lay like a stain on the bright white tiling, the scrappy red shoes lying discarded beside it.

With frustration attacking him from all angles, he dragged off his jacket and had to really fight the temptation to slam it down beside the red dress and shoes in a counter-declaration.

It was realising the childishness in the act that made him stop to wonder bleakly what was happening to him. Anger, frustration, childish acts of temper? These were not the scenes he expected to fill his home with! They lacked the sophistication with which he liked to run his private life.

And, on top of that, he was beginning to feel like a jealous husband without the official bit of paper that said he had to put up with this. Hot anger suddenly turned to ice, the mere suspicion that Antonia was digging her claws into him deeply enough to make him feel that way, literally horrifying the heat out of him.

Marco was draping his suit jacket on a hanger when Antonia came out of the bathroom. Wide shoulders, long body, tight behind, powerful legs and a sleek olive hue to his skin that made her fingers itch to stroke it. She wished so much he had the face of a Gorgon to offset the perfect rest of him.

But he didn't. So when he turned to face her, even looking as coldly remote as he did, her body stirred beneath the silk robe she was wearing.

She wanted to hate him for being able to do that to her. Especially when all he did was freeze her with a look of contempt before turning away again.

'You've been working with Kranst again,' he declared flatly.

Without bothering to answer, she walked over to pick up the red dress and shoes from where she'd stepped out of them, and carried them over to the wardrobe next to the one he was standing by.

She opened one of the doors as he flicked one shut. 'Answer me,' he commanded coldly.

'I wasn't aware you'd asked a question,' she tossed back with equal cold. 'It sounded more like a statement of fact to me.'

From the corner of her eye she saw his mouth tighten, ignored the stinging warning in his eyes, and placed the shoes on the shoerack before reaching up to pluck a hanger from the rail and begin hooking the thin shoulder straps of the dress onto it.

'Explain to me, then, what he was implying tonight, when he talked about something *interesting*.'

She shrugged as she re-hung the hanger on the rail. 'I have absolutely no idea.' Though she certainly had a few worrying suspicions.

'You must do,' Marco insisted. 'You know the man. You lived with him for over five years.'

Ten, she wanted to correct, but held back the information. 'And I've lived with you for all of one,' she pointed out as she closed the wardrobe door. 'But knowing what makes you tick is beyond me.'

'Oh, very trite,' he mocked. 'Now, answer my first question and tell me if you've been secretly working with him again.'

'For a man famed for the sharpness of his intelligence, you can be really dense sometimes,' she derided. 'Ask yourself—when?' she suggested. 'Have I had the opportunity to *work* or do anything else with Stefan?'

He didn't like the derision, his eyes darkened. 'For all I know the man might have a secret studio set up right here in Milan where the two of you meet on a regular basis.'

'So, I'm keeping the two of you happy?' Her laugh was scornful. But even Antonia was aware that her expression was suddenly guarded, because Marco had unwittingly drifted too close to a carefully kept secret of her own.

He saw the change. Of course he did. Reaching out with a hand, he drew her across the few feet separating them. His eyes were hard, his features grim and his grip on her wrist was firm. 'You're hiding something,' he gritted.

She refused to answer, her mouth set in a defiant pout. Marco formed his own conclusions, his expression darkening some more. 'If the two of you are plotting my embarrassment on Friday, then I'm warning you, you will regret ever knowing me!'

'Why won't you listen?' she snapped. 'I don't *know* what Stefan is planning for Friday!'

'Then why the shifty look?'

'You don't own the right to know my every secret!' she hit back bitterly. 'I'm your mistress, not your wife!'

This came hard on the fact that he had just reminded himself of the same thing, and his expression hardened into steel. 'The way the two of you were lost in deep conversation while you clung to him like a vine says to me that you were discussing something important while you made love to each other in front of everyone. And I want to know what that something is!'

'We were discussing you!' she flashed. 'And whether it was time for me to leave you or not!'

The claim had hit a nerve. Antonia actually saw it flick like the tip of a whip across his taut cheekbones. 'Are you saying he wants you back?' he demanded thinly.

'He will *always* have me back!' she flung at him recklessly. 'And when I'm ready to leave you, then I probably will go back to him!'

With that, she gave a tug at her wrist to free herself and walked proudly away, trying not to show how badly shaken she was feeling at this, the worst row they'd had to date.

Needing something to do in the drumming silence that followed her, she sat down on the stool in front of the dressing table and began to let down her hair.

'If there was the remotest possibility of you actually walking out on me, you would have done so without the warning,' Marco drawled in a voice loaded with derision.

'You think I'm a real push-over, don't you?' she muttered, tossing hairpins in an angry scatter across the dressing table top. 'You think that because you're as sexy as hell and so darn wealthy you can afford to buy anything, that I should be grateful that you decided to buy me!'

'I did not *buy* you,' he denied. 'I *chose* you. There is a definite difference between the two.' His arrogance, she noted, really showed no bounds. 'Whether or not you sold yourself to me, though, is a question I have no wish to hear the answer to.'

'Why not?' she challenged, via his reflection in the mirror. 'Are you afraid to discover that maybe your wealth is more appealing to me than your body?'

About to undo his bow-tie, she watched him stop and stiffen as if something really nasty had just stepped into the room. Antonia was very pleased to watch him do it. The man could be so insufferably conceited sometimes that it made her want to hit him where it would hurt the most!

'I sit here swathed in the finest silk,' she continued, to compound his momentary disconcertion, 'with my flesh pampered by the finest beauty products money can buy. I live in the kind of luxury most people only see between the pages of glossy magazines, and downstairs in the basement sits the kind of car most women only dream about owning—'

'The car belongs to me,' he inserted. 'You are merely permitted the use of it.'

'Permitted—!' A choked gasp brought her twisting round on the stool to stare at him. Then, 'Ah...' she said. 'So now we get down to the nitty-gritty. The car is yours. The luxury accommodation is yours. The expensive clothes I wear belong to you, as does the wonderful array of priceless jewels you keep carefully locked away in your safe until I require the use of them. So—yes,' she acknowledged, 'I suppose it is natural for you to believe that I sold myself to you.'

'I never said that,' he snapped, a deep frown suddenly darkening his features as fresh irritation flicked into life.

'Then let's just clarify the point, shall we, so that it can be done with once and for all?' Getting up, she went to stand right in front of him. Confrontation wasn't in it. 'If, let's say, I decided to walk out on you right here and now, what would I be allowed to take with me?'

'This is stupid,' he sighed, sliding the strip of black silk out from under his shirt collar. 'When we both know you have no intention of walking anywhere.'

'The car? No,' she continued, regardless. 'The jewels? Definitely no. What about all the designer clothes, then? Have I performed well enough to earn the right to take those, Marco?' she questioned provokingly. 'Or do you intend to let me walk out on you naked? If so,' she added, without giving him a chance to answer, 'then you surely can't say that I sold myself to you. For what exactly is it I am supposed to have gained from doing so?'

'A year of great sex?' he suggested nastily.

'Oh,' she pouted. 'I was hoping you would have the good taste to leave the sex thing out of this.'

'Why?' he asked tauntingly. 'When it is all I—'

Marco stopped himself—but not soon enough. And the black anger went flooding through him again as he watched her annoyingly provocative face blanch.

'You asked for that,' he insisted, wishing to hell he had never started this.

'Yes,' she agreed, 'I surely did.' But the fight had disappeared from her tone, and his jaw felt so tight it was in danger of snapping.

She went to turn away from him. It was sheer frustration with the whole sordid scene that made him stop her, he told himself. It had nothing to do with the sudden suspicion that if he let her turn away she would never turn back to him again.

So his hands found her shoulders and drew her against him, then, simply because he needed to do it, he lowered his head and his mouth took her mouth by storm.

At least she didn't fight him, but neither did she respond. She just stood limp and lifeless against his body while his mouth ravaged hers without receiving any feedback at all.

Not liking what was happening here, and liking even less the knowledge that she could stand there lifeless while his own body was reacting as fiercely as it always did to her, he went for the kill with a pride-staking vengeance aimed at demolishing her resistance.

For he knew this woman, he consoled himself grimly as he began covering her face with the kind of small light teasing kisses guaranteed to drive her wild. Her cheeks, her jaw-line, her firmly closed eyes, the length of her small straight nose. His kisses found all the right pleasure points while carefully avoiding her mouth even when, with a helpless whimper, she slackened its tense little line in sensual expectation.

Yes, he confirmed triumphantly. He knew her so well. The way her breathing quickened, and she began to vibrate to the feather-light stroke of his fingers. It was easy to urge the silk from her shoulders and leave it to slither down her body until the only thing holding it up was the belt knotted around her waist.

As she released a gasp in startled surprise he at last captured her mouth again. She fell into his kiss like a woman with a fever. When her fingers came up to clutch at his rock-solid biceps, he stroked her hair, stroked her body, and stroked her beautiful breasts with their sensitive points that simply begged for his further attention.

He gave it willingly, knowingly—ruthlessly, arching her over his arm so far that she had no choice but to reach up and hook her hands around his neck to maintain some control over her own balance.

Within seconds she was groaning. Eyes closed, head tilted right back so her long silken hair swung in a rippling swathe over his arm as he grimly tore through every veil of rejection she had dared to pull on against him. When the groans became hot little gasps of pleasure, he consolidated his success by gliding a hand along a silken thigh until it found the cluster of golden curls that shrouded her sexuality. The robe was no barrier; it had already slid apart to give him easy access. But the real triumph came when her thighs parted for him in all-out invitation.

The battle, in his mind, was surely over. Having won it, as abruptly as he had started it, he brought it to an end and watched with a grim detachment as she leaned weakly against him, dizzy and disorientated enough to find it impossible to support herself.

'You want *me*, Antonia,' he declared in a tough cold voice that made her shiver. 'Try dangling another man in front of me in an effort to improve on what we have, and you will find yourself having to learn not to want.'

It was an outright warning.

Standing there in his arms, Antonia said absolutely nothing. He'd done this to her merely to make a point. It was humiliating.

After a moment, he sighed and let go of her. She swayed a little, but found her balance, and remained exactly as she was while he strode for the door. And what was the picture he took with him? Antonia asked herself as she watched him go.

His suitably chastened mistress standing there with her seduction-red silk robe still hanging from her waist by the belt, and her breasts still taut and alive and throbbing. Like her mouth—like her sex.

She had never felt so sickened in all her life.

Sickened by herself—sickened by him. Sickened by the knowledge that really they were both as bad as each other. For Marco might take and take and take, but she had let him do it.

'I hate you,' she whispered, not sure if she was telling herself that or the wretched man striding out of the door.

Whichever, he heard it, paused and turned. There was contempt in that lean hard handsome face of his. Enough contempt to make her skin crawl.

'Take my advice, *cara*, and think carefully about on which side your bread is buttered. Beautiful women come in disposable packs of ten these days.' The cut of his cynicism was deep enough to draw blood. 'A poor performer can therefore be tossed onto the scrap heap and replaced as easily as—that.'

The snap of his long brown fingers made her flinch. Marco gave a curt nod of his dark head to acknowledge it, then left the room.

But he took with him the sight of her standing there still half stripped of her robe. It made him sigh again as he slammed into his study. For, no matter how ruthlessly he had just set out to demolish her, the way she had refused to cover herself seemed to give her the last word that was strangely demolishing *him*.

What was it exactly he had been trying to prove? he

asked himself as he made directly for the whisky bottle. That she *had* to love him more than she loved Kranst?

She'd left the handsome bastard for him, hadn't she? Marco argued with his own angry head. And why bring the love thing into it when he had never asked or wanted love from any woman?

But neither do you want to believe she could have the capacity to love another man, his conceited side answered the question. You're an arrogant swine, Bellini, he told himself. You want it all. You always have done. But you're never going to give that much back in return.

Snatching up the bottle and a glass, he took them over to his desk then threw himself down into the chair. Whisky splashed into the glass. He tipped it down his throat, swallowed, then sat back to glower darkly at nothing.

He'd never felt like this before, and he didn't want to feel like this now! Angry and guilty and—yes, he admitted it—riddled with confusion and jealousy. It creased his insides every time he heard Kranst's name leave her lips in that oh, so tender way she always said it. And seeing her clinging to the man tonight had forced him to trawl whole new depths of jealous resentment.

'He still wants her,' Louisa had said.

Well, so do I!

Another splash of whisky burned its way down to his stomach.

And he wasn't giving her up just to watch her walk straight into the arms of her ex-lover as if Marco Bellini had never even been there!

Was that it? he thought suddenly. Was that what was really bugging him? The idea that if he did send her packing she would simply go back to where she had been before she met him and pick up where she'd left off, with hardly a tear to say she was sorry to do it?

To hell with Kranst. Antonia was *his* woman! And Kranst could go and look elsewhere for his inspiration.

Which reminded him about the painting the guy had been taunting him with tonight. Getting up, he staggered, frowned down at the whisky bottle, and was amazed to discover how much of it had gone.

Drunk. He was drunk. Well, that was a first since his reckless youth, he thought with a grimace. Would Antonia be pleased to know what she had driven him to?

Concentrating on walking in a straight line, he went over to a door and punched a set of numbers into the security console, heard the lock shoot back and pushed the door open on the investment side of his art collection—the Rembrandt, the Titian, the Severini and the Boccioni, which his insurers insisted he kept housed in a secure room.

Would Antonia be pleased to know what else he had in here? he mused as, with glass in hand, he walked right past the masters, his attention fixed only on Stefan Kranst's *Mirror Woman*.

It was only one of a series the artist had produced over several years. Each painting was different, but the theme was always the same—perfection seen through the eyes of the artist via a mirror reflection.

What had Kranst really been trying to say when he'd painted Antonia like this? Marco pondered thoughtfully. That the mirror reflected her perfection where reality did not? Or had Kranst merely been the voyeur, capturing on canvas something he knew he could never have any other way?

Marco frowned as he always did when he tried to understand what Kranst had been trying to relay here. No suggestion he could come up with ever truly fitted. The idea of Kranst as the mere voyeur, for instance, was shot to pieces the moment you saw the two of them together. They *knew* each other *intimately*. Touch, taste, sight, sound. In fact he had never experienced intimacy like it between two people, unless he included himself with her.

As for the mirror-perfection versus reality: the painting didn't lie. Antonia was as perfect in real life as Kranst had portrayed her here.

The *Mirror Woman* was easily the best of the series—which was why Marco had bought it. It was also the most disturbing, because this was the only painting where Antonia stood in full focus. She was standing on a balcony—an *English* balcony, he mused with a grimace. Long and slender, naked and sleek, with an early-morning sunrise caressing her skin with pale gold silk. She was looking back over her shoulder towards the mirror with a terrible—terrible sadness in her beautiful eyes.

Frowning, he reached out to absently graze a fingertip over an unusually careless brush-mark blemish that shouldn't be there on her left shoulder. Then her eyes were drawing his attention again. Those dreadful, empty, haunted eyes. What was she supposed to be seeing when she looked into the mirror like that? Herself? The artist? Something else unseen by anyone else from this angle?

He'd once asked Antonia why the look. 'Life,' she'd answered flatly. 'She's seeing life.' Then she'd shuddered and walked away and never asked to see the painting again.

It had been an unexpected response from someone who refused to reveal any hint of embarrassment whenever she came up against her own nudity in one of the many other forms it had taken since Kranst had painted her. The signed prints, the calendars, greetings cards, etcetera, being the mediums by which the artist earned his real fame and fortune.

Only this painting upset her. Or was it the fact that *he* owned it that made her walk away? She refused to talk about it, and would be appalled to find out that to acquire it he'd had to convince his own mother to sell it to him.

The irony in that put a smile on his lips. 'Stefan Kranst is a worthy investment,' his mother had said. 'He has a gift for catching the inner soul of his subject. This poor creature, for instance, is dying inside that beautiful outer casing. I feel for her. I feel for the artist because he so clearly loves the inner woman.'

The word *dying* was a disturbing description. He preferred the word *empty*, because it soothed some part of him to know that Antonia had never looked empty while she had been with him.

But his mother had admired the woman in the painting *before* she had known Antonia had moved in with him. Now all she saw was a woman willing to expose herself for all to see and who possessed no conscience about doing it. She also despaired, because her son had not yet assuaged what she saw as his obsession with both the painting and the woman.

The smile turned itself into a sigh, because he was aware he hadn't assuaged anything where Antonia was concerned. Not his desire for the woman or his fascination with this painting.

Now Kranst was implying that there was another painting, like this one. Which meant what, exactly? That Kranst hadn't painted out *his* obsession with Antonia?

That this new painting was going to tell him things he didn't want to know?

If that was Kranst's motive, then Marco didn't want to find out, but he knew he needed to. He didn't want to go to Kranst's damned private viewing, but he would have to go.

And he didn't want to lose Antonia, but he had a horrible feeling he was going to lose her one way or another. By his own stupid actions or with the help of exterior forces like Kranst or his mother or the compelling pull of his sick father's need.

The whisky no longer had any flavour. The painting of Antonia suddenly did nothing for him. He wanted the real woman. The one he had just hurt for no other reason than a need to reassure his own ego.

But she was *still* the warm and pliant woman probably lying fast asleep in his bed now, he then added, with yet another kind of smile as he left the room and closed the door behind him. Then, with a walk that was almost unwavering, he rid himself of his glass and went to join her.

The bedroom was in darkness, the bed a mere shadow on the other side of the room. Making as little noise as possible, he stepped into the bathroom, silently closed the door to spend a few minutes trying to shower off the effects of the whisky, before going back into the bedroom and over to the bed.

He meant to surprise her awake with some serious kisses in some very serious places. She would be sulking, of course, but he could deal with that. She would fight him too, he would expect nothing less. And he would grovel a little because she deserved to have him grovel—

before he drowned himself in the sweetest pleasure ever created for a man to share with a woman.

Then he stopped and frowned when he found himself staring down at the smooth neatness of an untouched bed.

CHAPTER FIVE

A SHAFT of alarm went streaking down his backbone and massed deep in his abdomen. He spun, sharp eyes piercing the darkness to scan the room for a sign of her shadowy figure—curled in a chair, maybe, or standing by the window.

She wasn't there. The alarm leapt up to attack his heartbeat. She wouldn't, he told himself. She couldn't have quietly dressed and left him while he'd been busy drowning his sorrows—could she?

No, he wouldn't have it. He might have behaved like a rotten bastard, but Antonia would never just walk out and leave!

But then there was Kranst waiting on the sidelines, he remembered, and started moving, unsure, so damned unsure of himself that the uncertainty was actually making his legs feel hollow with fright!

It was the whisky, Marco told himself. But he was still going to kill her when he found her for scaring him like this, he vowed, as he began striding round the apartment opening doors and closing them until he came to the locked door belonging to one of the spare bedrooms.

Relief shuddered through him, followed by a shaft of white-hot fury at her whole attitude. Stubbornly forgetting his own bad behaviour. he banged hard on the door. 'If you don't unlock this door I'll break it down!' he shouted threateningly.

And kept on banging until the door flew open.

Antonia was already walking away from it even as it swung back on itself. Her hair rippled about her naked shoulders and his body almost screamed as it responded to the carelessly sensual sway of hers. And it was the turn of the red silk wrap to lie in a discarded blot on the floor.

'Don't ever lock me out of a room in my own home again,' he ground out as he strode forward.

'I have nothing to say to you,' she replied in a voice meant to freeze a man's nether parts.

A willingness to grovel was forgotten—ousted by a much more satisfying desire to remind her just who called the tune around here.

Arriving at the bed, she prepared to climb back into it. In two long strides he stopped her, by the economical act of scooping her off her feet. Her protesting shriek was ignored, as were her wriggling attempts to get herself free. Without a single word from his tightly clamped lips, he turned and began carrying her out of this bedroom and down the hall to *his* bedroom.

'You are such a primitive underneath the layers of breeding,' she sliced at him disgustedly.

He stopped dead and kissed her—so hot and so hard she was gasping for breath by the time he lifted his head again.

'Is that primitive enough?' he asked, not in the least bit insulted she'd called him that. In fact he liked the whole scenario, since he was feeling very primitively aroused right now.

Marco shut the door behind them with a very satisfyingly primitive kick. The bed waited. He dumped her on its pale blue cover, then followed with the long hard length of his body in a very primitive man-on-top-of-woman pinning down.

Her angry eyes shot amber bright warnings at him. Her beautiful hair streamed out above her head, and her clenched fists made a puny but determined effort to do him some damage. 'Get off me,' she insisted. 'You're just a big brute—*and* you taste of whisky!'

'And you taste of champagne and woman—*my* woman,' Marco growled back, enjoying this new primitive role that allowed him the rare luxury to completely dominate.

Her breasts heaved against the solid wall of his chest and her slender hips writhed delightfully beneath the pressure of his. She felt the rise of his passion and spat her utter contempt at him, while the mocking arch of his eyebrows asked her who was to blame.

She hit back with more than her fists, 'Stefan was right about you,' she lashed. 'You are a—'

Ducking between the flailing fists, he stopped the words with his mouth. Discussing Kranst was *not* going to happen in *his* bed! he grimly determined, and kept on kissing her until her hands stopped punching and began to anxiously knead his shoulders instead.

Triumph sizzled through his system; the red-hot heat of desire spun through his blood. He made love to her as if there was no tomorrow and, because there was still the heat of an angry fear burning behind the passion, he drove her to the edge more than once before ruthlessly drawing back again.

'I hate it when you do this to me,' she sobbed in frustration.

'You would hate it more if I didn't do it at all,' he threw back.

Her breath broke on a whimper because she knew he was right. The helpless little sound did things to him no woman could ever begin to understand. He thrust into her with the force of absolute possession.

'You belong to *me*. Just remember that next time you feel like wrapping yourself around another man.'

If he'd expected her to respond at all, it was not the way she did. With the slick roll of her body he suddenly found he was the one pinned down and she the one most definitely on top. For the next few minutes he experienced what it was like to be utterly seduced by a woman hell-bent on making him embarrass himself.

It didn't happen. He was no one's easy victim. But Antonia in this mood was irresistible. She was the true sensualist born to pleasure man. She kissed him and stroked him and rode him towards heaven. And when his body began to tighten and his heart began to pound, she gave him back a taste of his own medicine by pulling away to rise up and stand over him.

Feet planted either side of his body, hands resting in the delicious groove of her slender waist, and her wonderful long golden hair spiralling around the face of an absolute wanton, she asked, 'And who do *you* belong to, Marco?'

The little minx. The beautiful, outrageous little minx! he thought, and, with a laugh of appreciation, he jack-knifed into a sitting position, clamped his hands to her hips—and gave his mouth the pleasure of bringing her to heel again.

The battle progressed to a different level. She gasped and protested and tugged at handfuls of his hair in an effort to dislodge him, and eventually lost the ability to stand. She was groaning and trembling but still in there fighting, matching him kiss for kiss, caress for caress, intimacy for exquisite tortuous intimacy, which had them crossing a few boundaries they'd never attempted to cross before in their quest to get the better of the other.

By the time he was back where he belonged—on top and deep inside her—he had lost the will to pull back again. Hot, bathed in sweat and no longer on this planet, they rode the fiery dragon with a focused compulsion that blocked out everything else.

He climaxed first—she was so damned determined to make him do that. But she followed a half-second later, urging him on with the convulsing tug of her muscles towards the kind of prolonged orgasm that laid them both to waste for long minutes afterwards.

Yes! he thought with a deep satisfaction as he lay heavy on her, fighting for breath. This was it, the elixir of life, and to hell with the covetous Kranst. To hell with his disapproving mother! he added fiercely to that—he couldn't bring himself to repeat the dismissive curse regarding his father, but inside he was aware that the need to hold on to what he had here was beginning to overshadow everything else.

Lying there beneath him, almost completely engulfed in his body and his scent and the glorious weight of his utter satiation, Antonia wondered ruefully if she would ever find the energy to move again. Her bones felt like liquid and certain muscles were trembling in the aftermath of something pretty spectacular, even for them.

What she couldn't understand was how it could be like that after what had gone before it. She should have been repulsed by his touch. She should have lain like a stone beneath him. But she hadn't—she hadn't…

Weak, you're weak, she derided herself miserably, and made a move to remind him that she was still here, just in case he'd forgotten while he basked in sexual bliss.

With a kiss to her brow, he acknowledged her presence, then relieved her of his weight by rolling them onto their sides so he could wrap her against him.

'You move me like no other woman,' he murmured huskily.

Did he think that was a compliment? she asked herself. Because it wasn't. She had no wish to be tagged and sorted according to performance. In fact, if she had the energy she would take serious offence and get up and leave!

But she didn't have the energy. And, in truth, lying here against him in the soft darkness of the summer night, with one of his hands gently stroking the curve of her hip while the other absently grazed over her left shoulder, she could think of no other place she would rather be.

Weak, she repeated. It was her biggest problem. She needed to be with him though she didn't *want* to need. He was arrogant, self-motivated, insensitive and…

Her sigh warmed his throat. Dipping his dark head, he caught the sigh with the kind of kiss that squeezed the heart dry. When it was over she reached up to touch his lips with her fingertips, unable to believe that a mouth could be so tender and not feel something deeper than desire for her.

'I wish I'd never met you sometimes,' she quietly confided.

'Only sometimes?' he threw back.

Tipping her head, she expected to find him smiling. But he looked quite sombre as he gazed down at her through swirling smoke-blue eyes set between kohl-black lashes in a polished bronze framework no gifted sculptor could improve upon.

'Do you want me to apologise for my earlier behaviour?' he asked her. Huskily spoken, sincerely meant.

No, she thought sadly. I want you to love me. Then had to swallow the lump of tears in her throat as she gave a shake of her head. 'I just want you to promise never to do that to me again,' she replied.

Smoke-blue eyes darkened with repentance. 'On my life,' he vowed, and sealed it with a kiss, then repeated it again and again until both the vow and the kiss became yet another seduction.

It was his way, a willingly humble side to his proud character, which had the power to demolish her resistance far more easily than the ruthlessness he had meted out before.

Her fingers began trailing tender caresses across hair-peppered, muscle-hard, satin-tight flesh. He was built to worship, she thought mistily. Built to make any woman melt with desire. It was she who deepened those soft penitent kisses into one long sensual banquet. She who slid onto her back and drew him over her, then slowly relaxed her thighs so he would settle between. In a wonderful intimacy that had her long legs tangling with his and her body arching to a sensual rhythm, they indulged in a different kind of kiss.

His mouth left hers to taste other parts of her, and she sighed in pleasure as it closed on her breast. Fingers trailed into his hair, stretched out to glide down the satin smoothness of his back. He shuddered in response and drew on her nipple until she felt the needle-sharp pleasure reach deep down into her very core.

As quickly as that, it all began again. No tormenting this time, no battle of wills. In only seconds he was feeding his powerful arms beneath her so he could lift her into closer contact with the pulsing length of his sex.

Dragging his mouth from her breast, he requested, 'May I?'

'Oh, yes,' she invited, aware that they were both more than ready for this.

This time he came into her with the gentle force of a man who was very mindful of his own power. She willingly accepted him, and wasn't surprised to hear them both utter those exquisite sighs of pleasure because, quick though this was, they were perfectly in tune.

Can I walk away from him? Antonia found herself questioning as not just her senses but her whole world began to quicken. Can *he* really want this to end?

As if he could sense that her mind had strayed, Marco was suddenly rearing up and over her. His eyes were like two dark circles of passion, his mouth warm and moist and hungry for hers. 'This is special,' he said roughly. 'And it is ours.'

'Sometimes it feels as if you hate me,' she whispered.

'No, never,' he denied, and crushed her mouth beneath his and crushed all thoughts from her head by other means.

The next morning, the light brush of his lips on her cheek awoke her. Opening her eyes, she smiled sleepily at him.

Clean-shaven and smelling deliciously vital, he was already dressed for his busy day in a dark grey suit and pale blue shirt that did sensational things to his golden features.

'Get up, get dressed and come and join me for breakfast,' he invited. 'I have a surprise for you.'

'A surprise?' she repeated, yawning while stretching.

'Mmm,' he murmured, and it was the sexiest murmur Antonia had ever heard in her entire life.

It brought an invitation to her eyes and a hand reaching up for him. 'Show me now,' she commanded in a tone which was demanding something else entirely.

He caught the hand, kissed it, then firmly replaced it back on the bed. 'Not on your life.' He grinned. 'You have to come downstairs looking prim for this surprise.'

And with that thoroughly intriguing statement he turned and strode out of the room. Antonia watched him go with a smile in her eyes, quietly amazed at how a night of loving could turn their relationship around. The man was an enigma of complicated mood codes: one minute looking as if he wished to see the back of her, the next almost dying with pleasure in her arms. Now he wanted to please her with surprises—though how he'd found the time to come up with anything to surprise her with at—she checked the bedside clock—seven o'clock in the morning was completely beyond her.

Innovative, that was what Marco was, she thought indulgently as she climbed out of the bed and went off to shower and dress, as instructed, in something prim. Her choice was a white tailored linen suit teamed with amber accessories that almost matched the colour of her eyes.

On her way to the breakfast room, she popped her head into the kitchen and was surprised to find no housekeeper there to exchange the usual morning greetings. Still frowning slightly at Carlotta's absence, she entered the sunny breakfast room to find her favourite breakfast bowl of fresh fruit and a steaming pot of hot coffee waiting for her on the table—and her favourite man reclining in his chair reading his morning newspaper.

But he paused to watch her walk towards him with his

eyes narrowed in male appreciation. '*Perfezione*,' he murmured, as she leant down to press a morning kiss to his ready lips.

'*Grazie*,' she returned in mocking relief. 'For this is about as prim as I get.'

The sun caught the strawberry highlights threading through her neatly pleated hair, and played sultry games with the amber colour of her conservatively styled silk blouse. On her feet she wore classically plain court shoes and a simple string of pearls she had owned for ever and didn't warrant locking away in Marco's safe circled her slender throat. Her make-up was so natural there was barely any sign of it and her smile said everything was right in her world.

'Where's Carlotta?' she asked as she sat down next to him.

'Called in sick,' Marco explained. 'I found her message waiting with our answering service, along with a hundred and one others…'

Antonia's hand froze momentarily on its way to pick up the coffee pot. Stefan, she remembered. Stefan had said he'd been leaving messages for her all last week. A small silence began to vibrate with the hum of expectancy while she waited for what Marco was going to say next.

But he said absolutely nothing, and when she dared a glance at him, he was behind his newspaper again. He wasn't going to mention Stefan's calls, she realised. And she was damned if she was going to mention them and put at risk all this wonderful harmony they had managed to recapture.

So, 'Did Carlotta say what was wrong?' she enquired instead.

The newspaper twitched, long brown fingers flexed

slightly, as if he was aware that she was aware of Stefan's calls and those fingers were reacting to the fact that she too was going to pretend they had never happened.

'Summer flu,' he replied. 'She does not wish to pass it on, so she expects to be away for the rest of the week.'

'Poor Carlotta. I must send her a get-well card,' she murmured, and finished pouring her coffee before transferring her attention to her bowl of fruit. 'Did you prepare this?' she asked.

'Mmm.' It was not quite the sexy *Mmm* of before. Was he angry? Was he annoyed that she wasn't going to ask about Stefan's calls?

'*Molti grazie, mi amante,*' she returned, determinedly keeping her tone light. 'This unusual act of servility is most definitely your biggest surprise to date.'

The husky dark tones of a very male laughter flipped her heart over, then it flipped again with relief when he folded the paper away and she was able to see the humour also reflected on his beautiful face.

He wasn't brooding about Stefan. He wasn't going to let this newly attained harmony spoil because of a few silly messages. 'Eat your fruit. Drink your coffee,' he advised indulgently. 'We have approximately ten minutes before we have to leave.'

'Leave?' She frowned. 'Why? Where are we going?'

'*I'm* going to Venice,' he replied as he got to his feet. 'And you, *mi bellisima*, are coming with me.'

With that, he dropped a casual kiss onto the top of her head and began to stroll arrogantly for the doorway.

But this time no warm smile followed him. No feeling of delight that he was planning to take her along on one of his business trips for the first time since she'd entered his life.

So much for protecting harmony, she mused grimly as she felt it all wither away. 'When did you decide this?' she fed quietly after him. 'Before or after you played back the messages?'

He stopped walking and turned, an almost saturnine figure with his features suddenly cast in bronze. 'Before,' he replied, earning himself a flash of scepticism. 'It was learning that Carlotta would not be around to play chaperon that clinched your fate for you,' he answered that scepticism. 'For no woman plays Marco Bellini false while he is safely ensconced elsewhere, *capisce*?'

Oh, she understood all right. He didn't trust her to be alone in Milan with Stefan in the same city. 'So the surprise you promised was never intended as a pleasant surprise,' she concluded, and smiled cynically. 'How typical of you to give with one hand and take back with the other.'

'On the contrary,' he argued. 'The trip to Venice could be a pleasure for both of us. It really depends on whether you want to make it so.'

'Or not, if I decide to stay here instead,' Antonia pointed out.

The threat had him walking back to her. When he reached her side, he bent to place one hand on the back of her chair, the other flat on the table. The way he loomed over her hinted at menace. Placing her fork in the bowl of fruit, Antonia refused to let her fingers shake as she placed them down on her lap, then sat back in the chair to face his hard gaze squarely.

'You prefer to stay here?'

His eyes held hers, and were loaded with challenge. Answer *yes* and she would be lying, not to mention confirming his suspicions about her motives. Answer *no* and she would be feeding his ego with something she had no wish to feed him now.

She went for the compromise. 'Stefan is my *friend*. Why can't you accept that?'

His eyes didn't waver, not for a second. 'Do you prefer to stay?' he repeated.

Hers did, though; they flickered away on a frown of irritation. 'Of course I would rather be with you,' she sighed. 'But not under duress, and *not* because you feel it's your only option!'

'I could throw you out. That's another option.'

'I could walk!' she lashed back. 'That's an even better one!'

'Are you coming?' The wretched man wasn't fazed in the slightest.

'Yes!' she snapped, and dislodged his hand by pushing back her chair and shooting to her feet with a jolt of anger.

He just sent her a mocking look. 'Then eat your fruit and drink your coffee,' he suggested, and with a wave of a hand walked away again. 'Come and get me from my study when you're ready to leave.'

'I'll need longer than ten minutes to clear up here before we go,' she threw impatiently after him.

'For you, *mi amante*, I will delay our flight!'

Magnanimous in victory, he left her standing there not sure whether to smile or scowl. The smile won, twitching impulsively at the corners of her mouth as she sat down to finish her fruit. Twenty minutes later she was annoyed again because he hadn't told her until just before they were leaving that they were going to stay over in Venice, so she hadn't bothered to pack a bag.

'Shop for what you need when we get there,' said the man to whom money had a different meaning.

'For want of a further five minutes it seems terribly extravagant,' she complained.

'Time is money to me, *cara*,' he pointed out.

'Then I'm sorry for costing you money while you waited,' she said primly. 'What a problem I am to you.'

Sarcasm or not, he slashed a grin at her. 'My biggest problem is going to be keeping my mind on business when I know you're within easy reach of me,' he murmured lazily.

'Then I hope you spend your meetings in a state of permanent distraction.'

'While you do what?'

'Spend your money as fast as I can produce the credit cards,' she answered.

He laughed, and kissed her until the lift arrived. After that it didn't really matter any more that he was only doing this to keep her and Stefan apart. The harmony was back, and she was happy to bask in it. Happy to bask beneath the amount of care and attention he paid her throughout their short flight to Venice and the ensuing journey along the canals until they came to their hotel.

Heads turned, people stared. She basked in that also. For being with a man like Marco Bellini was a bit like walking alongside royalty: paths were smoothed, people deferred. He was rich, he was known, he was handsome and single. Women envied her place in his life. Men envied all his many advantages.

Having safely delivered her to their hotel, he left her to her own devices while he went off to keep his appointments. She shopped till she'd dropped, and spent the rest of her time trailing around some of the tourist sites amongst the thick summer crowds and the heat that melted.

By the time she arrived back in their suite she was so exhausted it was all she could do to run a bath and sink into it. On the bed lay the smart designer bags to go with her new smart designer purchases. On the floor lay the scatter of her discarded clothes.

Letting himself in a few minutes later, Marco smiled at the evidence of her occupation. Antonia was untidy by nature, though she would make the effort to try not to be because she thought it must irritate him. Being brought up to strict rules set by a succession of nannies meant that regimental neatness had become second nature to him.

But it didn't irritate him. In truth, he liked to walk into a room and see instant proof of her presence. The bathroom door stood ajar, and from behind it he could hear the lazy slap of water which told him what she was doing now.

It was the easiest thing in the world to strip off his clothes and go in there to join her. Up to her neck in bubbles, she smiled as he approached, lifted her knees to allow him room to sit down opposite her, then, on a contented sigh fed her feet up his chest as he stretched his long legs on either side of her.

'Long day?' he enquired.

'Spent your money. Played tourist. Got too hot. Killed my feet. Came back here to die peacefully. And you?' she returned the enquiry.

'Made a few lira, invested a few lira.' His accompanying shrug said it was par for the course. 'Threw my impressive weight around a bit. Came back here to make love to this woman I know.'

Her eyes began to gleam. 'Is she any good?'

So did his. '*Molti bellisima*,' he softly confided, and picked up one of her feet to begin an expert massage to its slender sole. She liked that. Closing her eyes, she simply lay back and let him indulge her.

In fact Marco indulged her in many ways during the next few days. They dined in quiet out-of-the-way places where the tourists didn't go, walked hand in hand through narrow streets like dark caverns, and made love for most of the night. When he had to leave her to attend his meetings he made it brief, and secondary to what was really going on here in Venice.

Which was the steadily strengthening realisation that she was becoming more and more important to his happiness than he had ever allowed himself to believe before.

By the time they caught the flight home to Milan, on Friday afternoon, he knew he was almost ready to make the ultimate commitment. Only—

He wanted to see what Kranst had planned before he laid himself open. Antonia hadn't mentioned Kranst. *He* hadn't mentioned him. But had she been in touch with him? Did she know what Kranst was up to? Did she know that Marco was worrying about it?

Did she care?

He needed to know the answers before he made any kind of commitment because, damn it, he had his pride to protect here!

It was a hesitation that was going to cost him, though Marco couldn't have any way of knowing it then.

They arrived back at the apartment late on Friday afternoon, to find Carlotta back at her post and smiling her usual welcome. She thanked them for the postcards Antonia must have sent her, then went on to relay a series of messages, most of them business, but some from his mother wanting him to call her as soon as he got in.

'My father?' he questioned sharply.

But Carlotta shook her head. 'I asked,' she said. 'Your *mamma* assured me he was pleasingly well.'

So he nodded, and decided to leave any calls home until after this evening was over.

That was another mistake.

There were also several calls for Antonia from Stefan Kranst which, from their content, told him that Antonia had held faith and not attempted to contact Kranst while they'd been away. He wanted to wrap her in his arms and kiss her for that, but good sense warned him not to make an issue of it—just as she was sensibly asking no questions about that other taboo subject, his parents.

Franco rang as they were sharing a pot of coffee while relaxing for an hour in front of the TV before they needed to start getting ready to go out. Marco felt fine, very at peace with himself and the beautiful creature curled up beside him. He and Franco chatted as best friends do. He was thanked for the painting they'd given the de Maggios as an anniversary present, and for the thought which had gone into it, and tried to pass the whole thing off as if he knew exactly what Franco meant. But he didn't, and his gaze was sardonic when he remembered how easily he had let Antonia off without answering that little bone of contention between them. Then he suggested dinner somewhere after the Kranst showing.

It was at that moment that the tension began to creep in. Antonia sat up and away from him. Studying her profile, he heard Franco telling him that he and Nicola were not going tonight because they were spending the weekend up at Lake Como with her parents. Franco suggested Wednesday instead. Marco agreed, then hurriedly rang off.

'What's wrong?' he asked instantly.

'Nothing,' she replied. 'I think I'll go and get my shower now—'

But he wasn't so easily fooled. 'Kranst can only hurt you if you let him,' he said quietly.

'It isn't me Stefan hurts, Marco,' she replied, smiled a sad smile and walked away.

She was referring to him, of course, and it was a strange experience to acknowledge that she was right. Kranst did have the power to hurt him. He hurt Marco's pride and his ego, because the artist had a part of Antonia he had never been able to touch. What part that was exactly he had not been able to work out, but it had something to do with the way she refused to accept any hint of criticism where Kranst was concerned, whereas Marco she could find fault with very easily.

CHAPTER SIX

THE Romano Gallery claimed prestige position in the famous Quadrilatero. It was double-fronted in plate glass, with black steel framework, and Rosetta Romano's name made its point with eye-level modesty in black lettering on the door.

Class wasn't in it. Only people of substance dared place their fingers on that door. A black-suited lackey did it for Marco and Antonia, pulling it inwards with panache and a crisp, '*Buon giorno*, Signor Bellini—*signorina.*'

The interior was an artistic exhibit in its own right— white walls, white floor and a white stairway leading up to the main gallery rooms. Its only decoration was a single black spot, strategically placed on one wall to offer perspective.

Marco's hand at the base of her spine kept her moving towards the stairway. They took it together, climbing towards the two black-clothed waiters stationed at the top, holding trays loaded with glasses of champagne. Neither took a glass. To swallow right now would be an impossibility, with the tension rising steadily since they'd left the sitting room back at the apartment.

She had thought of ringing Stefan and insisting he explain about the painting so she could then decide whether to come or not. But two things had stopped her. One had something to do with a complicated thing called loyalty. To speak to Stefan just now seemed to be putting her loyalty to Marco into question. And the second was because she knew Marco would insist on coming here to-night no matter what she wanted to do. It was a male pride thing. Stefan had thrown him a challenge and Marco would rather slit his own throat than decline it.

But that didn't mean she hadn't spent time on her own, going over every painting from her days living with Stefan, looking for the one he had not shown in public before. As far as she could recall there wasn't one—which worried her all the more, because he had to have some-thing up his sleeve or he wouldn't have thrown down that teasing gauntlet to Marco in the first place.

Dressed from neck to toe in black, at least she blended in with the status quo tonight, she then observed, as her gaze flicked around a semi-packed ante-room that fed into the main viewing rooms. Her hair was up, caught in a twist of black velvet, and her only adornment was a gold chain necklace with a single tear-drop diamond that Marco had placed around her throat just before they left the apartment. The diamond nestled against the black of her dress and sparkled as she moved.

'Stunning,' Marco had called her. 'Too lovely to resist. Too perfect to touch.'

But she still didn't deserve his surname, she mused, with a mockery that was a long way from humorous.

'Ah, *buona sera*!' Rosetta Romano came to greet them with all the extravagance of an Italian hostess. 'Marco, *mi amore*…' Both elegant hands touched his face, then were replaced with kisses to both cheeks. 'Do you realise it must be over a year since you visited me here?'

It was a scold issued in the nicest possible way. While Marco said all the right things in reply Antonia studied Rosetta Romano, who had been a legend in her time for choosing husbands by the size of their wallets. Now that her beauty was fading she preferred to be known for her artistic eye. All the big names had exhibited here. Two years ago Stefan would not have stood a chance. Now—?

Rosetta turned her attention to Antonia. Her eyes sharpened, then narrowed searchingly. 'Yes.' She nodded. 'I see it. Stefan assured me I would. *Buona sera*, Signorina Carson,' she greeted with a slightly wry smile. 'It is a pleasure to meet you at last.'

Kisses on both cheeks were compulsory in Milan. The whisper Rosetta placed in her ear was most definitely not. 'Stefan is such a wicked man. I do hope you are prepared for this.'

No, she wasn't, and keeping that from showing on her face took a lot of self-control. But she wasn't able to stop the small anxious shiver from chasing down her spine. Marco felt it, and his hand moved on her waist to draw her closer to his side.

'What did she say to you?' he questioned when Rosetta floated away to greet her next arriving guests.

Antonia didn't even try to dress it up. 'She wanted to know if I was ready for whatever is coming,' she told him.

'And are you?' he asked curtly.

She flashed him a look. 'The point is, are you?' she coolly countered. 'Since you seem to believe that anything to do with me and Stefan is deliberately engineered to reflect badly on you.'

She was right and he knew it. A muscle flexed in his jaw. Then he was forced to offer an amiable smile to some friends who immediately accosted them. After that it was other friends. Progress towards their main objective became a laboriously slow affair. With his hand never leaving contact with her, Marco conversed lightly with acquaintances while Antonia stood beside him, eyes constantly looking around the steadily thickening crowd in search of Stefan. But still he hadn't put in an appearance.

What was he up to? Why was he piling on the tension like this?

People began filtering off into the adjoining rooms. With the smoothness of a man in no kind of hurry, Marco manoeuvred them into doing the same.

Antonia held her breath, Marco's hand pressed her just the bit closer to his side as they stepped through to the main gallery. Together they paused, together they took stock of what was presented—and together they began to frown.

For there was nothing on these walls that could warrant the challenge with which Stefan had lured them here—if you didn't count the evidence that Stefan had seemingly found himself a new subject to occupy his genius.

She was tall, she was dark, she was exquisitely different, and her rich African beauty could not have been further removed from what had gone before her. The long slender line of her body laid bare a sensuality that curled around the senses, the silken quality of her skin set fingers twitching with a need to reach out and touch. But, as usual, with Stefan, it was her eyes that drew you.

No hint of mirrors or ghosts anywhere, but a luxurious darkness that seemed to hold all the secrets of the universe.

Understanding came, trailing gentle fingertips over her emotions in the heart-rippling realisation that here, in these frames, was Stefan's salvation.

He had set himself free.

'Are you all right?' Marco asked gruffly.

'Yes,' she whispered. But he knew that she wasn't. He could feel her fighting a battle with tears as they walked from frame to frame. 'She's incredible, don't you think?'

'*Bellisima,*' Marco quietly agreed. And he knew he should be pleased by what he was seeing, but in truth he wanted to wring Kranst's selfish neck for choosing this way to tell her he had finally found someone else who drew this depth of emotion from him.

'I presume by your response that you knew nothing about her?'

'Not a thing,' she replied, having to swallow the tears again.

'Maybe you should ask him,' he suggested, and drew her attention to where Stefan Kranst was standing, not far away, watching her responses with an intensity that made Marco's blood boil.

Her head twisted round, her breath caught for a second, then her slender waist was sliding away from his hand. Without another word to him, she crossed the room to-wards a man who had always held too much power over her for Marco's peace of mind. Grimly he watched her pause a step away, watched her head tilt to one side as it tended to do when she asked a question. He saw Stefan Kranst's handsome face break into a rakish grin, and wanted to hit the self-obsessed bastard!

'Who is she?' was the question Antonia had put to Stefan.

'My saviour,' Stefan had grinned.

'Her name?' she demanded.

'Tanya,' he provided.

'Tanya…' Antonia repeated, and let her gaze drift to the nearest painting, where Tanya's smile held the rich knowledge of all men's needs. 'It suits her,' she murmured, then on a burst of soft laughter she went into his arms. 'Oh, I'm so happy for you!' she cried.

Across the room, Marco turned away from that embrace to continue to view the painting in front of him as if he had no problem at all with his woman falling into her ex-lover's arms once again. Someone sidled up beside him.

Of course it had to be Louisa. 'I do admire your confidence in those two, Marco,' she drawled lightly. 'Now, if, for argument's sake, *he* belonged to me, I would be over there scratching *her* eyes out by now.'

'But he doesn't belong to you—he belongs to her,' he said, indicating the beautiful black woman whose naked form exuded sexual contentment from every gifted brushstroke. 'And Antonia,' he then added very softly, 'belongs to me.'

With that he walked away, in no mood to play tit-for-tat word games tonight. He wanted his woman back, and he wanted her now!

'When do I meet her? Where is she?' Antonia was demanding of Stefan.

'Back in London, hiding away from you,' he drawled lazily. 'Just in case I was wrong about you, and you are secretly in love with me.'

Catching her soft burst of laughter as he approached, Marco also heard Antonia's amused reply. 'Of course you told her that I will always love you?'

'Hello, Marco,' Stefan greeted, a trifle drily. 'Come to claim Antonia?'

The man could read minds.

'We have to be leaving soon,' Marco answered smoothly. 'Another engagement, I'm afraid,' he invented with bland ease.

The moment he began speaking Antonia moved to his side and slipped her hand into the crook of his arm. She was making a point here, Marco recognised. And it should feel good.

So why did he feel as if she was taking second best by coming to him like this?

Irritation flicked to life. What the hell was he talking about? He scorned his own crazy imagination. He had never played second best to anyone in his life!

'Dare I ask the expert for an opinion?' Kranst reclaimed his attention. His expression was slightly wry, slightly challenging Marco to do his worst.

But Marco found he no longer wanted to play tit-for-tat games with Kranst, either. He just wanted to get Antonia somewhere private so he could make her forget Stefan Kranst's name!

So, 'You must know you've done it again,' he said easily. 'Have you sold the reproduction rights yet?'

'Still negotiating.' Stefan smiled. Then, 'Thank you, Marco,' he added seriously. 'Your opinion means a lot to me.'

And to your reputation, Marco added silently. Though anyone with eyes should be able to see that the man was about to make his second killing here.

Glancing down, he found Antonia was smiling up at him as if he had just bestowed the greatest accolade he possibly could. It made him want to shake her for still caring so much about Kranst's precious ego when it was clear the man didn't give a damn about hers!

'It's time we were leaving,' he told her, wishing they hadn't bothered to come here at all. The man was a menace—to him and to Antonia!

'Before you do that,' Stefan Kranst inserted, looking at

Antonia, 'I have something for you, my darling, if you remember…'

Beside him, Marco felt her stiffen. 'You mean this isn't surprise enough?' she laughed, in a voice strapped by strain.

'No.' The artist's smile was rueful. 'Special gifts come in solid form.'

Marco frowned at the answer, because it wasn't true. Not where Antonia was concerned. It was a lesson he had learned himself only last week via the red Lotus. Then he remembered Kranst's remark about the *Mirror Woman*, felt his own tension rise up to meet Antonia's, and realised that she had remembered a whole lot sooner than he had done.

'I have it waiting in Rosetta's office,' Stefan Kranst said smoothly, and turned away to stride purposefully towards Rosetta Romano's private office.

It really left them with no choice but to follow. 'This had better be worth the build-up,' Marco muttered, unable to stop himself.

'I hope not,' Antonia mumbled in reply, which just about said it all for both of them.

Rosetta Romano's office was a large white space of modern stylism. The only thing, therefore, that stood out in the room, was the giant black easel holding a large frame covered by a piece of fine black muslin.

The moment she saw it Antonia released a gasp of recognition, 'Stefan…no!' she shot out.

But Stefan was not willing to listen. He was already standing beside the easel and, with an agonising smoothness he trailed away the fine sheet covering.

Total silence arrived in starbursts of pain-bright recognition. Antonia began to tremble. Marco simply left her standing there and moved on legs suddenly in danger of collapsing to stand right in front of the painting.

It could have been a copy of the *Mirror Woman*. Certainly it was the same balcony, the same morning half-light touching that same sensual hint of gold to her silk-smooth skin. And it was certainly Antonia standing there naked, looking back over her shoulder in much the same way as the Mirror Woman did.

But it wasn't the same painting. For this was no mirror reflection, there was no emptiness in her beautiful eyes. Instead they were filled with the truth.

Antonia was held paralysed by exposure, static eyes fixed on Marco's hardening profile, static heart threatening to burst in her breast. She wanted to run, but she couldn't. She wanted to say something in her defence, but she couldn't do that because the evidence was so terribly damning.

Stefan came to stand beside her. His hand took hold of her hand and gave it a comforting squeeze. But she didn't feel comforted. Standing here watching the man she loved grimly coming to terms with the knowledge that she had been deceiving him filled her with the kind of dread that made every nerve-end she possessed scream in agony.

'I can't believe you've done this without my approval,' she managed to breathe out fraily.

'If I had asked, you wouldn't have given it,' Stefan gently replied.

'But *why* have you done it?' It seemed such a betrayal from the one person in this world she trusted completely.

'It was time he knew,' he said simply. 'You've let it go on too long. You must know that by now, my darling.'

Knowing it and wanting *this* were two separate issues! 'You should not have done it,' she whispered, and felt her eyes start to burn as Marco reached out to touch the painting. A long finger gently grazed across a perfectly formed, blemish-free shoulder. Antonia felt that graze as if he'd reached out and touched her. Response shuddered through her on an electric spasm.

'I'll never forgive you,' she told Stefan, and stepped away from him with the intention of going to this other man who was so very important to her—

Only to freeze yet again, when Marco chose the same moment to turn.

His face looked as if it had been chiselled out of marble. 'You didn't paint this.' He honed his cold eyes directly on Stefan.

It was a clearly defined accusation. 'There speaks the voice of an expert,' Stefan smiled. Then, 'No,' he admitted. 'This was—'

'Mine,' Antonia put in unequivocally. 'It belongs to me!' She looked at Marco for understanding. 'It isn't even Stefan's to give to me! I *own* it! No one is supposed to—'

Marco's hard-eyed narrowed look silenced her. 'Who painted it?' he demanded.

'Does it matter?' she begged. 'It has never been put on public display and it never will be, Marco! I never—'

'I didn't ask if it had been shown,' he cut in. 'I asked you who the hell painted it!'

His fury was spectacular. Antonia drew back a step in dismay. 'I think you're missing the point, Marco,' Stefan put in quickly. 'I didn't show you this to—'

It happened so quickly that Stefan had no time to react to it. With a smoothness of movement that gave no indication whatsoever of what he was intending to do, Marco took two strides and, with a lightning move of his long lean body, he floored Stefan with a punch to his jaw.

With a grunt, Stefan landed in a sprawl in front of him. Antonia's cry as she lurched towards them filled his ears. 'Why did you do that!' she choked as she bent down beside Stefan.

'For messing with your life. For messing with *my* life!' he ground out violently, then just turned and strode out of the door.

Antonia watched him go with her heart in her eyes. On a groan, Stefan sat up and put a hand to his jaw. He was shaking his head as if he couldn't quite believe he had allowed that to happen.

'What have you done to me?' Antonia sobbed out.

'Fulfilled one of your dearest wishes and got him to punch my lights out,' Stefan very drily replied.

Not the least bit in the mood for his kind of dry humour, she came upright then bent to help him get up. 'Has he hurt you?' she asked.

'Don't sound so sympathetic.' He mocked her frosty enquiry. 'Split my lip, that's all,' he then answered, only to really infuriate her by suddenly beginning to laugh!

'Stop it!' she choked. 'How dare you laugh at a time like this? What have you *done* to me, Stefan? *Why* have you done it?' The tears began to swim as she stared at the closed office door. 'He's never going to forgive me for this. You do know that,' she told him thickly. 'He's even left without me!'

'Not that man,' Stefan stated confidently. 'Give me a minute to put some ice on this, and we'll go out there and find him. I promise you,' he assured her pained white expression, 'he's going to be there...'

But Marco didn't want to be found for, having walked out on one ugly scene, he now found himself standing outside Rosetta Romano's door, flexing his abused fist and staring directly at the looming threat of yet another scene.

His mother had arrived. God alone knew where she had come from—and God alone knew why, when he'd believed her safely ensconced in Tuscany. But there she was, holding court in the middle of the ante-room surrounded by a host of delighted old friends and acquaintances.

In the black mood he was in, he actually contemplated pretending he hadn't seen her and getting the hell out of there before she saw him!

Only he was not leaving without Antonia, he determined, with a grimness that promised a glimpse at hell for someone. And it took only a thin sliver of common sense to get through his anger, to tell him that he couldn't avoid speaking to his own mother, for goodness' sake!

But a meeting between her and Antonia? His blood ran cold at the very idea of it. It was a sensation that forced him to work hard at pulling a smooth mask down on his bubbling anger and then striking out towards his mother with the grim intention of getting the mother-son reunion out of the way *before* Antonia decided to put in an appearance with her famous ex-lover in tow!

But lady luck was not working in Marco's favour tonight. The room was pretty crowded with Milan's best. People who more or less knew each other on first-name terms. Isabella Bellini was known and liked by many. Her son even found an amused smile as he approached and saw just how many people were gathered around her slender form.

She saw him coming, and her lovely face broke into a welcoming smile. His smile became a rakish grin as he took this beautiful, delicate creature he adored into his arms and let her shower kisses all over his face.

Hands replaced kisses, followed by remarks to the crowd on how handsome he was, how cruel he was to his mother for not returning her calls. It was the Italian way. He accepted it and even enjoyed it. His apologies were profuse, his enquiries about his father sincere.

'He is having a good week,' his mother informed him— and the smiling circle. 'So he threw me out and told me not to come back for at least two days. He says I fuss too much, but in truth,' she confided, 'he plans to play cards, drink wine and gamble with his friends without me around to disapprove.'

The laughter was warm and appreciative. From the corner of his eye Marco saw the door to Rosetta Romano's office open; his skin began to prickle.

Isabella looked back at her son. 'And this one,' she announced, 'cannot even find the time in his busy life to answer his mother when she calls to him! I get his housekeeper,' she informed her audience.

Antonia was approaching him from his right. She looked pale, she looked anxious. She had no idea what she was going to walk into.

'I get the message service,' his mother was continuing. 'I have to ring his friends to discover where he might be this evening!' Marco smiled the expected rueful smile, and wondered which friend it was who had dropped him in this mess.

Antonia had now come to within a few paces of his right. Beside her was Stefan Kranst, wearing a bruise on his lip and a crooked smile. It was decision time, Marco accepted heavily. He either drew Antonia towards him, introduced her to his mother and risked offending his mother's outdated ideas on what was acceptable in polite society, or he ignored Antonia standing there and offended her. It was a lousy choice to have to decide.

Someone arrived at his left side, diverting his mother's attention. Her face broke into a beatific smile. 'Ah, Louisa,' she greeted. 'There you are! And looking so beautiful, as always. I was just telling everyone how I had to call you up to discover where my own son would be tonight…'

Louisa. It had to be Louisa, Marco noted grimly. The knowledge tipped the balance of his decision away from his mother. For no one had the right to try manipulating either him or his life, and maybe it was about time that his mother and Louisa realised that!

Louisa was being welcomed with the usual kisses from his mother when Marco turned the half-inch it required to catch Antonia's gaze. He saw the uncertainty there, the knowledge that she had recognised whom it was holding centre stage. His heart turned over. She was so beautiful. So much his woman, no matter what secrets she had been keeping from him, that it was suddenly no decision at all to smile and hold out his arm in invitation for her to come to him.

Her relief shone like the diamond at her lovely throat as she took the final irrevocable step which brought her beneath the protection of his arm and into the smiling circle.

Slender-boned, exquisitely turned out in matt-black crêpe, her satin-black hair sleek to her beautiful head, Isabella Bellini was just emerging from her embrace with Louisa when she observed this little interplay—and her eyes began to cool.

'Mother,' Marco said formally. 'I would like you to meet—'

As if he hadn't spoken, and Antonia wasn't there, Isabella Bellini simply turned her back on them. The deadening silence that followed was profound.

It was such a blatantly deliberate act, that it was all Antonia could do to remain standing there, with her stinging eyes lowered, hiding the deep gouge of humiliation that was tearing into the very fabric her pride was made of.

While Marco emulated a pillar of stone.

How many people actually witnessed what had just happened, Antonia didn't know. But it really didn't take an audience for her to understand that the cuckoo had just been devastatingly exposed.

The hum of conversation suddenly rushed into overdrive as people attempted to cover up the dreadful moment. Someone gently touched her arm. It was Stefan. 'That—' he growled, 'was unforgivable.'

She began to shake. Stefan glanced angrily at Marco, who still hadn't moved a single muscle. Then, 'Come on,' he murmured gruffly. 'Let's go back to Rosetta's—'

'No,' a hard voice countermanded. And with it Marco broke free from his stone-like stasis. 'We are leaving,' he announced.

The hand tightened on her shoulder. Antonia could feel the anger in its biting grip and clenched the muscles beneath it.

'I'm coming with you,' Stefan declared, still gripping Antonia's arm. 'I have no wish to—'

'No.' Once again Marco cut him short. 'We appreciate your concern, but this is not your problem.'

'It is when it's Antonia who has been insulted,' Stefan said angrily.

'And *my* mother who did the insulting,' Marco coldly pointed out.

'Excuse me,' Antonia whispered, and broke free from both of them. She needed to get away from here, and she needed to do it now. Fighting tears, fighting the crawling worms of humiliation, fighting to keep her head up high as she went, she walked quickly for the stairs.

If she'd cared to look back, she would have seen that Marco's mother was already feeling the discomfort of what she had done. She was touching her son's arm, trying to get his attention. But Marco didn't even offer her a glance as he strode after Antonia. His hand found her waist and clamped her close. Together they started down the stairs. In her haste Antonia tripped over her own spindly shoes. Marco grimly held her upright, and kept her moving while the throb of his anger pulsed all around her like the heartbeat pound of a drum.

They reached the plate-glass door at the same time as the doorman pulled it open. Neither realised the door was being opened to allow someone outside to come in. There was a bump of bodies.

'*Scuze signor—signorina,*' a deep, quietly modulated voice apologised.

It was automatic to glance up. Automatic to attempt the polite reply to the apology. Antonia looked into the stranger's face, he looked into hers, and any attempt to speak was thoroughly suffocated beneath yet another thick layer of appalled dismay.

Black hair spiked with silver, grey eyes with a hint of green. As tall as Marco, but more slender than Marco, he was a man in the autumn years of his life.

Still, she knew exactly who it was she was staring at—and, worse, he knew that she knew.

'*Madonna mia*,' he breathed in shaken consternation. 'Anastasia.'

Anastasia... It was too much in one short evening for Antonia to deal with. It was all she could do to shrink back into the only solid thing she could rely on right now.

Marco might be immersed in the red tide of anger, but he saw the exchanged looks, heard the name shudder from the other man's lips. Knew there was yet something else going on here that he wasn't privy to, and felt his anger switch from his mother and back to the woman now shrinking into his side.

'You are mistaken,' he clipped at the other man. 'Please excuse us,' he added coldly, then got them the hell out of there before anything else smashed into them.

Outside, the Quadrilatero was busy with window-shoppers. Marco's car was parked in a side street not far away. Holding on to his temper until he got them there was a case of clamping his mouth shut and saying nothing.

Opening the passenger door, he helped her into the plush black leather seat, then squatted down to lock home her seat belt. She didn't seem to notice. With yet another lash of anger, he grabbed her chin and made her look at him. Her eyes were almost black, her skin paste-white and her lovely mouth completely bloodless. She looked as fragile as a piece of fine Venetian glass, likely to shatter without careful handling.

But he didn't feel like handling anything carefully. In fact, he wanted to shatter her into little pieces so he could reach the real woman, because this one had become a complete stranger to him!

With a harsh sigh he released her chin, stood up and closed the car door. He got in beside her, then fired the engine. Jaw locked, teeth clenched, he set them moving, bullying his way into the nose-to-tail traffic clogging up Milan's crazy one-way road system, then took an amount of pleasure in doing the same thing in his quest to forge them the most direct route home.

Car horns blared at him in protest. Headlights flashed. Abuse was thrown at him in colourful Italian. He didn't care. He was so angry! Angry with Kranst and his little party piece. With his mother and her unforgivable behaviour! And he was angry with Antonia for allowing him to believe the painting he had in his apartment was of her!

And then there was the man in the gallery doorway, he added to his long list of grievances because, despite appearing otherwise, he'd recognised him. His name was Anton Gabrielli, a wealthy industrialist turned recluse, who had rarely been seen in public since his wife died several years ago.

And he might have called Antonia *Anastasia*, but the error had been irrelevant. He *knew* her! And, more to the point, Antonia had recognised him!

'How do you know Anton Gabrielli?' he demanded.

It was like talking to a puppet. 'I've never met him before in my life,' she answered woodenly.

'Don't lie to me!' he rasped. 'He may have got your name wrong, but you knew each other all right. The mutual horror was all too revealing.'

'I said I've never met him before!' she shouted. It was so out of character that he threw a sharp look at her. No puppet now, he noted. She was shaking so badly that it made the diamond at her throat shimmer. On a choked little gasp, she turned her face right away from him so he couldn't read it. It was the act of someone caught in a lie.

Without another word, he turned his attention to getting through the traffic, while a new filthy suspicion began to tear into him. Anton Gabrielli was about the same age as Kranst. If she'd enjoyed Kranst as a lover then why not Gabrielli? After all, what did he actually know about Antonia's life before Kranst?

Nothing, he realised. Absolutely nothing.

As the ugly green stuff began to replace his blood again, he finally managed to reach his goal and pulled them to a screeching stop in the basement car park of his apartment. He switched off the engine—then clamped a hard hand on Antonia's thigh as she released her seat belt.

'Stay,' he gritted. It was a dire warning. She wasn't going to make him kick his heels down here for a second time while she rode the lift alone.

The fingers fluttered, then went to rest on her lap, her body melting back into the seat. With a tight hiss of satisfaction he got out, swung round the car, opened her door then bent to help her alight.

The lift took them upwards, with her shaking like crazy and him with his fists clenched to stop him taking hold of her and shaking her some more! When they reached the apartment door it was Marco who opened it; Antonia didn't seem capable. But, once inside, the few seconds it required for him to deactivate the alarm system gave her the chance to get away from him.

She headed straight for the bedroom. He stayed where he was long enough to utter a few choice curses before grimly striding after her. If she'd locked the bedroom door on him then she was in for one hell of a shock! he vowed.

But the door wasn't locked. And what he found when he tossed it back on its hinges stunned him to a complete standstill.

CHAPTER SEVEN

'—What the hell are you doing?' he raked out incredulously.

But he could see what she was doing. A suitcase already lay open on the bed and she was tossing things into it like a criminal on the run.

'Antonia!' he demanded when she didn't answer.

'I'm l-leaving,' she stammered, then froze within the midst of what he realised was full-scale panic to stand with body stiff, arms straight, fists tightly clenched, while she fought a battle with whatever emotion was suddenly trying to overwhelm her.

'The hell you are,' he grimly countered, but his own voice no longer sounded quite so steady.

He began striding towards her, and the act jolted her back from wherever she'd gone to and she turned on him, paste-white, stark-eyed—he had never seen an expression like it in all his life.

'*Cara…*' he murmured hoarsely. 'For goodness' sake…'

'I'm leaving you, Marco!' She almost screamed the words at him she was so out of control. 'Now—tonight! I n-never want to see you again.'

The fact that he could see it had almost killed her to say that didn't make him feel any better, because he could see she actually meant it—and that was scaring the life out of him.

She turned back to the suitcase. With a swipe of his

hand he sent it flying to the floor. Clothes scattered everywhere. Silly things like a couple of sets of underwear, a couple of skirts, a couple of simple cotton tops.

He tried swallowing and found he couldn't. He tried making sense of the evidence he was looking at. He couldn't do that either. For no woman—*no woman!*—left Marco Bellini with only the clothes she'd come to him with!

No woman left Marco Bellini.

'You aren't going anywhere until you've answered some questions,' he growled, and grabbed her hand. 'Maybe once you've done that I'll be glad to see the back of you!' he threw in for furious good measure, and began trailing her behind him out of the bedroom and down the hall while she tried her best to get free of him.

No chance, he vowed silently. No damn chance.

Throwing open the door to his study, he strode them over to the locked door. Still holding her hand prisoner, he stabbed in the security pin-number, hauled her inside, then over to the *Mirror Woman.*

'Now, let's start right here,' he gritted. 'Who is *she*?'

Anastasia, Antonia thought tragically, and began shaking all over again, fighting a battle with tears that reached right down to her abdomen. Sad, tragic—beautiful Anastasia.

'Mirror—mirror,' she whispered thickly.

'What is that supposed to mean?' Marco said harshly.

It was no use lying, no use trying to pretend that she didn't know what he was talking about. The game was up. She had been exposed as the fraud she was.

'This,' she said, 'is Anastasia...'

It took a few moments, then it hit him. 'My God,' he rasped. 'Are you saying that she is your twin?'

A laugh left her throat on a strangled sob. Her amber eyes shimmered with tears and a pained kind of humour, because Anastasia would have *so* loved to have been here to hear this big handsome Italian say that.

'No, not my twin,' she murmured softly. 'She was my mother…'

My poor, wretched, haunted mother, she silently extended, while the silence grew thick all around her.

'Mother,' Marco repeated, as if he had to do so to understand the concept. 'You mean, you and Kranst actually….'

The words stopped. Antonia turned to look at him. For once he was literally floundering on the rocks of shock. And he looked white. He looked horrified.

'What?' she snapped as anger began flooding up from the depths of a bitter knowledge of where they were about to go with this. 'Did we collaborate to deceive everyone? Yes.' She openly admitted the charge. 'Did I pose nude for Stefan so he could pretend I was my mother? No, I did not,' she denied that. 'Stefan and my mother were lovers for ten years! He adored her. And no *again*, before the cogs inside your head start turning to something nasty,' she sliced at him. 'Stefan did *not* bed-swap between my mother and myself!'

'I was not about to assume—' Marco began stiffly.

But angrily she cut in. 'You've *always* assumed!' she cried. 'From the very beginning you assumed we were lovers. But Stefan is my *friend*!' she threw at him. 'My dear, dear friend who arrived in our lives when we really needed someone warm and loving and endlessly giving like him! Between us, we nursed my mother through a long and miserable illness. And the result of those dark years?' She gestured with a trembling hand towards the painting. 'How my mother *wanted* Stefan to remember her. Not the withered and worn-out shell she became towards the end!'

Tears flooded her eyes. She looked away from him, her whole torso heaving with the fight for control.

'So he painted a lie,' Marco said grimly.

'And what if he did?' she replied. 'What does it matter to anyone else that the image they see isn't the gruesome reality?'

'Hence the mirror.' Oh, he was very good, she had to give him that.

'It reflects what was,' she confirmed. 'Stefan could pick up a paintbrush even now and paint her looking exactly like this. He loved her so very much...'

'Yet he was quick to sell these when opportunity knocked,' Marco pointed out cynically. 'And he was quick to let you masquerade as her to add a bit of juicy notoriety to the sales!'

'I didn't say he was perfect,' she snapped. 'And the paintings went on show *before* my mother died!' she pronounced. 'At *her* request! For *her* pleasure! It *amused* her when people mistook me for her! And *anything* that made her happy, Stefan and I gave her!' Her eyes flashed, tear-bright but unrepentant.

His hardened into bitterness. 'That's all fine for everyone else. But don't you think you owed it to me to tell me the truth?'

'Why should I have done that?' she gasped out in angry bewilderment. 'You got what you came looking for, Marco,' she told him. 'You got the woman in the painting. You had no interest in me as a living breathing human being!'

Two streaks of colour hit his cheekbones, his whole body stiffened in affront. 'That's not true,' he denied.

'Yes, it is,' she insisted. 'Take away the kudos in being able to lay claim to Stefan Kranst's notoriously sexy model, and it would take away the desire; I always knew that.'

He didn't answer. For her, his silence said it all. Looking back at her mother for one last time, Antonia touched a gentle finger to the tiny birthmark on her shoulder, smiled a sad 'I love you' smile, then withdrew again, curling her fingers into her palms as she turned for the door.

'Where are you going?'

She paused, but didn't look back. 'Home,' she whispered. 'I'm going home. There's nothing left for me here.'

'I'm here,' Marco murmured gruffly.

'No, you're not.' Antonia shook her head. 'You're standing aloft in a place I can never reach you. It's called the social ladder. You don't mind coming down to the bottom rung to enjoy life with the masses now and then, but when it comes to elevating someone up to your top rung—no chance.' She laughed. It was a bitter sound. 'Élite marries élite. Darling Mamma expects it.'

'Leave my mother out of this,' he rasped back angrily.

'But why should I?' she spun round to demand. He looked so grim and remote it was almost as if he was already climbing back up that ladder and away from her. 'In truth,' she said, 'I'm actually grateful for what your mother did tonight. Because she forced me to take a good look and see just how I had been wasting my life living here with you.'

'Wasting it because I haven't asked you to marry me?' he threw back with contempt. 'Is that what your year-long investment in me has really been about, *cara*? Give a man what you think he wants. Lie to him, cheat him if necessary, in the wild hope that the dividend will give back the jackpot billionaire with all the luxury trimmings?'

He saw himself as the *jackpot*? 'You arrogant bastard,' she said scornfully, 'I invested in *love*!' she cried. 'As in my love for you being strong enough to ignite some love back by return! But it never happened, did it, Marco?' Her eyes began to shine like the diamond at her throat. 'And even after a whole year of living together you can still freeze up in dismay when confronted with the disapproval of your mother, *and still stand here* and toss your contempt at me for actually daring to think myself fit to marry you!'

'I did *not* freeze in shame because of *you*!' he raked back angrily. 'I froze in shame of my wretched mother!'

But he was shouting it to an empty space. Antonia had already walked away. For all of five seconds he remained where he was, wanting to just let her go and stew in her own dignity. But then he remembered the suitcase on the floor of the bedroom and calculated how quickly it would take her to repack it.

Anger shot through him. Curses rattled from his tense lips. But alarm set his feet moving. He hated it—*hated feeling like this*!

Sure enough she was in the bedroom, standing over the bloody case. 'All right!' he lashed out. 'Marry me! If that is what it takes to stop this—craziness. Marry me—*marry me!*'

She turned to look at him. It was like watching snow cover a mountain her skin turned so white. Then the rain came, flooding into those beautiful amber eyes and her lips erupted with an agonised quiver.

Shaken to the roots by his own proposal, stunned beyond movement by her response, he watched one of her hands come out and give a flick in a bitter throw away gesture. Then she began walking towards him. His skin came alive to a million bee-stings; his heart lost the ability to beat. When she reached him she paused, and those awful tear-washed eyes looked right into his.

'May you go to hell, Marco,' she whispered thickly, then pushed him out of the way so that she could get past him.

It took him several moments to gain the will to move again. By then, a door further down the hallway had shut and the key had been turned. Staring round the chaos she had left behind her, he suddenly felt like a man standing in the middle of a ruin. Helpless, hopeless, unable to come to terms with how quickly it had all come tumbling down around him.

His legs eventually managed to take him forward, his feet picking their way through the debris of her clothes. Sitting down on the bed, he leant forward and clasped his head between long tense fingers.

He could have played an old scene again and gone charging after her, but it didn't even come up as an option this time. She needed to cool off, and he needed to get a grip on what had just happened because at this precise moment he didn't have a single clue!

One minute he had been the one with all the grievances, the next Antonia had been spilling hers out all over him. His sigh was heavy, shot with a residue of anger and frustration because so much of what she had thrown at him was true!

Her mother…he remembered, and got up with a swing of his body that responded to a sudden clutch of dismay.

His feet took him back to his study, took him back to the *Mirror Woman* where he stood gazing into a face he'd believed he knew. But the differences were already manifesting themselves, as if someone had come along and altered certain brushstrokes. The curve of her eyebrows, the tilt of her jaw, the way her slender neck blended into her slender shoulders. The birthmark he'd assumed was the artist's carelessness with his paintbrush. All very subtle differences that only an expert eye would ever notice.

He'd thought he had that expert eye. He'd believed he was a great connoisseur, when in actual fact Antonia was right and he was merely one of many, seeing only what he wanted to see.

Now he could look at this sad creature and pick out a hundred differences between her and her beautiful daughter—if he could bring himself to look at the rest of her, that was. It felt like a sin to do so now. He'd always thought Kranst the voyeur in this painting, and it didn't sit comfortably to realise that the real voyeur had been himself.

It made him want to turn the darn thing to the wall and forget he'd ever seen it. But—

This was Antonia's *mother*, he reiterated bleakly. Antonia loved this woman. It had been there in every word that she spoke! To turn her to the wall would be a rejection of someone who was as precious to Antonia as his own mother was to him.

Though he didn't want to think about his own mother right now, he accepted with an angry hardening of his jaw.

And Antonia had never been uncomfortable with the nudity in this painting. Her discomfort had been in looking at someone she had loved and lost, not the nudity itself.

Not her own nudity—or her mother's, he extended, as many things began to make sense. She had lived for ten years with an artist who specialised in the naked female form. He had a gift—no, a genius—for the genre, therefore it was only natural that she would learn to see nudity as something to appreciate in its own right, and not something to turn away from in shame. As it had been to him until he discovered who it was he was actually looking at!

Since when had he developed a bigot's view of something this special? Marco asked himself. This was art! Master-class art! If he'd been in a better frame of mind, he would have been purchasing one of Kranst's latest offerings. And not just for the investment, but because he *liked* what Kranst painted on the canvas!

But *who* had painted Antonia's nude image? he then asked himself, and felt his whole sophisticated outlook tumble like a house of cards. Anger enveloped him, spewing forth from a strange place inside him that could now accept Kranst as her painter—but not some other man!

How the heck had she managed to divert him so thoroughly that he hadn't demanded some answers about him? And there was Anton Gabrielli lurking in the shadows.

Behind Marco the telephone started ringing. If it did nothing else it diverted his attention away from what was beginning to flood his veins again.

He walked over to his desk and stood there making no attempt to pick up the receiver. His mother? he wondered. Wanting to voice her disapproval in more detail? Kranst, wanting to know if Antonia was still alive?

He let his answering service take over. By the time it

had silenced the telephone ring he had closed the door on the study. He didn't want to talk to anyone, and he certainly didn't want to listen to them prose all over him.

What he wanted was Antonia. But not yet, he grimly reiterated. And not at all tonight, until all of these ugly feelings rattling around inside him had been given a chance to calm down.

Antonia's insides were shaking, the fight to hold back the tears strangling the ability to breathe. Without really knowing what she was doing, she walked over to the bed and began tugging at the back zip to her dress as if it was perfectly natural to undress—when in actual fact she should be getting away from here. Not hiding behind a locked door which only extended the agony!

The zip snagged between her shoulderblades. She struggled with it for a while, with her head lowered and her eyes concentrated on the diamond at her throat. The zip wouldn't budge. It seemed a kind of justice, after the night she had just had, that it should do so at a point where she had no hope of wriggling out of the dress. On a trembling sigh of frustration she diverted her fingers to the necklace, removed it, then just stood there staring at nothing.

Had he really had the gall to offer to marry her, then stand there looking as if he'd just committed a mortal sin?

'Oh.' She choked on a tear that managed to escape. I should hate him. I should hate him for saying it the way he did, she told herself. But it wasn't hate she was feeling, it was hurt, because he hadn't meant it. He had merely been determined to grab the higher ground in an argument which made little sense to begin with! What a dreadful night, she sighed out bleakly. What a terrible, eye-opening, miserable night.

Beginning with Stefan springing that painting on them without warning. Then moving on to Marco's mother's neat little snub that was still managing to crease her up with pained mortification.

And, if all of that wasn't enough, she had to come face to face with Anton Gabrielli. A shiver ripped through her as something hard and cold turned pain to anger. How he dared to even whisper her mother's name after what he had done to her, she would never know!

But to do it in front of Marco of all people, was the ultimate sin she would never forgive Gabrielli for. *He* had been the final ruin of everything. *He* was the reason she had to leave here or risk the kind of scandal Marco would never forgive her for.

Did Anton Gabrielli know? Had he guessed by now that he had just come face to face with his daughter?

Then—no. She denied that. She was *not* his daughter. His was merely the seed which had formed the base of her conception. She'd never known him, never met him and didn't want to. In fact, she would rather remain the notorious Mirror Woman than lay claim to a father who had deserted her mother as soon as he'd known she was pregnant.

And what immortal words had he used to do it? 'Men like me don't marry their mistresses. It is not your function.'

God, she hated him.

Therefore she should hate Marco too, since he had used similar words to her not that long ago. What would his mother say if she knew about Anton Gabrielli? 'The sins of the mother,' would be oh, so appropriate. The same looks, the same paintings, the same attraction to tall dark handsome Italian billionaires!

Bitterness welled. Tears still cut her throat in two. She turned for the door with the intention of keeping to her original decision and just getting away from here!

Yet when she reached the door she just couldn't do it! Oh, what was to become of her if she couldn't even bring herself to walk away now, when there was nothing left for her here? Nothing!

'I'm here,' Marco had said to her.

Wrapping her arms around her body, she hugged that gruffly spoken statement to her for all she was worth as her restless feet took her the other way, over to the huge floor-to-ceiling windows which gave access out onto the terrace.

Sliding one of them open, she stepped outside in the vague hopes that some fresh air would clear her confusion. But it was stifling out here after the air-conditioned interior. Still, rather than go back inside, she moved over to one of the sun loungers, slipped out of her shoes, sat down and curled her knees up so she could rest her chin on them.

The terrace was a very impressive part of the apartment, which wrapped round two full sides of the building. When Marco threw one of his extravagant parties all the doors would be opened so every room leading in from the terrace could be used for one function or another. And the sound of music and life and laughter would follow you everywhere.

But tonight it was more silent than she'd ever known it. Even Milan's constant traffic way down below her seemed to have stopped running.

Or maybe it's me who's stopped, Antonia mused bleakly. The way fate had come along and hit her with just about everything tonight, it could be its way of making her stand still and face reality.

But she didn't want reality, she thought with a sigh that sent her brow onto her knees. She wanted things back the way they used to be—lies, uncertainties and all...

CHAPTER EIGHT

IT WAS around two o'clock in the morning when Marco slid open the door to the terrace and stepped outside. Behind him lay the rumpled bed he had just given up on. He couldn't sleep. The bed felt strange without Antonia sharing it with him. So he'd pulled on a thin black robe and gone to the kitchen to raid the fridge before deciding to come out here to eat his sandwich, drink a glass of soothing red wine—and brood.

Making for one of the loungers, he adjusted the backrest into its upright position, sat down, then stretched out his long legs with an accompanying sigh.

It was a hot humid night, but anything was preferable to that bed without Antonia in it with him. In fact, he might just spend the rest of the night out here.

It was either this or he convinced Antonia to open her door for him. And since he'd lasted this long without giving in to that particular urge, he could last until dawn, he told himself, and made his shoulders more comfortable against the cushions, took a sip at the wine, then closed his eyes.

It was peaceful, he noticed. Pleasant, if you didn't count the heat. And the darkness was acting like a shroud, holding at bay all of those things he didn't want to think about.

Shame a soft sound had to disturb him. In fact he would have ignored it if there hadn't been something very familiar about it, like one of those sensual soft sighs Antonia had a habit of making when she was sleeping.

Opening his eyes again, he turned his head.

She was less than ten feet away, lying on her side with her back towards him. If it hadn't been for the oatmeal colour of the lounger cushions he wouldn't have seen her through the darkness, but the black dress outlined her slender shape.

The muscles around his heart contracted, knocking its even rhythm onto a different beat. Getting up, he put the plate and the wineglass down on a nearby table then began walking towards her with the silence of bare feet. Rounding the end of the lounger, he stood for a moment gazing down at her. There was a painfully vulnerable look about the way she was lying on her side, with her arms crossed over her breasts and her head turned downwards so her hair covered her lovely face.

Squatting down beside her, he gently lifted her hair up and brushed the silken spirals over her shoulder. The first thing he noticed was how hot she felt to the touch; the next was the evidence of tears on her cheeks.

His heart pulled a different trick by actually hurting. He didn't like to think she had been alone out here crying. He didn't like to know that she had probably been crying because of him.

She must have sensed his presence because her eye-lashes fluttered, her soft mouth parted on another one of those sighs. Then her eyelids lifted to reveal sleep-darkened beautiful eyes—and she smiled at him.

When had she ever opened her eyes and *not* smiled at him like this? Marco asked himself painfully. And those eyes were awash with love for him. Always love. *Why* did he find it so impossible to return the words? Because he felt the emotion—*Dio*, he felt it. In fact he had been feeling it for ever, only he'd refused to acknowledge it to himself.

A set of slender white fingers came up to touch his cheek. They moved to his eyebrows then dropped to run the length of his half-smiling mouth. For a man who had been used since birth to having his face lovingly touched like this, this was touching like no other touching he had ever experienced. It was like being anointed with the sweetest blessing ever.

Lifting his hand to capture those fingers, he made his own loving gesture by pressing a kiss to her palm. Her eyes flooded with warmth and his began to gleam. They had always been able to make love with the smallest of intimacies. It was what made their relationship so special.

'Hi,' he murmured softly. 'What are you doing sleeping out here?'

It was then that she realised where she was—and, more to the point, *why* she was out here. The hand was withdrawn, along with the smile and the love. Looking away from him, she slid her feet to the floor so she could sit up. It was his cue to stand up and give her some space, but he was damned if he was going to withdraw now he had her within touching distance. So he remained squatting there in front of her while she made a thing of finger-combing her hair and trying, he supposed, to regroup her defences.

'What time is it?' she asked.

Irritation sparked to life. What did it matter what time it was? 'You didn't answer my question,' he prompted.

'The zip caught on my dress,' she replied, as if that should explain everything.

But it didn't. 'And you couldn't come to me for help with it?'

Of course she couldn't, and her expression told him that. On a sigh he stood upright. So did she, then went to move around him, but he stopped her with a hand on her shoulder.

'Don't go, *cara*,' he said. 'At least not until you have asked me what *I* am doing out here.'

The prompt made her hesitate. She glanced up at him warily. He smiled a wryly self-mocking smile. 'The bed was too empty without you in it beside me,' he confessed. He felt the tension easing out of her shoulder and added huskily, 'Come back there with me?'

She wanted to. He saw it written in her eyes before she lowered them again with a small shake of her head. 'I don't think it would be a good idea,' she murmured.

'Because we argued?' he said. 'We always argue. It is a part of who we are.'

But this was different. He knew it was different. And by the shake of her hair, Antonia did too. 'Too much has happened...'

'Nothing we cannot work out, *cara mia*,' he gently certified. And if she shook her head again, he swore he would use other methods to persuade her!

She didn't shake her head. 'I don't want to talk about it—'

'I never mentioned talking,' he murmured drily.

Her eyes came back to his. 'I don't want to do *that* either,' she flashed.

That assumption earned her a lazy grin—until he felt her begin to tense up again. 'Sleep,' he offered. 'Where we both prefer to be. In our bed, curled around each other. Nothing more, nothing less. What do you say, *cara*, hmm?'

What did she say? Antonia asked herself wistfully. She

said *yes* to him because she had never been able to say *no*. And she was tired and miserable, so she might as well be miserable curled up against him than miserable out here on her own, she justified her weakness.

So with a small nod of her head she gave him his answer. His arm came about her shoulders. It felt so good to feel it there that she released a sigh, gave in and leaned closer. They didn't speak again as they walked the terrace towards their bedroom. Marco was keeping silent because he had got what he wanted and didn't want to chance spoiling it. Antonia was silent because she knew she should not be letting him this close again, yet couldn't bring herself to turn away.

He was her weakness. He always would be.

The first thing she noticed when they stepped through the open window was the room had been swept clean of her clothes and suitcase. The next was the rumpled bed, which told its own story.

Still maintaining the silence which this short truce had been built upon, when they reached the bed Marco turned her so he could deal with the snagged zipper on her dress. Her hair was in the way. She reached up to gather the silken tresses over one shoulder. It was as dark in the bedroom as it had been out on the terrace. The dress was black, the zipper was black, so it took a little while for him to untangle the teeth from the snagged piece of fabric. By the time he sent the zip sliding free Marco had a feeling Antonia had stopped breathing. And the first moment she could she stepped away from him, to remove the dress herself.

He grimaced, and contained the urge to finish a job he had always found a pleasure. Instead he turned his attention to straightening out the crumpled evidence of his restless hours alone in here. When he turned back to her again the dress had gone, to reveal black silk underwear that did wonderful things to her pale skin. And, though he couldn't be sure in the darkness, he had a suspicion she was blushing, which made him frown, because he could not remember a time that she'd ever been shy in front of him, other than the first time they'd made love. And then, if he hadn't known better, he'd have sworn he'd been her first ever lover.

But there was worse to come when she actually tried to get into the bed without removing anything else. The fault of those paintings? His mother? Or was it *his* fault that she wanted to hide what she had always been so comfortable with?

'No,' he said. Then, 'No,' again, with a completely different meaning placed in the word. The first had been a protest, the second a plea.

When she hesitated, he used the moment to step behind her and unfasten her bra strap. Black silk fell away from pale satin flesh, her beautiful breasts were set free. She removed the rest herself without comment then slipped between the sheets—all without once letting him see her face.

Grimly he stripped off his robe and joined her. In silence he drew her into the curve of his body. She settled as she always did, but he could feel the guard she had placed on herself that was stopping her from melting against him.

The urge to say something got the better of him, even at the risk of causing yet another scene. 'I don't like to fight with you,' he admitted as he nuzzled his lips into the scented flow of her hair.

'I know,' she replied. And she did, he realised. He

found it rather disturbing to have to admit that she knew him a whole lot better than he actually knew her. 'But this changes nothing, Marco,' she obviously felt compelled to add.

Was she talking about leaving him? On that dark thought, one of his hands found her breast, one of his legs hooked over hers to keep her close, with the curve of her lower body nestling into the cradle of his hips. 'Go to sleep,' he said on a heavy sigh, while willing himself not to challenge that final statement and just take his own advice and go to sleep.

It was a crazy idea. You didn't sleep when you'd both been through the emotional mill as they had tonight. You didn't sleep when it was all still churning round in your head.

And you didn't sleep when the woman in your arms was implying that she intended to leave you.

What you did was move closer to that same woman. You let your hand increase its pressure on what it was holding. You buried your face in the sweet scent of her hair.

Beneath his palm he felt the tightening of her nipple, lower down, his own natural response caused the muscles in her body to flex sensually. He allowed his thumb to replace his palm and began a slow circling of that pretty rosebud tip. Her pulse began to quicken, her breathing altered pace. On a muffled groan he nuzzled deeper into silken tresses until he found her nape.

Her response was to twist around until she was facing him. Their eyes met. He knew what his were saying, but hers were still trying to fight it.

'You don't play fair!' she protested.

'*Grazie,*' he replied, as if she had just paid him a great

compliment, and claimed her mouth with a kiss aimed to kill any kind of argument.

What followed was an in-depth demonstration as to why what they had was too special to throw away. It was hot and it was good, and as his body hardened with masculine arousal hers began to soften to a sensual pliancy that invited any intimacy.

She was beautiful. He adored her. No other woman had ever made him feel this deeply. He kissed every sweet sensational inch of her until she gave up trying to hate what he was doing and, on a helpless sigh, began to join in. What she found she couldn't reach with her mouth, she touched with tender knowing fingers. By the time he took final possession she was his entirely; there was no doubt about it. He watched her build towards her climax, he watched her reach and tumble into it, and he held her there. With gritted teeth and burning loins he held her, held her in magical suspension for as long as he could possibly manage it. Only when she eventually opened her eyes to look at him in dazed astonishment did he surrender and give her back what she had just given him.

Himself. He gave himself.

It really was the perfect moment to glide past everything that had gone before it and just be content to drift into sleep on the soft cloud of knowledge that neither of them was going to throw this away.

Lying there, with her cheek resting in the hollow of his shoulder and her hand covering the steady beat of his heart, escape into sleep was certainly all that Antonia wanted to do.

But Marco didn't agree. He was basking in self-confidence again, and that set his brain working. 'Tell me what Anton Gabrielli is to you,' he said, and very effectively shattered the peace.

'You just can't stop yourself, can you?' she snapped, pulling away from him to sit up with a sigh.

'I don't like mysteries,' he explained. 'And you knew the man, *cara*, no matter what you try to say.'

Knew him? A short laugh accompanied the weary shake of her head. Well, she mused bleakly, did she tell him and get it over with, or was this one secret better kept to herself? 'My mother was his mistress years ago.' She went for the compromise with part of the truth. 'He set her up in an apartment in Naples, visited her regularly, and took her out with his friends. He adored her on the face of it—but forgot to tell her he was married. When she found out, she left him.' That seemed the simplest way of saying it.

'You were around to witness this?' Quiet though it was, huskily gentle though it was, Antonia knew what he was thinking.

Learn by example.

'Yes, I was around,' she answered, while her fingers plucked at pale blue sheeting. Then, with a toss of her head, she made herself look at him. 'So you see, it was just another case of mistaken identity,' she explained bitterly.

'Then we will make it a priority tomorrow to correct the mistake.'

It was just so typically arrogant of him. 'Are you planning to put an ad in the newspaper, Marco, announcing to the world that your mistress is not the Mirror Woman? And do you honestly think anyone will believe you if you do?'

'We can at least try to set the record straight.'

'For what purpose?' she asked. 'To make *you* feel better? Your mother? *Me?* Don't you see? It doesn't matter who the model is; people will always look at me and see the same woman! I can't change that. I *look* like her! In every way but name I could *be* her! Either you have to learn to accept it or we have nothing left here to—'

Firm hands toppled her back down to him. 'Shut up,' he gritted. 'I know what you were going to say, so just shut up!'

'You started it,' she sighed.

'And I am finishing it!' And he did, by launching into a second seduction.

It was all very fierce, intense and possessive, but sex didn't solve everything. Okay, so in bed they were as compatible as any two human beings could be. But out of it?

Nothing could change. He wanted to fix what couldn't be fixed. Which was why she hadn't told him the full truth about Anton Gabrielli. She might love Marco, but some secrets you could only trust to someone who would love you enough not to care what you had to tell them.

And Marco didn't love her that way.

This time her drift from satiation to sleep was allowed to happen uninterrupted. But Marco lay awake, frowning into the darkness until dawn eventually began to filter into the room, when, carefully untangling himself from Antonia, he slid out of the bed.

Two hours later he was in a helicopter heading for his parents' Tuscany home, intent on an interview with his father. And Antonia was just awakening to find the place beside her empty—if you didn't count the written note waiting on the pillow.

'Don't worry me, *cara*,' it said. 'Be here when I return.'

Don't worry me, she read again. *Be here…*

Such emotive words, she thought sadly. But what did they tell her, except that he didn't want her to go? They didn't solve anything. They didn't put right what his mother had done to her self-esteem. She would have to be really brazen to go amongst his friends after last night's public humiliation and boldly outface their new perception of her.

And she wasn't that brazen. Though she didn't think Marco would understand if she tried to explain it to him. He would probably think she was angling after another marriage proposal. When in actual fact the one he'd given her had been more than enough for her.

So was she going to 'be here' when he got back?

Her indecisive sigh told its own story. She just couldn't make up her mind. To go was going to hurt. To stay was going to hurt. Her problem was deciding which one was going to hurt more.

Getting out of bed, she showered and dressed in a simple dusky-mauve skirt and a cerise top, then went to search out Carlotta to see if she knew where Marco had gone.

It was Saturday, after all, and she had rarely known him to work on Saturdays. He preferred to laze around and do as little as possible.

Carlotta was just placing a pot of coffee, a bowl of freshly sliced fruit and some toast down on the table for her when she arrived in the sunny breakfast room.

No, she didn't know where Marco had gone.

The smell of the toast made Antonia realise that with last night's drama she hadn't eaten a scrap since late afternoon yesterday and she was hungry, which was a much simpler problem to solve.

Or was it that she didn't really want to look for the answer to where Marco had gone? she wondered as she sat down. He'd threatened to go and see Anton Gabrielli. He also had to smooth things out with his mother. Who else? she asked herself. Confront Stefan with what she had told him? Demand his money back for the *Mirror Woman*? The list could go on and on.

Any interview between Marco and Anton Gabrielli did not sit comfortably with her, although the man could only tell Marco more or less what she had already said, she attempted to reassure herself.

As for an interview with his mother—the outcome of that depended entirely on which one of them was the more committed to his or her offended senses. Either way, it did not promise to be a pleasant conversation. Nor did it sit comfortably with her that she was the cause of dissension between mother and son.

Then there was Stefan. Annoyingly unpredictable Stefan, who was likely to say anything if Marco pushed hard enough. And, since he knew just about everything about her, it was yet another confrontation she would prefer didn't take place.

Which leaves you with what? she asked herself as she poured a second coffee. All of these people discussing you as if you didn't have a voice of your own? When all it would take is for you to face the man and tell him everything, warts and all, then stand back and see what the full truth brings you back by return.

Maybe she would. Maybe she would wait around after all, do just that, and tell Marco everything.

Carlotta appeared. 'A Signor Gabrielli is in the foyer, *signorina*,' she informed her. 'He is asking if you can spare him a few minutes of your time?'

Signor Gabrielli. Her stomach turned over. The coffee suddenly lost flavour. He couldn't know—could he? No, she told herself firmly. He couldn't know. He was here to ask about Anastasia, probably. Wanting to find out how his ex-mistress had faired in the twenty-five years since they'd last met!

Well, she was ready to tell him that, Antonia resolved, and came to her feet. 'Let him come up and show him into the small sitting room, Carlotta, if you please.'

The sheer formality of her words set the housekeeper frowning. The way Antonia's face had suddenly turned so cold caused a hesitation before Carlotta turned away without saying whatever had been on her mind.

Alone again, Antonia made herself sit down, made herself sip at the coffee and eat a piece of toast. And she made herself ready for a meeting that was coming twenty-five years too late.

CHAPTER NINE

HE WAS wearing a dark suit, white shirt and dark tie. And Antonia's first impression as she stepped into the room was—stiff. In the single grainy newspaper cutting she had of him he didn't look stiff. He looked young and vital— very much as Marco looked.

But that had been taken twenty years ago. In twenty years maybe cynicism with life could change Marco into this man's image. Though she hoped to goodness that it didn't, she thought with a distinct shiver.

'Good morning, *signor*,' she greeted him in cool English. 'I believe you wanted to see me?'

Gracious, polite, giving no hint that she knew anything at all about him. She was leaving it up to him to give away as much—or as little—as he knew about her.

He didn't return the greeting. In fact he didn't do anything but narrow his eyes and look her over like something in a specimen jar. Her nerve-ends began to tighten. He had a face cast from iron and a thin-lipped mouth that appeared to have forgotten how to smile. Already predisposed to dislike him, what she was feeling bouncing back from him gave her no reason to alter that view.

'You are Anastasia's daughter,' he eventually announced, as if he'd needed that detailed scrutiny to make absolutely sure before he committed himself to the statement.

'Yes,' she confirmed. 'Is it about my mother that you wish to see me?'

He shifted his stance. It wasn't by much but it was enough for her to know that he was intensely uncomfortable at being here. '*Si,*' he replied. 'And—no,' he added. 'By your response, I have to assume that you know about me?'

'Your affair with my mother? Yes.' She saw no reason to hide it.

He nodded in acknowledgement. 'It was perhaps unfortunate that we should meet as we did last night.'

Unfortunate? 'I think I shocked you,' she allowed. 'And I'm sorry for doing that.'

His eyes contained a distinctly cynical glint at her apology. 'Until I saw you I believed the Stefan Kranst paintings were your mother. But then,' he said curtly, 'I did not know that you existed.'

For the first time someone had made the correct assumption about Stefan's model. It was ironic that he was now changing his mind to suit what everyone else believed.

'We were extremely alike,' she said. 'Few people could tell the difference.'

'Were—?' he picked up sharply.

'My mother died two years ago,' she explained.

'I'm sorry for your loss,' he murmured politely.

'Thank you,' she replied. This couldn't become any more formal if they tried.

Shouldn't she be feeling something? Antonia asked herself curiously. Shouldn't she at least sense a genetic bond, even if it was only a small one? Realising she was still standing by the door, she began to walk forwards, gauging his tensing response as a man very much on his guard. What did he think she was going to do—physically attack him?

'You even walk like her,' he uttered.

Antonia just offered a brief smile. He wasn't telling her anything she didn't already know. She looked like her mother. She moved like her mother.

'Would you care to sit down?' she invited politely, 'Can I offer you a drink—espresso or ?'

'I am your father,' he ground out brusquely, bringing her to a breathtaking stop. Then, with a slash of a hand, 'There,' he said. 'It is now in the open between us. So we may stop this civility. What do you want?'

'I b-beg your pardon?' Antonia blinked in astonishment.

'You heard me,' he said. 'I want to know your price.'

Antonia could not believe she was hearing this. 'But you came to see me,' she reminded him. 'I didn't—'

'It is called pre-empting your intentions,' he cut in. 'I decided that it would only be a matter of time before you came after me. So here I am.' He gave a shrug. 'All I want to know is how much your silence is going to cost me.'

Her silence? Antonia stared at him in disbelief. He had come here to face her because he thought she was about to start blackmailing him? 'But I don't w-want—'

'Your kind always want.'

Suddenly it hurt to breathe. His voice held contempt. His eyes held contempt. He hated the sight of her! He didn't even know her yet he was judging her to be mercenary. And, *her kind*? A flashback came to her of Marco's mother wearing the same expression, showing the same arrogant superiority that they thought gave them the right to treat her like this!

Glancing up, he caught her expression; his own turned graven. 'Anastasia let me down,' he ground out bitterly.

'You should not be here. It is most unfortunate that we have to have this conversation at all.'

Was he saying what she thought he was saying? Sickness began to claw at her stomach. 'You thought my mother would go back to England and rid herself of me simply because it was what you expected her to do?'

'Anastasia demanded money,' he explained. 'I automatically assumed she meant to use it to—rectify the problem.'

The *problem*? 'I was not my mother's problem!' she cried. '*You* were that! She needed money to survive!' God, she felt so disgusted. 'You walked away, closed the lease on her apartment, bank accounts, *everything*!'

'It is the way these things work.' He was callously unrepentant. 'As you will find out yourself, no doubt, when your moment arrives.'

Was this how he had treated her mother on that final confrontation? Was this the reason why she never really recovered her self-esteem? How could she have loved this man? How could she have *not* seen through him?

'You make me feel sick,' she breathed.

'Don't take the high moral ground with me, *signorina*!' he suddenly barked at her. 'For here you are, living with a man who makes you the scornful talk of all Milan!' His face was hard again, his accent cold and his opinion of her set in stone. 'Think before you speak, whether you would prefer *me* to announce to the world that Marco Bellini's mistress is Anton Gabrielli's bastard daughter! And the Mirror Woman is actually her cheap slut of a mother!'

She slapped him—hard. For which part she wasn't sure, but the hand flew out when he insulted her mother. Standing there facing each other, both emanated intense dislike, and she did not feel even a small hint of remorse for that slap. His hand came up to cover his cheek and his eyes burned vows of revenge on her.

'I heard what Isabella Bellini did to you last night,' he said. 'The whole gallery was buzzing with talk of the incident.' And he smiled that thin smile again when she turned white. 'Do you think you will still be here if this situation ever becomes public?' he posed. 'Do you think because you can lay claim to a father worth as much as the Bellinis they will turn a blind eye to what you actually are?'

'How can you stand there and preach over me when your own sins are staring right at you?' Antonia gasped. 'And why come here at all, if you don't care if I speak out? You have a wife. Don't her feelings count for anything?'

'My wife is dead,' he said. 'You cannot hurt her. But I can most certainly hurt your present position here in this place of luxury if you dare to make our connection public.'

'But I don't understand why you should think I'd want to!' The whole thing had become so bewildering, she couldn't follow his logic at all.

'I don't,' he said. 'I merely wanted to be sure that you understand your position here. For you don't have one.' He made the point plain. 'I am no use to you as a lever towards marriage to Bellini. In fact I am most probably your biggest danger to that goal. But I am willing to accept you possess a certain right to lay embarrassment at my doorstep,' he conceded. 'And, bearing in mind that one day in the future Bellini is going to tire of you, I accept I owe you some—incentive to keep your silence about me when that time comes.'

'I want you to leave,' she announced, beginning to shake on the inside.

'This is not your home to order me out of,' he replied, and at last his thin lips did what she suspected they had been wanting to do since he arrived here and twisted into bitter dislike. 'Just name your own figure...'

Staring at him, she realised he'd had the absolute gall to reach into his inside pocket and take out his cheque-book! He was expecting to pay her off! Anger returned, and she was glad to feel it rise up inside her because it saved her from bursting into tears.

He was standing there with book and pen, waiting for her to say something. So she did. It was really too irresistible not to. 'Everything you're worth,' she announced, then folded her arms and watched his face turn to plastic. Money, it seemed, was all-important to him. Oh—and his reputation, she added, since he really couldn't cope with the idea of having a twenty-five-year-old mistake come back to haunt him!

Irritation flashed across his face. 'I don't think you understand—'

'My own worth?' she put in. 'Or how much *you* are worth *signor*?' She took delight in watching him stiffen. 'Well, let me put that question straight before there is any more confusion here. You are worth precisely *nothing* to me—*capisce*?' She even used Marco's way of saying it. 'So you may write on your cheque "I give my illegitimate daughter Antonia Carson exactly *nothing*!"' Her eyes flashed with disgust. 'Now excuse me,' she said, and turned and left the room.

If Marco had been there to watch her do it, he would have recognised the move as Antonia showing her contempt.

But Marco wasn't here. And neither did she intend to be by the time he arrived home. If her own father could view her like that, what hope did she ever have of gaining the respect of anyone while she continued to stay with Marco?

She had to go—and right now, she decided. Before Marco had any chance of convincing her otherwise! And the saddest thing was she knew he could do it. One word, one touch, and she was as weak as a kitten where it involved him.

Carlotta was hovering in the hallway. Her face looked concerned, which made Antonia wonder if the housekeeper had overheard what had been said in the sitting room.

But, 'Will you see Signor Gabrielli out for me, please?' was all Antonia said to her. Then walked past her and into the bedroom...

At about the same time that she was confronting her father, Marco was confronting his own across the desk in the family library. All around them stood the results of centuries of time-honoured collecting. The house itself was a national treasure. And out beyond the window spread a whole valley strung with the vines which made the wine the Bellini name was as famous for as its centuries-old corporate leadership.

'I need your support,' Marco was saying grimly. 'I have no wish to feud with my own parents, but push me and I will.' It was both a threat and a warning.

'You are expecting me to dictate to your mother?' the older man asked, then released a laugh of fond derision. 'Sorry, Marco. But I am too sick and too wise to accept the task.'

But he wasn't as sick as Marco had expected to find him. 'You're looking better,' he remarked—perhaps belatedly.

'Thank you for noticing.' His father thought it belated too. In height, in looks, in every way there could be, Marco was his father's son. But a few months ago a virus had sucked the life out of Federico Bellini. By the time the doctors had managed to stabilise him he had halved his body weight, lost the use of one lung and damaged his heart, liver and kidneys.

'New drugs,' the older man dismissed with the same contempt with which he had always treated the medication which kept him living. 'Who is this woman your mother sees as such a threat that she publicly offends her?'

Subject of his health over, Marco noted. It was his father's way. It would be Marco's way, given the same circumstances. 'You know who she is,' he sighed. 'She's been living with me for the last year.'

'You mean you're still with the same one?' Federico pretended to be shocked, but Marco wasn't taken in by it. Though he did allow himself a wry little smile of appreciation for the thrust. 'No wonder your mother is in a panic.'

'It isn't her place to panic.'

'Then I repeat,' his father incised, 'who is she?' And the accent was most definitely on the *who*.

Dipping his hand into his inside pocket, it was not a chequebook that Marco retrieved, but a photograph, taken at his best friend's wedding. He dropped it on the desk in front of his father. Federico picked it up, studied it.

'Your good taste has never been in question,' he drawled.

'But—?' Marco prompted.

'I might have been out of circulation for the last year, but I have seen the painting,' Federico said. 'She has an exquisite body and sad eyes.' The photograph came back across the desk.

Odd, Marco noted, that when he could have challenged that comment with the truth he did nothing of the kind

Because Antonia was right, he realised. Look at the naked mother and you see the naked daughter. So it didn't really matter what people were told.

And anyway, there was a point of honour here he was determined to hold on to. He had a right to choose his own future, and Antonia had a right to be accepted for that choice. If his parents could not bring themselves to do that, then...

Then what? he asked himself.

'Nice to own. Nice to sip,' his father murmured. 'But that's about all, Marco...'

It was a refusal of support. Marco picked up the photograph and placed it back in his pocket. 'Is that your final word?'

His father sent him a grim look as he stood up to leave. 'Is she pregnant?' he asked.

Now there was an interesting concept, Marco mused cynically. A Bellini child, born out of wedlock. A wry smile touched his mouth 'No,' he replied. 'But I could easily make it so.'

Ah—now he was actually being taken seriously, he saw with grim satisfaction as his father's expression sharpened dramatically. 'Sit down,' Federico commanded.

Marco complied, but only because it was what he had expected to be told when he'd stood up in the first place.

'Now, explain to me why *this* woman, when you could have any woman you wanted?'

Arrogance abounded. Antonia would have just loved to hear his father say those words. 'She's what I want.' He stated it simply. Then he sat forward and looked his father directly in the eye. 'She is what I intend to have,' he extended with deadly seriousness. *'Comprende…?'*

The silence lasted for all of thirty seconds, the sabre fight with their eyes an evenly matched thing. Then Federico Bellini sat back in his thick brown leather chair, huffed out a short laugh, gave a shake of his head and said, 'Next weekend. Here, I think. We will keep this official, above-board and on the right side of the sheets, if you don't mind.'

'Grazie,' Marco thanked him, and not by a flicker did he wallow in his triumph.

But his father hadn't finished. His eyes suddenly took on a devilish gleam. 'Now all you have to do is get your mother to see things your way…'

Carlotta had already been in and returned the bedroom to its usual pristine smoothness, Antonia found. Nothing out of place, nothing to show that the room had been used at all. Walking over to a built-in closet, she took out the small leather suitcase again. She wasn't really surprised to find that Marco had neatly returned her clothes to their appropriate places in the room. It was the way of the man. The way of his housekeeper. Everything neat and in its place. This bedroom was Antonia's place. Last night should have reminded her of that.

This time no angry male strode in to halt the process of packing. The suitcase closed with a snap. But as she set the case down on the floor a knock sounded on the door and Carlotta stepped inside.

Of course, she had to see the suitcase. Her eyes shot to Antonia's. 'No, *signorina*, you—'

Something stopped her. An awareness of her place in the order of things? Acceptance that, for Antonia at any rate, leaving was perhaps the wise thing for her to do?

Looking away again, she walked forward 'Signor Gabrielli asked me to give you this,' she said, and handed Antonia a cheque, then turned and left again without uttering another word.

It kind of said it all. Without so much as glancing at the cheque to see how much money her father considered his daughter's silence worth, she ripped it into small pieces and deposited it in the waste-paper basket, then, simply because she needed to do it, she walked over to the terrace window and stepped outside.

Milan shimmered in the blistering heat of yet another hot summer's day. Way down there below her the traffic made up for its unusual silence of the night before. And one of the first things her eyes fell upon was the imprint of Marco's body still hugging the cushions on the lounger he must have used. Carlotta had obviously not got around to coming out here yet, because a sandwich and a glass of red wine were standing on a table close by.

When he hadn't been able to sleep last night, he must have gone to the kitchen to make himself a late night snack and brought it out here to enjoy. But he'd seen her lying asleep on the other lounger. Food and wine had been forgotten in favour of other forces.

Like the recovery of his woman, she mused. The putting her back where she belonged, in his arms, and in his bed.

Her eyes glazed over. She had to turn away to stop the tears from flowing. It was then that she remembered the tear-drop diamond necklace, and set her feet moving further down the terrace to find it still lying exactly where she had placed it beneath the lounger. Recovering it, she took it back into the bedroom and was about to put it down on her dressing table when she noticed the note from Marco folded there.

'Don't worry me, *cara*,' It said. 'Be here when I return.'

It came without warning. The first sob, followed quickly by another—and another. Dropping onto the dressing stool, she covered her face with her hands then simply let go and sobbed her heart out.

When it was over, she stood up. Took a moment to compose herself and decide what she needed to do before she left here for the last time...

Marco was standing alone in his father's library, using the landline telephone to connect him with the Romano Gallery. He wanted Stefan Kranst. He got Rosetta Romano.

'Where is he?' he demanded.

'He flies home to England this afternoon,' Rosetta told him. 'I thought you must know that he never meant to stay longer than the first-night viewing. What do you want me to do with Signorina Carson's painting?' she asked. 'Stefan never said, and Signorina Carson rang off before I could ask her when she called looking for Stefan not ten minutes ago.'

The painting. Marco frowned. He'd forgotten all about it. 'Have it packed up and delivered to my apartment,' he instructed. 'Did Antonia say why she wanted Kranst?'

'No. She just asked where he was staying and rang off, that was all.'

Marco rang off too. It wasn't that he was worried any longer about Stefan Kranst, he told himself. But his feet took him in search of his father to wish him a quick farewell before he was heading outside and to the waiting helicopter. It didn't occur to him, until he was in the air again, that he could have rung Antonia before leaving, just to check that she was okay.

Okay, he then repeated drily. You want to check that she's actually there! He didn't trust her. Could he trust her? 'This changes nothing,' she had told him in the depths of a night of loving. Impulsively he fished out his mobile. One glance from his pilot and he was reluctantly putting it away again.

Antonia was arguing with Stefan. 'You have to do this for me, Stefan—please,' she begged him. 'You *owe* it to me after last night's fiasco!'

'Isabella Bellini was contrite afterwards, if that helps you any,' he told her.

'I don't care what she was!' It was almost a sob. 'It doesn't make any difference. My mind is made up. I'm leaving Milan.'

'And Marco?' he included.

She swallowed and nodded. 'These are the keys.' Her fingers shook as she held them out to him. 'All you need to do is pay off the lease then get my things and bring them with you back to London.'

Stefan refused to take the keys. 'What in heaven's name happened after you left with him?' he demanded impatiently.

But she shook her head. 'I'll tell you another time. I have a plane to catch.'

'Does he know you're going?' Stefan asked.

She didn't answer. He released a sigh. 'My darling, I've

told you something like this before but I am going to say it again. Marco Bellini is not a man to cross swords with.'

Her chin shot up, jewel-bright eyes sparkling with something he had never seen there before. It was bitter, blinding, gut-wrenching cynicism. 'Is that your way of saying that *you* don't want to cross swords with him?'

'My God,' Stefan breathed, and took the keys. 'Go,' he said. 'Go!' he repeated. 'I'll follow on tomorrow if I can get a flight. But go if you must.'

'Thank you,' she whispered, kissed his cheek and left his hotel suite without looking back again. If she had done she would have hesitated, because Stefan was wearing a look fit to slay any dragon that might be threatening her.

And she didn't want Marco slayed. She needed to know he was alive and happy. In fact, it was essential to her own sanity that he remained exactly the way she wanted to remember him. Tall and lean and suave and sophisticated, but wearing one of those lazy grins that oozed sex appeal. She wanted to remember him laughing with his friends. Talking seriously about art. Or lying on a sun lounger in the middle of the night with a glass of red wine and a sandwich—missing her.

Oh, yes, she needed him to miss her, she admitted, as her taxi began a battle with Milan's mad Saturday traffic.

She had managed to reserve a seat on a flight out of Linate airport, which was only four miles outside Milan. But it was tourist season and the roads to the airport were as busy as she had ever seen them. As the taxi eventually made it to the perimeter of the airport compound she glanced outside in time to catch the sun sparkling on a helicopter as it hovered just before landing.

Marco's preferred form of transport to his parents' home, she recalled, with a sad little smile, and turned away quickly, not wanting to think about Marco right now when she could still weaken and change her mind.

Marco saw the traffic as he came in to land, and cursed it. It was going to take an age to get back into the city through all of that. With a quick thanks to his pilot he got out of the helicopter and strode off towards the airport building. Any other time he would be heading for the executive car park and jumping into his car. But the Ferrari had been booked in for a service this morning, so he'd had to come here by taxi. Which meant he now had to walk right across the airport concourse to find the nearest taxi rank.

If he'd thought about it, he could have used the Lotus and saved himself a lot of hassle, because he had things to do, people to see, before he could get back to Antonia.

Which reminded him. Taking out his mobile, he tried getting a signal. It was only when nothing happened that he realised he'd forgotten to put the battery on charge the night before. The damn thing was dead. Sighing, he pocketed the phone again.

It was beginning to turn into one of those days.

The airport lounges were busy, packed to bursting with newly arriving tourists. Taking the direct route towards the exit doors, he had to squeeze between people and their luggage. There was a moment when he paused though, half considering going to check in the other lounge to see if Stefan Kranst was there. But he decided he didn't have the time and kept on going towards the exit.

Outside again, the queue for taxis was long. Frustration bit into his patience while he waited with the rest of them. As one cab drove off another took its place. The constant circling of people to and from Milan must be a very good earner, the banker in him decided.

At last he got his turn. Diving into the back of the cab, he gave his destination, then closed the door. As he sat back, he experienced the strangest sensation when he picked up the scent of Antonia's perfume.

On his clothes, on his skin? he wondered. Or was it so impregnated into his senses that it was always there? He liked that idea. It made him smile and relax while he let the driver take on the battle to get him where he needed to go.

To Buccellati's first, to find something that bit special for Antonia to wear on her finger. Then the less palatable task of taking on his mother...

By the time Antonia discovered that her flight had been delayed she was beginning to have second thoughts about running away like this. She didn't want to go. She didn't want to stay. She didn't know what she wanted to do!

Yes, you do, she told herself. You want to have everything go back to how it was. But it can't. Too much has happened.

I love him, though!

She lowered her head, glad she'd left her hair down because it helped to hide the tears swimming in her eyes. Her bag lay across her lap. She opened it up to hunt for a paper tissue. But what she came up with was a photograph taken at Nicola and Franco's wedding. She was standing next to Marco and he had his arm around her. She looked so happy. So did he, though not in the same way. Her happiness shone through with love, his shone with—

Sexual contentment.

She was right to go, she told herself.

But her mouth began to quiver, and the tears were beginning to spread.

Stefan thought she was making a mistake. He had been angry—disappointed with her, even. 'He'll strike back hard,' he'd warned her before at the de Maggio's anniversary party.

Oh, yes, please let him do that, she prayed, like the weak little fool that she was. Let him come for me, lock me up and throw away the key—I don't care! I *like* being his mistress! It's everyone else the job seems to offend!

Think of your mother, she grimly told herself. Think of Anton Gabrielli and how you could actually *see* Marco becoming like him in years to come! Then, no, she denied. That isn't true. If I was pregnant Marco wouldn't—

How do you *know* he wouldn't?

She didn't know, and that was the ugly little truth which kept her pinned to the chair in the airport lounge instead of getting up and running back to him. Anton Gabrielli had planted a lot of ugliness into her heart, she realised. The contempt, the accusations, the automatic belief that she must be out for all she could get. He'd despised her mother just for *being*! He despised her in the same way. So did Marco's mother.

Her chin jerked up. It was a strange sensation, but her heart suddenly felt as if someone had walked past and wiped it clean as a slate!

Only a mother could do that. Only a mother had the power to wipe another woman clean of any aspirations towards her son. So maybe it was because of Isabella Bellini's contempt that she was still sitting on this chair. For, without her blessing, any relationship with Marco would be sordid from now on.

It hadn't felt sordid last night. It had been beautiful last night. It had been special. Marco had made it special. 'Don't worry me,' he'd written. 'Be here when I return.'

Her heart gave a squeeze. As the muscles relaxed again, all the warmth and feelings of love came flooding back in. Glancing down, she saw the photograph still clutched in her hands. The tears came back. The indecision. She wished they would call her flight. She needed to go—get away from here!

Marco strode into the apartment building and headed directly for the lift. He'd had a good day in a lot of ways. A real *coup d'état*! But it had taken too much time, and now he was anxious to see Antonia, begin to put things on a proper footing for them at last.

As the lift took him up with its usual smoothness he found himself smiling when his hand coiled round the small ring box in his pocket. The lift stopped, the doors slid open. He strode out. This was it, he told himself as he opened the apartment door. The most important few minutes of his life were about to happen!

Strangely, he'd never expected it to feel this good.

Stepping inside, the first thing he saw was the large brown cord-wrapped package leaning against the wall— Antonia's portrait he'd had delivered from the Romano Gallery. The next thing was Carlotta. She was standing there wringing her hands. Ice cold struck right through to his heart.

'Antonia?' he rasped. 'Where is she?'

The housekeeper's eyes were filled with dismay. 'She's gone, *signor*,' she whispered. 'She's gone…'

CHAPTER TEN

His legs took him down the hall, into the bedroom and straight to the built-in cupboard. The suitcase had gone. Through the eyes of a man who was still not prepared to take in what was happening to him, he turned to scan the rest of the room.

What had once pleased his eye, with its uninterrupted use of space, now looked cold and spartan, as if someone had come along and wiped it clean of its heartbeat.

So the few small items carefully placed on the smooth bed caught his attention. Walking over to them, he just stood staring down at the set of keys to this apartment, the tear-drop diamond necklace, the stack of credit cards and the mobile telephone.

His skin suddenly felt as if it didn't fit his body any more. Was that all she felt she was worth to him? Even the bed was playing its part here. He began to feel sick. If she'd tossed down a set of scarlet underwear she could not have made her feelings more clear.

The phone gave a beep. He looked at it, saw there was a message written on it in text. Picking it up he stared at the words she had left for him. 'I'm sorry,' was all that it said.

In English too. He sometimes forgot she spoke English her Italian was so good. But, maybe in this case *I'm sorry* said it better for her than *mi despiace* did.

It didn't for him, because *sorry* wasn't enough! He

wanted to know more. He wanted to know *why*! Could she not have held faith with him for just one more day?

'When did she leave?' He was aware of Carlotta standing in the doorway, watching him with anxious eyes. She obviously had something to tell him or she wouldn't be there invading his private moment like this.

'Just after the *signor* left,' the housekeeper answered.

Signor. Marcos swung round. 'Signor Kranst?' he demanded.

But Carlotta shook her head. 'A Signor Gabrielli,' she informed him. 'I think they argued,' she added, looking uncomfortable for saying so. 'The *signorina* had me see him out. It is when he gave me the cheque to give to Signorina Antonia.' Her eyes flickered, then dropped to the waste-paper basket standing by the dressing table. 'She was very upset,' she added, as Marco's gaze followed hers to the basket.

A bell sounded then, saying that someone was in the foyer wanting to come up. 'I don't want to see anyone,' Marco grimly instructed.

With a nod, Carlotta left, leaving him alone to walk over to the waste-paper basket.

About the same time that Stefan was using tough talk on Carlotta to gain his way into the apartment, Antonia's flight was being called at last.

It was now two hours late and her nerves were completely frazzled. Gathering her things together, she stood up, then paused to take in a careful breath. This was it, she told herself. She could leave now. No more arguing with herself. No more agonising over what she really wanted to do. It had to be better to go while she still had the strength to do it, rather than wait until she was thrown

out then spend five years pining for his return, as her
mother had—wasn't it?

So move, Antonia, she told her feet. Follow the general
exodus towards the gate as if you're just another tourist
on her way back home.

'No luggage slip, *signorina*?'

She looked down at the cabin-weight suitcase which
suddenly seemed a pathetic judgement on her year in Milan. When she'd packed it, in London, she had meant to
send for her other things once she was settled with Marco.
But he had done away with the need by buying her new
things. Anything else of value to her would be coming
back to London with Stefan.

She shook her head at the attendant who was checking
her boarding pass. 'This is all I have,' she said. And a
heart full of tears, she added silently.

Marco was leaning against the open window, which led
out onto the terrace, when Stefan Kranst had the arrogance
to stride into the room.

'I want words with you,' he insisted grimly. 'I don't
know what happened last night after you left Romano's
with Antonia. But—'

'Anton Gabrielli happened,' Marco inserted, without
bothering to turn.

The name met with silence. Not the blank, who-are-
you-talking-about kind of silence. But the dear-God-in-
heaven kind, that throbbed with grim recognition.

'What did he want?' Stefan asked him.

'I see you know the man,' Marco drily responded.

'What did he want?' Stefan repeated harshly.

His anger jolted Marco enough for him to wave a hand
towards the bed. 'See for yourself,' he invited. And turned

to study Stefan Kranst's face as he walked over to look down at the neat row of items set out on the bed. The diamond, the keys, the credit cards, the phone still displaying its message. And the cheque, carefully pieced back together. Stefan stared at it for a long time before he spoke.

'I saw him at the gallery last night,' he admitted. 'I hoped you'd got Antonia away before he arrived.'

'They came face to face. He called her Anastasia...'

Other than for a tightening of his lips, Stefan made no comment. 'When did this arrive?' he asked grimly instead.

'The man delivered it himself this morning,' Marco told him, 'while I was out,'

'No wonder she left in a hurry. He threatened her, didn't he?' Hard eyes lifted to Marco. 'Do you know who he is?'

The question earned him a grimace. 'Her father, at a guess.'

'She told you that?' Stefan looked so surprised that Marco couldn't hold back the wry smile.

'No,' he admitted. 'I managed to work it out.' She didn't feel able to trust me with it, he added silently, and sent his gaze flicking back to the view beyond the terrace. She hadn't really trusted him with anything, when he came to think about it. Not the truth about the *Mirror Woman*. Not the father he hadn't known she had. Even her innocent relationship with Kranst had been kept a titillating secret.

Out there, above the city, he saw a flash of light as the sun caught the tips of a plane as it took off. 'Do you know where she is?' he asked quietly.

'Not on that flight, if that's what you're thinking,' Stefan Kranst replied. 'She left for England hours ago, Marco,' he added almost gently.

The gentleness was almost his undoing. Moisture dared to slide across his eyes. He stiffened up, shoved his hands in his pockets, heaved in a deep breath. Felt the ring box, felt some other emotion wreak havoc with the wall of his chest.

'I'm going after her,' he announced, keeping his face turned away from Kranst as he shifted towards the bedroom door.

'I came here for a reason,' Stefan reminded him.

Marco paused. 'To gloat?' he suggested.

Stefan released a heavy sigh. 'Give me a break for once, Marco,' he begged wearily. 'I *care* about Antonia more than her real father does. That means I *care* about what's been happening here! She came to see me before she left,' he went on tightly. 'I didn't like the way she looked. Now I know why, if Gabrielli's been here,' he added cynically. 'But the point is, she gave me something I think you should know about…'

Marco spun around.

'Keys.' Stefan took them out of his pocket. 'And an address in Milan. I came to see if you were as interested as I am in finding out what the hell she has been keeping from *both* of us!'

She couldn't do it.

Standing here at the departure gate, with her boarding pass in her hand and only a short walk to freedom, she couldn't take another single step!

Tears clogged her throat, burned her eyes, hurt her stomach. I love him! she cried inside, and just couldn't go!

'Are you all right?' someone asked her. Someone else pushed impatiently past. 'You don't look well, *signorina*...'

I'm not. I'm sick with love. 'I've just r-remembered s-something,' she murmured shakily. 'I have to go back to Milan.' She swallowed at the attendant's shocked expression. 'Can you take my name off the f-flight register, please? I have my luggage here with me so you d-don't have to have it removed from the plane.'

Maybe that was why she'd used the smallest suitcase she could find. Maybe she *never* intended leaving Marco! Maybe she'd needed to get this far before she could finally accept that the man was her other half! You couldn't go anywhere with only half of you! It just wouldn't let you.

Dropping the tickets and the boarding pass on the attendant's desk, she turned and started running. She needed to get back to him—fast! 'Don't worry me,' he'd said. 'Be here when I return!'

He wanted her. What more could she ask of him, for goodness' sake? He *cared* that his mother had upset her! He had even asked her to marry him so that she wouldn't leave!

Oh God, why did clarity have to come this late? Why couldn't she have just waited until he got home and then faced him with Anton Gabrielli, instead of running away without giving him a chance to respond? And he *wasn't* like Gabrielli! How dared she compare the two of them?

The taxi queue was huge. Strange therefore, after a half-hour wait, she should get the same driver that had brought her to the airport. She gave the address for the apartment. He raised his eyebrows at her via the mirror as he drove off. 'It is a popular address today, *signorina*. I collected you from there this morning,' he remembered. 'Then I took another person there this afternoon. Now I take you back. Do you think the gentleman will be waiting to catch my taxi for the return journey here?'

He thought it was funny. Antonia didn't. 'Do you know the man's name?' she questioned huskily.

'Sure,' he shrugged. 'Everyone knows Signor Bellini. He tips well too...'

Marco paid off the driver and got out of the taxi to wait for Stefan to join him. The Ferrari wasn't back from its service and he was damned if he was going to drive Antonia's Lotus. That was staying exactly where it was until *she* came back to claim it.

'What the hell has she been doing in a place like this?' he demanded.

Stefan didn't answer. Going to the door, he used the key, then stepped inside. With Marco crowding behind him he took the stairs floor by floor, passing by the doors bearing nameplates of a suspect nature.

'You do know that this is part of the red-light district?' Marco growled into Stefan's back.

'I do now,' the other man answered and, though he had a fair idea what it was that Antonia did here, he was beginning to feel a trifle edgy—just in case he was wrong.

They arrived on the top landing. Neither spoke as they stepped up to the only door. Stefan turned the key, the tension riding high as he walked inside first.

Therefore he had those few split seconds to just stand looking around him before murmuring, 'Well, that's a relief.' Then he added a rueful grin.

Not for Marco it wasn't. How long had he known this woman? he asked himself as he stood there beside Stefan Kranst and stared at what might euphemistically be called an artist's studio. Light streamed in through a wall of windows, setting dust motes dancing in the air. The room smelled of old wood and oil and turpentine thinner, and everywhere you looked stood the paintings. Some drying, some framed, some waiting to be framed. Piazza del Duomo. La Scala. Pusteria di Sant'Ambrogio. The bustling Brera, with its trendy little shops and people, and the gardens at Villa Reale.

Over by the window stood a huge trestle bench stacked with pencil sketches. On the easel waited a half-finished view from his own terrace, looking out over the top of Milan.

Marco hadn't known Antonia had ever picked up a paintbrush, never mind possessed the capacity to produce work like this.

'Look at these,' Stefan murmured. He had moved towards the window and was now sifting through the sketches.

Sketches of life drawn with a quick sure hand. Sketches of people going about their business. Something caught in Marco's chest as he had a sudden vision of her sitting on a bench or a low stone wall just sketching—sketching while he had been safely out of the way in his office playing in the big league, believing her to be doing what the women of wealthy men did, which was basically nothing.

Then—no. He amended that notion, and didn't like himself for admitting that he hadn't really given much thought to what Antonia did when he wasn't there.

Stefan lifted a sheet of paper to one side, then went still enough to catch Marco's attention. Marco's own face looked back at him. It almost took his breath away, at the accuracy with which she had caught his mood of the moment.

The shark on his way to hunt prey, he named it with a wryness that didn't hold any humour. Picking it up, he found another—and another. All revealing his different moods in accurate detail.

Then something else caught his eye to divert his attention. It was a half-finished painting of Franco and Nicola about to leave on their honeymoon. Antonia clearly had not been pleased with the result because she had tossed it onto the bench and left it there. But that wasn't why the painting held him. It was the realisation that, in size, it would have fitted exactly the painting she had wrapped for the anniversary gift.

Yet she hadn't thought to show him, ask his approval. In fact she hadn't sought his approval on anything she had been doing in here.

And it hurt. 'Why not tell me?' he murmured out loud.

Turning from where he had wandered off to, Stefan Kranst looked at him—just looked—and he knew the answer. She would have had to feel safe from his mockery to tell him about all of this, and she hadn't.

'I am no ogre,' he growled out angrily—angrily because this was just another area she hadn't trusted him with.

Antonia had changed her mind at the very last minute. She didn't know why she had done it, but some instinct had suddenly spoken to her and said, Better stop Stefan from emptying your studio if you're intending to stay here. So she'd redirected the driver and realised only after she had let him go that she no longer had any keys to get into the building.

Fortunately another tenant was just coming out. He recognised her and, with a smile, stood back to allow her inside. 'You have visitors,' he told her.

Stefan. She smiled. *'Grazie,'* she said, and let him close the door behind her.

Her case wasn't heavy, but she was puffing a bit by the time she reached the top landing. The door was open a little. Pushing it wider, she paused to put down her suitcase just as Marco growled out harshly, 'What did she think I was going to do—laugh in her face?'

Her breathing changed from an out-of-breath pant to a trembling stammer, her mouth ran dry, her eyes glazed. Marco was here, with Stefan, of all people. It felt as if fate was still controlling her actions like a puppet on a string.

'Well,' she managed to whisper, 'are you?'

He spun round to face the doorway. Silence roared, tension sung, the sunlight shone on his black silk hair. He was wearing slate-grey. Slate-grey suit, slate-grey shirt, darker slate-grey tie. His skin had a polished gold cast to it, and his eyes were the same colour as his tie—dark with anger and passion and hurt pride.

She wanted to break down and weep at the sheer beautiful sight of him. She wanted to go to him, wrap her arms around his neck and cling so tightly that he would never *ever* be able to shake her free.

But instead her chin went up, it simply had to. No matter how desperate she was to feel his touch, or how shaky she was feeling inside, or even how afraid she was of hearing his answer to the question—she had to challenge him with it. It was a matter of her own pride.

'You're on a plane,' he said. It was really stupid. It was the very last thing she'd expected him to say.

'I couldn't go.'

'I'm not laughing.' He answered her question.

'What I do here is important to me,' she told him.

'I can see that,' he answered. 'Why couldn't you go?'

Her eyelashes flickered. Everything felt as if it was coming to her through a confused mist. She wet her lips with her tongue, linked her fingers together in a trembling pleat across her trembling stomach.

'Y-you didn't want me to,' she murmured unsteadily. 'Y-you trusted me to stay but I didn't trust you to...' The words trailed away on a wash of distraction. 'Th-that s-sketch you're holding isn't a good likeness.' Her fingers unpleated so she could point to what he was holding in his hand.

He looked down at it like someone who had no idea that he was holding anything. 'You think I'm a shark,' he murmured as he looked back at her.

'Sometimes.' She nodded.

'Are you coming in, or are you thinking of running again?'

'Oh.' It was her turn to glance down as if she didn't know where she was or what she was doing. She was still standing on the threshold, with her case sitting beside her and her bag swinging from one of her shoulders.

She went to pick up the case. The moment she moved, so did Marco. He came across the bare-board floor at the speed of lightning. The case was lifted out of her reach. Her arm was imprisoned in long fingers. Before she knew what he was about she was fully inside the room and the door was being firmly closed behind her.

That was when she saw Stefan, leaning against a wall with his arms casually folded and his expression—interested. 'Hi,' she murmured self-consciously.

'Hi, yourself,' Stefan softly replied. 'I don't suppose you would like to explain what's been going on here?' he drily requested.

'She doesn't need to explain anything,' Marco put in tensely, and his hand tightened on her arm as if he expected her to break free and run, when in actual fact she was already hanging on to his shirt at his waistband and had no intention of letting go of it.

Stefan sent the dry look Marco's way. 'She does if you want me to get out of here,' he replied, without bothering to hide his meaning.

Marco grimaced and remained silent, conceding Stefan's right to demand an explanation.

Still shaking too much, and not thinking straight, it needed a few attempts at breathing properly before Antonia could find some semblance of intelligence.

'Y-you know I paint. You taught me to do it,' she reminded Stefan.

'You taught yourself,' he drily corrected. 'By being a pain in the neck and insisting on placing your easel next to mine every time I worked so you could copy my every damn brushstroke.'

'I *learned* from you then.' She sighed at the play with semantics.

'Not this kind of stuff,' he said with derision. 'This is chocolate-box art they sell on street corners.'

'It's art,' Marco sliced back at him in her defence.

It was sweet of him, but Stefan was right. 'Shops,' she corrected. 'I sell them to the shops on the Brera. They sell them to the tourists. It—it makes me a nice little living...'

'So that's why you hardly ever touched the money I gave you,' Marco said bleakly.

'And your serious work?' Stefan asked, refusing to be sidetracked.

She tensed up; so did Marco. 'What serious work?' he demanded.

'You saw an example of it last night,' Stefan informed him, without taking his eyes off Antonia's suddenly angry face.

'*Dio mio,*' Marco breathed, his eyes wide with surprise as he stared at her. 'You mean *you* painted your own nude study?'

'Sometimes I hate you,' she hissed at Stefan.

Stefan just shrugged, moved out of his lazy stance against the wall and began walking towards them. 'Ask her about the one she has stashed against the wall over there,' he suggested to Marco as he passed by them. Then he paused, leaned over to kiss Antonia's angry cheek. 'Pack the chocolate-box stuff in before you ruin yourself with it,' he warned seriously, then pulled open the door and left them to it.

Or left Antonia to stand there on her own while she watched Marco stride across the room to the large canvas Stefan had so kindly pointed out to him.

Her cheeks began to heat, her body to stiffen in readiness for what was to come. She tried to divert him. 'Marco, we need to talk…'

But it was already too late. 'Now, just look at what we have here,' he drawled lazily. And with a deft flick of his hands he scooped the painting up and took it over to her easel.

She struggled not to gasp. Her cheeks were on fire. Standing back, he proceeded to study the nude painting of himself with the all-seeing eye of the complete connoisseur.

When he started to grin, she felt like following Stefan. But the way he reached out and touched the lean shape of a sleek male thigh was pure infuriating conceit.

'It's all wrong,' she snapped. 'The proportions are out. Your nose looks like Caesar's and your torso is too long!'

'I think it's perfect.'

He would, she thought with an angry frown. 'I *hate* people looking at my work until it's finished!'

'You mean you hate *me* looking at it!' His mood changed so swiftly she wasn't prepared for it. From lazy conceit he was suddenly pulsing with fury. '*Why*?' he demanded, walking back to her. 'Why couldn't you tell me that you can paint like this? I thought I knew you! But I've been living with a stranger! Your mother sits on my wall but you don't bother to tell me that! Your ex-lover has never been your ex-lover! In fact, I bet you never even had a lover before me—did you?' She blushed and shook her head, which only infuriated him more. He continued heatedly, 'You have a rat for a father. And you have a gift at your fingertips that I would have thought you would have been *proud* to let me see!'

'You own a Rembrandt!' she fired at him defensively.

'I own a Kranst!' he threw right back. 'Many works by totally unknown artists. *And* the Rembrandt! Are you saying I am an art snob on top of all my other failings?'

'Your opinion meant too much to me!' she cried. 'So it was safer not to seek it!'

He grabbed her and kissed her. And about time too, she thought as she fell into the kiss like a woman starved.

'*Dio mio,*' he rasped against her clinging lips. 'Do you have any idea what it did to me to come back and find you gone today?'

'I cried all the way to the airport,' she confessed, as if that should make it easier for him.

It didn't. 'Don't *ever* leave me like that again!'

'I won't,' she promised.

He sunk them into another hot deep hungry kiss that didn't last long enough before he was pulling right back. 'No, you won't,' he agreed. 'Because I am going to make sure that you don't!'

His hand went into his pocket and came out again, holding a small black leather box.

The moment Antonia saw it she knew what it was. And on a choke of dismay, she said, 'No,' and snapped her hands behind her back. 'You don't have to do that.'

She even started backing away.

He followed. 'Of course I do.' He reached for her.

'No!' she cried, and almost bounced as her shoulders hit the wall behind her.

Marco started frowning. '*Amore*, this is what *I* want. It is what we *both* want!'

But she kept on shaking her head. 'I came back,' she repeated. 'I don't need this to keep me here! A ring will just make everything more complicated! I would rather—'

'It's okay,' he said soothingly. 'I squared it with my father. He—'

Her eyes shot to his. Her mouth trembled. 'You told your father about me?' She looked so horrified it hurt. 'But you had no right to upset him with this when he's ill!'

'Ill,' Marco agreed. 'Not incompetent! And it is out of respect for his illness that I sought his approval. But do you honestly think I am the kind of man who requires the approval of anyone?'

'You require mine,' she pointed out. 'And I am not

prepared to come between you and your parents. I don't *need* to do that. I am perfectly happy with things as they were.'

'Well, I'm not,' he announced, his eyes narrowing on the sudden leap of anxiety that claimed her eyes. His teeth began to glint like a tiger preparing to take his first bite. 'So I made my father an offer he couldn't refuse,' he slid in silkily—and followed her until his arm could rest against the wall near her head. 'I said it was either done this way—' he lifted the box close to her nose '—or I used less—conventional methods.'

'There aren't any.'

In reply he swooped on her mouth. She died for that kiss. Of course she did. 'An illegitimate Bellini child is just not acceptable,' he murmured as he drew away again. 'My father saw my point and—'

'You mean you threatened to make me pregnant?' she gasped. Then her expression hardened. 'Do you honestly think I would allow you to do that to me?' His eyes began to gleam with a taunting message: You haven't got the will-power to stop me.

But she had. On this point, if on no other, she had the power to say no to him. 'A child isn't a pawn, Marco,' she said, stepping sideways and away from him. 'You don't play Russian roulette with its future just to win an argument.'

'Is that the voice of experience?' His expression had turned curious. She flashed him a wary look. 'Anton Gabrielli,' he announced. 'And a cheque for a serious amount of lira. He was either paying off a mistress or buying your silence,' he explained with a shrug. 'And as I was sure you've only ever been *my* mistress, I came to the conclusion he was buying the silence. You won't believe how good I felt about it.'

He might but she didn't. She was seeing the glimmer of a chance at an old Italian name making the difference between unacceptable and acceptable. 'I won't acknowledge him as my father, you know,' she warned him. 'If he announced it to the world I would deny the charge. He will not be walking me down any church aisle just to make me respectable. And if he left me his millions, I would give them straight back again. So if this—' she flicked an expressive hand at the ring box '—honour you are now prepared to bestow on me is built on those assumptions, you're backing a losing horse here, Marco.'

'His *billions* will go to his son and heir,' he informed her levelly, and saw her flicker of surprise. 'I see you didn't know about him.' Marco smiled. 'Handsome guy. Likes the ladies. Plays the field with relish—much like his father did. Married,' he added succinctly. 'Two children—a boy and a girl. The wife lives with her father-in-law on their private estate on the island of Capri, while her husband enjoys himself elsewhere. As for the Gabrielli name, he can keep it since you will be taking the *Bellini* name. And if you don't want him as a father, then fine.' He shrugged. 'Because I have one worthy of taking on that role for you. And, despite your natural opinion of both my parents, they are really quite nice people. Their biggest problem is that they love me too much. But in time I am hoping to spread that around a bit to other, newer members of the family.'

'Your mother hates me—'

'My mother,' Marco took up. 'Was so repentant when I saw her this afternoon that she wanted to come back to the apartment to tell you so. Fortunately—' he grimaced

'—I talked her out of it. Or she would have been witnessing her son's complete downfall. Interested in that?' he quizzed her softly.

Her eyes filled with guilty tears. Her mouth began to tremble. He wanted to kiss it until it was warm and red and too full of him to tremble ever again. Instead, he pocketed the ring. She watched him do it, and he was very pleased to see her eyes darken and the way she had to turn and walk away in an effort to hide her disappointment. She might make all the claims in the world about not wanting the ring, but she was lying; she wanted *it* almost as much as she wanted *him*.

But now she could wait. He had handled it badly anyway. And this was not the setting in which he preferred to commit himself to marriage. So they were leaving— now, he decided. Except first...

He spotted everything he required and went over to collect a sheet of brown paper and a roll of sticky tape. She was standing by the window, staring out on the kind of view of Milan that gave this scruffy room reason. Ignoring her, he went over to the nude portrait of himself and, with the efficiency of one who knew exactly how to handle an unframed canvas, he started to package it ready for transportation.

Glancing at him over her shoulder, she didn't even attempt to protest at what he was doing other than to say quietly, 'It isn't finished.'

'You may have all the time in the world to do so back at the apartment,' he replied. Sticky tape screeched as he stretched it over brown paper. 'We will convert one of the guest bedrooms into a studio.' Sharp white teeth neatly sliced through the tape, long fingers smoothed it into place.

'Marco—'

'Is there anything you want to take with you now, or can the rest wait until we are more able to receive it?' he cut in smoothly, then lifted the canvas down and finally looked at her.

Although the sunlight might be wearing the warm-gold of the late afternoon, the way it touched her hair and her skin reminded him of her own self-portrait. But the expression in her eyes could have been her mother's. Sad. It was sad. She didn't believe there was any hope for them.

'You came back, *cara*,' he reminded her soberly. 'But you did so to a new order of things. That order cannot be returned to what it used to be because you are afraid of what the change may mean.'

'It can if you let it,' she argued.

But he shook his dark head. '*I* no longer want what we used to have,' he explained, so succinctly that Antonia had no choice but to understand his meaning.

Her eyes grew so dark that his heart hit his ribcage. It was obvious she saw the choice he was giving her—between leaving him again or facing their future with all its complications—as equal to standing between a black hole and oblivion.

But she *had* come back, he grimly reminded himself. It was the only thing that stopped him from going over there and promising her anything so long as she agreed to stay with him.

It was a strange sensation, this fear of losing her, he noted as his eyes—and his bluff—held firm. 'Ready?' he prompted.

She lowered her eyes, turned away, ran her fingers up her arms to her shoulders as if she was trying to hug something to her. Courage? The chill of fear? The love he knew she felt for him? The need to believe that he felt the same about her?

It was time she began trusting in that word 'love', he thought grimly. Time she began to trust *him*.

'Yes, I'm ready,' she said quietly.

Relief almost floored him. He had to turn away to grimace at the way his legs had just turned to nothing.

'Let's go, then.' Still holding the painting, he went to collect her bit of luggage. As she approached he silently handed over her shoulder bag, then just as silently turned to the door.

CHAPTER ELEVEN

THE apartment had a hushed air about it after the taxi ride across the noisy city. A large flat brown card package leant against one of the walls with the Romano Gallery name printed on it. Marco went to place his new find beside it, then walked away down the hall and into their bedroom with her suitcase.

He was making some statement about ownership, Antonia recognised that as she followed him. Strange, then, that stepping into the one room where she'd always believed she truly belonged she should suddenly feel as if she was entering alien territory. Yet nothing had changed, the room looked exactly as it should do—if you didn't count the absence of her few personal possessions.

Marco was already putting the case away in the cupboard. There was a statement in the way he did that, also, because the case had not been unpacked and he was shutting the door, turning the key in the lock and even went so far as to remove the key and pocket it.

Try running off with only what you came here with, now, the action yelled at her.

Unsure how to respond, Antonia was still considering her options when he came back towards her, shut the bedroom door with one hand and removed her bag from her shoulder with the other then simply let it drop. And every action was so deliberate that he set her nerve-ends tingling. Her hand was caught next. He used it to trail her behind him over to the window where he touched the switch that sent the vertical blinds sliding across the glass.

The room became shrouded in a soft half-light. Seduction suddenly eddied in the air. Turning her towards him, he looked down at her, searched her whole face as if he had forgotten what it looked like, then sighed a small sigh.

'Why the closed blinds?' she asked him. He had never bothered to do that before.

'Ambience,' he replied. 'A desire for your full attention,' he added. 'And the need to shut the rest of the world out while we remind each other what it was we almost lost.'

'I'm sorry,' Antonia said. 'I—'

'Don't *ever* use those words to me again,' he cut in harshly. 'Especially *not* in English.' He even shuddered. 'They will always represent to me the coldest little good-bye a man could experience.'

He was talking about her text message. Her heart found her throat and blocked it as she gazed into his pain dark-ened blue-grey eyes. *I'm sorry* hovered on her lips again. She converted the words into a tender-sweet kiss meant to convey the meaning for her.

Pain-dark changed to passion-dark. '*Si*,' he whispered in approval. The kiss was most definitely preferable to words for him.

So one tender kiss led to another, until tender became hungry and hunger converted itself into desire. Desire stripped clothes away in a slow precious reacquainting with what she had put at risk today.

This was it. All she needed, she told herself. This man looking at her like this, touching her like this—*needing* her like this. Anything else he cared to bestow was merely a bonus. Because she could feel the love emanating from him even though he had never said the words to her.

But, as she had just demonstrated, words weren't necessary when there were other ways to relay your feelings. It was special. What they had was special. So they made love as if this was their first time. And as one day slipped harmoniously into another, Antonia began likening it to a honeymoon, where neither was seemingly prepared to allow anything to spoil what they had together.

Who wanted a betrothal ring? Who wanted a marriage proposal? This was so much more comfortable. So much more her perception of what real love was about.

On Monday, Marco slipped back into his work routine without so much as hinting that he couldn't trust her to be there when he came home again. And Antonia began converting one of the guest bedrooms into her studio. Tuesday was the day she remembered the two paintings that had disappeared from the hallway and made a note to ask Marco where they had gone, only to forget completely when he arrived home that evening with a letter from Anton Gabrielli. It was an acknowledgement that she was indeed his daughter, apologising for his behaviour, and offering to announce her as such if she wished him to do so.

'Did you bully him into this?' she asked Marco.

'I merely made him see the error in his judgement of you,' he replied. 'I thought you deserved that. What you do about him now is, of course, your own decision.'

'So you aren't going to persuade me into making his relationship to me public?'

It was a challenge, and Marco recognised it as such. 'I don't need him, *cara*,' he stated it quietly. 'But I wondered if you might feel the need to know him better one day.'

'I won't,' she said adamantly. 'It turns me cold just to look at his name.'

'Then put the letter away,' Marco advised, 'and forget about him. He won't trouble you again, I promise you.'

Which made her wonder what influence he had brought to bear on a man like Anton Gabrielli that he could sound so sure about that. But she didn't ask, didn't want to spoil her new grasp on happiness by contaminating it with questions she really didn't want the answers to.

Wednesday, they went out to dinner with Franco and Nicola, who were just back from their visit to Lake Como. Nicola looked radiant. Her eyes shone with pleasure because it was so very obvious that Antonia and Marco had sorted out their differences. Everyone enjoyed themselves. It was just as it used to be.

Thursday and Friday she devoted to overseeing the transfer of her artist's studio to its new location, and not once... Well, maybe once or twice she found herself thinking wistfully back to a certain ring box she had last seen disappearing into Marco's pocket never to see again. But then she would pull herself together and get on with whatever it was she was doing. She was content. She was happy. Marco was making her a permanent part of his life and he loved her; she was sure of it. Or becoming more sure of it as the days went by.

Then he ruined it.

It came so unexpectedly that it just hadn't occurred to her how she had been living the last week, cocooned in her own sweet dream-world constructed around a comfortable self-denial, until, over breakfast on Saturday, he murmured casually, 'We are going out tonight. A party. I think we will go shopping for something really special for you to wear…'

A party, she repeated. A party meant people. People meant facing her public humiliation from the week before. She couldn't do it. 'No,' she breathed.

Lifting his eyes from his ever-present morning newspaper, he narrowed them on her paling face. 'Red,' he murmured softly. 'I think we will go for something truly outrageous in red. Long. Slinky. Strapless and backless to show off your wonderful skin.'

'I'm not going, Marco,' she announced more firmly.

'Wear your hair up,' he continued as if she hadn't spoken. 'Let everyone see your beautiful neck and know that the only man allowed to put his lips to it is me…'

'I said, I'm not going!' She jerked to her feet.

'And I will drip you in diamonds.' He refused to take any notice of her. 'Ears, throat, wrists—even a sexy anklet sounds really irresistible.'

'Why don't you just hang a sign round my neck saying *Scarlet Woman*?' she flashed at him angrily.

Sitting back in his chair, he grinned at the image. 'Red-painted mouth. Lots of black mascara. And I think a red carnation in your hair might just make the whole ensemble perfect.'

He even kissed the tips of his fingers. Antonia had never felt so hurt in all her life. 'I can't believe you're talking like this to me, when you *know* what happened the last time you took me into company!'

She was pulsing with hurt, with fright, with indignation, Marco observed ruefully. But he didn't question any of those emotions. In fact he absolutely understood her right to feel them.

But as for the rest? 'Are you ashamed of who you are, *cara*?' he queried curiously.

Her chin went up. 'No,' she denied.

'Ashamed of being my woman, then?'

'I won't be pilloried a second time.'

Which was a neat way of getting out of giving him the answer to his question. He stood up. She made to spin away. He held her in place with the firm grip of his hands on her waist. Trapped by the table, their chairs, and his hands, she had no choice but to remain exactly where she was. But the tension in her body was enormous, the need to run again so palpable he could actually feel it dancing along every muscle she possessed.

'We made a deal a week ago,' he reminded her.

'Deal?' Her eyes flickered restlessly to his, then away again. 'I don't know what you're talking about.'

Liar, he thought grimly. 'You returned to me wanting the same as what you almost left behind.' He spelled it out to her anyway. 'I told you you couldn't have that.'

'But we've been so happy this week!' she cried. 'Why do you want to mess with something that's working fine!'

'This week I've played it your way. I've allowed us to hide and pretend everything is *fine* because you seemed to need to do that. But I don't want *fine* I want *perfect*,' he added. 'And perfect comes at a price, *cara*. The point is, are you prepared to pay it?'

She clearly didn't like the sound of the word. It was like holding a tiger by its tail. 'And what is this price?'

'Your trust,' he announced. 'I want you to *trust* me to make this work for us. And, just so you understand how serious I am, I must warn you that I will accept nothing less than your total trust.'

Nothing less—as in *nothing*. No Marco at all was what

he was saying here. Antonia shivered at the mere prospect. 'And this trust comes in the colour red.' Her sigh turned itself into a grimace.

'In your face, knock them dead red,' he confirmed. 'Will you do it?'

Trust him not to hold her up as an object of scorn? No, she didn't. For you didn't dress your woman up, as he had just described, without having some ulterior motive for doing it. But to demand to know what that motive was had now been denied her by that word *trust*.

So, 'Yes,' she said.

His soft laugh said he was aware of how difficult she'd found it to say that word. But, 'Good,' was all he replied. 'Because I've seen the perfect dress on Via Monte Napoleon. Let's go and buy it...'

It was certainly red, Antonia confirmed, as she stood looking at herself in the bedroom mirror. In your face *and* knock them dead. A quiver of anxiety went shivering through her. In fact, Marco had described it perfectly. Long and slinky, with a heart-shaped boned bodice that defied gravity and a back that wasn't there at all. Pinched-in waistline, a long skirt that clung smoothly to every detail of her shape as it made its way down to her ankles, and a kick-back pleat that began at the back of her knees to give her the ability to walk—and her figure an hour-glass shape that was so damn sexy it couldn't be more 'in your face'.

Her hair was up, as requested, and she truly did drip with diamonds. Diamond choker, diamond bracelet at her wrist, diamonds dangling from her ears. Glancing down at her high-heeled strappy red shoes, she caught a glimpse of the diamond anklet he had insisted she wear. In fact the only thing she had been able to refuse, and get away with it, was the red carnation to dress up her hair.

Her lipstick was red, her eyeliner so much more pronounced than she would usually wear it that, as she looked into her own eyes, she didn't recognise them. She looked lush, she looked sexy, and she looked like a wealthy man's possession.

Which she was, she acknowledged.

And if this wasn't dressing up to brazen out whatever was coming, then she didn't know what was.

'If I come near, will you attack me?' a deep voice quizzed her.

Her eyes flashed to him via the mirror. Big and lean, too darn handsome for his own good in conventional black dinner suit and bow-tie, he was looking at her as if he wanted to eat her alive as she stood there.

'I wonder how many propositions I will get tonight?' she mused by way of getting a hit back at him without the suggested physical attack.

Stepping behind her, he slid his hands around her narrow waist, his thumb-pads gently stroking against her bare skin. She quivered in response, despite not wanting to. The sensation centred itself deep in her abdomen and refused to budge.

Sex, it was called. Give it to me. He saw it reflected in her eyes. 'They can try, *mi amante*, but we both know to whom it is that you belong, hmm?'

Yes, she thought, and for a moment actually hated him for being so sure of himself. It could not go unchallenged, though. So she turned in his grasp and stroked a hand up his dress shirt, found his warm throat, trailed her fingers up to his ear. This man might know her inside out, but she knew him also. The pleasure point behind his ear only needed the lightest of caress to send a shudder through him.

'And you know to whom it is that *you* belong, hey, *mi amore*?'

He caught the trailing fingers, kissed them with a wryly mocking bow, his eyes dark with promises as he straightened again. It was only then that she saw the colour of his jacket lining. It was glossy silk, matador-red.

He was most definitely out to make a very big statement tonight, she realised. 'Where are we going?' She frowned up at him.

'So you thought to ask at last,' he smiled. 'Well, wait and see. It's a surprise.'

Opening her red-painted mouth to tell him that she didn't like surprises, she felt the dark eyes challenge her. She held her breath, thought about that wretched word *trust*, and closed her mouth again.

He rewarded her with a kiss that required his mouth to be wiped clear of lipstick later and her to do a quick refurbishing job on her own.

After that they left the apartment and went downstairs to climb into the back of a chauffeur-driven limousine, which meant that Marco intended to enjoy a drink tonight. It wasn't late, which was unusual here in Milan, where most parties tended to begin way after ten. But she didn't begin to understand why they had set out so early until they arrived at Linate airport, to a waiting helicopter.

'Tell me where we are going,' she pleaded, unable to stop herself.

Helping her into the rear of the helicopter, and making sure her dress was neatly folded around her ankles as she sat down, he joined her, closed the door, gave the pilot the nod to get them into the air, then turned and announced very casually, 'We are going to my parents' home in Tuscany…'

Nothing—nothing had prepared her for that announcement. Marco could see that as her face went perfectly white. She didn't speak, didn't even gasp in shocked horror; she just sat beside him and died a thousands deaths in total silence.

His instincts were telling him to say something—anything to reassure her that this night was going to be fine. But that word *fine* wasn't enough for him. And the word *trust* was demanding he make her give him that unequivocally. It was a pride thing; he knew that. For, although he might have forgiven her for keeping so much of herself hidden from him, he still hadn't come to terms with how little she had trusted him with any of the important issues in her life.

Shallow. She'd thought him shallow. An arrogant snob who was quite capable of loving a woman senseless in his bed but could actually despise her for what she was. Well, tonight, she was going to learn a few harsh lessons. And one of them was to spend the next hour stewing in her own anxieties. He felt she owed him that.

And anyway, he was excited. He was out to make an impact tonight, and not just on his family and friends but on Antonia too. So, with the smoothness taught to him from the cradle, he began talking, filling in the trip with innocuous discussion about innocuous subjects that forced her to think and answer but did not detract from the tense expectancy that built up the longer they were in the air.

They arrived as darkness was falling. It was the perfect time to get her first glimpse of the Casa Bellini. The vine-covered valley, the house in its centre lit from the inside

by electric lighting while the final drape of the sun coloured a blush against its outer walls.

Waiting for the helicopter blades to go still before he
jumped out, Marco turned to lift Antonia down. She slid
through his grasp like smooth bone china, no weight, no
substance, nothing but fairness and beauty and an anxiety
that kicked at his gut.

'I love you,' he murmured, and placed a kiss on her
brow.

It was the first time he had said it out loud. Impact was
what he had been out for; impact was what he got. Her
eyes washed with moisture, and he felt his own want to
do the same.

'I just wanted to be sure you knew that before we went
inside,' he added very huskily—so huskily, in fact, that
he didn't know his own voice.

She didn't say anything. He didn't think she could. So
he took her hand and walked her towards his parents'
house and in through the huge French windows left open
to the evening air. Her fingers clung so tightly to his he
knew—*knew* this woman, this beautiful woman was his
for ever now.

The first people they saw as they entered were his
mother and father, waiting to greet them on the huge ex-
panse of brown and white chequered floor that gave their
home such a grand entrance that led right from the front
to the back of the house.

This was it, he thought. Show time...

Dressed in statutory black, but breathtakingly elegant in
it, Signora Isabella Bellini walked forwards. She was
smiling at her, Antonia noticed. It was an uncertain,

slightly wary smile, but at least it was a smile. She tried a smile in return.

'Welcome,' Marco's mother greeted, and leaned forward to place a kiss on each of her cheeks.

Her fingers tightened their grip on Marco.

'Th-thank you.' Antonia wasn't sure why she offered those words in English. It simply seemed appropriate. 'It was good of you to invite me here.'

'No.' Signora Bellini did not accept that. 'It should have happened a long time ago. I apologise for my rudeness and hope you can learn to forgive me for it. We Bellinis can be too arrogant for our own comfort sometimes.'

It was so gracious, so kind, Antonia felt the tears threaten again. 'I understood, really I did,' she assured the older woman. Well—maybe it was a lie, but it was a *kind* lie.

It was a good point for Federico Bellini to step smoothly into the breach. 'Now I see why my son lays threats at a sick man's door,' he remarked, softening the censure with a lazy grin which hit Antonia right in her solar plexus because it was so like Marco's smile.

He was tall like his son, dark-haired like his son—if a little peppered with silver. But it was also clear that, beneath the sophistication of formal black and white clothing, the rest of Signor Bellini had seen better times.

Opening her mouth to voice her concern for his illness, the man himself pre-empted her by bending towards her. 'Don't say it,' he confided. 'It is not necessary.' Then he kissed both her cheeks, raised his head and smiled his son's smile again. 'It's an honour to meet you at last, Miss Carson.'

Then he turned his attention to Marco. 'This is your

night, Marco. Your guests await. Therefore I suggest you get this started.'

With that hand still firmly clasped in his, Marco felt Antonia's instant tension, the shock in realising that this was more than just a formal introduction to his parents.

His father's eyes were glinting with sardonic knowledge. His mother was displaying no expression at all. She had not been against what he had set up here, but she had not been sure it was the right way to go about settling the issue of Antonia.

'Hurt her with this and she will never forgive you,' she'd warned him only yesterday.

'You don't know her as I do,' he'd replied. 'I have confidence in her. I *trust* her to understand.'

Trust. *Dio*, but that word was playing a major role in his life right now, he acknowledged as he started walking towards the doors which led into the family's formal reception room.

Antonia clung to his side. His parents fell into step behind them. As they reached the doors a waiting servant smoothly pushed them open to reveal a vast room lit by huge mountains of crystal. Marco paused on the threshold, so he could give Antonia a moment to absorb the sheer grandeur of the room and the people who were already present and waiting for their entrance.

The hum of conversation dropped into silence. Faces turned, people stared. Beside him, Antonia's pulse began to quicken as she took in the full impact of the whole assembly. And Marco did nothing, just waited for her restless eyes to finish making a full inventory of what he had set up for them here tonight.

Then at last she saw them, standing out like a pair of statements. Bold, brash, utterly scorning any hint of discomfort. Her warm soft red-painted mouth slackened, her ensuing gasp audible only to him. Surprise tingled from her fingers into his, then she simply stood there so breathless and still that he actually began to wonder if he had made a big mistake.

This just wasn't happening, Antonia tried to tell herself. She was having a dream. A very weird dream. She had to be. In a minute all of these people were going to start laughing in gruesome mockery, telling her to get out and never come near them again, which was how dreams like these usually finished. It was the only answer she could form to what it was she was looking at.

But it wasn't a dream. She knew it because she could feel Marco literally vibrating with waiting tension beside her. She tried swallowing and found she couldn't. She tried turning to look at him, but she couldn't do that either because her eyes were refusing to move from what they had frozen on.

For right there, hanging on his parents' wall for everyone to see, were two nudes painted in oils and mounted in matching frames. One was herself, looking slender and sleek and coyly seductive. The other was Marco, looking as bold and arrogant in his nakedness as she'd always perceived him to be.

Heat roared into her cheeks, then faded away again. Her heart began to thunder on the total shock of seeing the two of them so brazenly presented like this. And suddenly the dress began to make sense, the desire to drip her in diamonds. Marco was taking them all on—his parents, his friends, all those mocking doubters who didn't believe he could love this woman who could expose her body like this.

If you can't beat them, join them, he was saying. If I

can't make them believe, then—what the heck? Throw these two paintings in their faces and let them think what they like!

'If you can hack it then I can too,' Marco murmured beside her, and his voice was soft, layered with warmth and humour and a lazy challenge.

She found the strength to look at him, saw the humour reflecting in his eyes, plus something else—a plea, maybe, for her to understand what it was he had been trying to achieve when he'd decided to do this.

A short laugh rippled from her. It spilled into her eyes and turned his smile into a grin. She looked frontward again—and continued to smile, because she understood. She *knew*! This was his way of levelling the differences in them. It was *him* coming down his lofty ladder. It was *her* climbing up to meet him.

The hand he placed on her lower spine threaded electric sensation across her naked skin as it began drifting up her spine to her slender nape in an act of sensual possession.

'More to come,' he warned softly, and urged her into movement again.

Her legs felt like rubber. Her pulse was racing, and her mind was lost in a haze of shock and some dismay and a whole lot of sinfully delicious elation. He took them past smiling faces, past rueful faces, past familiar faces like Franco and Nicola. She saw, through what felt like a misted glaze, Stefan grinning knowingly at her, while the woman at his side looked on curiously. She was tall and dark and so beautiful it made Antonia halt for a second to offer her a warm smile.

'Tanya.' She whispered the woman's name.

'Later,' Marco advised, and pressed her into movement again.

At the other end of the room, he finally paused. It was a staged arrival, which placed them exactly in between their naked images. Lights sparkled, diamonds flashed, faces observed curiously as he turned her towards him.

Holding the whole room captive, he looked deep into her eyes, then dropped his gaze to her mouth and allowed it to linger there until the pulse of anticipation became an energy charge all of its own.

'Right,' he said huskily, 'now, this is the deal...'

'Another one?' she whispered back, aware that he was deliberately holding her balanced on a pin-head of expectation with the warmth of his eyes and the promise of his kiss, and the touch of his fingers on her—

She glanced down and had to blink several times before she could focus on the ring he was carefully sliding onto her finger. Made of gold and platinum, it was an intricate twist of finely worked metals forming the clasp for a diamond. And not just any old diamond, she realised, as she watched its flawless quality sparkle with a deep yellow lustre which told her instinctively that this was a very rare diamond indeed.

'What do you think?' Deep, dark, disturbingly husky, his voice made her senses sparkle like the diamond.

'It's—beautiful,' she breathed.

'At the risk of sounding really corny, it reminded me of your eyes,' he drily confessed. 'But it comes with a price-tag attached to it,' he then added.

'Another one of those also?' she murmured in an attempt to mock. But it didn't come off, for she was just too filled with the wonder in what he was creating for her.

It was pure romance tied up in bows of spicy sensation. The kind of thing you remembered for ever and relayed to your children and your grandchildren.

'Mmm,' he murmured, and it was one of the really sexy murmurs that she loved so much. 'Because with this ring, *mi amore*, I am about to commit you to a solemn promise that you will trust me to love you for the rest of your life...'

It was too much. Without a care for who was watching, she reached up on tiptoe and kissed him. Not shy and light, or tender and sweet, but with every ounce of love she had in her.

A camera bulb flashed. They were caught for posterity locked in a heated embrace with two oil paintings framing why they were kissing like that...

The villa in Portofino was the ideal setting for their honeymoon, Marco thought with a sense of warm satisfaction. They'd flown in by helicopter direct from their wedding reception at his family estate in Tuscany. And though it was dark outside the air was fresher here, so close to the ocean, so Marco had no problem leaning against the balcony rail while he watched his bride come towards him.

She was naked, of course. But then so was he—if you didn't count the rich cream-satin waistcoat she had made him put back on before she would allow him to make love to her. It was meant to make a statement, like the fine tulle veil she still had pinned to her beautiful hair, that floated around her exquisite face and shoulders as she moved towards him.

Sexy. Very sexy. He allowed himself a lecherous grin. 'When are you going to take it off?' he asked lazily.

'When I feel married,' she replied.

He arched a brow. 'And you don't feel married yet?'

'No.' The pout was very spoiled and sumptuously kissable. And, since they'd already made love several times since they'd arrived here, it was also a slight on his virility.

'Watch it,' he warned.

She had the audacity to look down. He laughed—what else could he do when he was being bewitched by a teasing little temptress with only one thing on her mind.

Dio, she made him feel good. She made him feel like the only worthy man on this earth.

Her fingers came out, stroked the cream satin lapel up to his shoulders, then made their way back down again. When she reached the open buttons she began to slowly close them. The cutaway edges of the waistcoat suddenly put a whole new meaning on erotic fantasy.

'If you're looking so intent because you're thinking of painting me like this, then take my advice, *cara*, and change your mind,' he advised.

Lightly said, lazily delivered, but still he meant every word of it. Her chin came up. The pout had gone; the seductress had switched back on. Stepping that tiny bit closer to him, she held his eyes for a long moment and caught his mouth with a kiss aimed to take the legs from under him—while her hands went in search of other weaknesses.

His eyes drew shut, his breath escaped on a thickened sigh as she unleashed her magic upon him. If he died right now, at least he would go taking this image with him.

Man and wife, belonging to each other.

'You have no inhibition,' he censured darkly.

'I love you,' she answered simply. 'It *is* uninhibited.'

She was right, and it was. The warm, red, kiss-swollen mouth he claimed with his own mouth. The woman he claimed in other ways.

A MARRIAGE PROPOSAL FOR CHRISTMAS

BY
CAROLE MORTIMER

CHAPTER ONE

'I KNOW no one is available to take my call at the moment, and no, I will not leave a message after the tone!' the man's voice snarled. 'I've already left four messages, and I'm sick of talking to this damned machine. I intend coming round there in person in the hopes that I can talk to a human being!'

Cally stood arrested in the doorway of the office as she heard the disembodied voice on the message her sister Pam was playing back on the answering machine. 'Not a dissatisfied customer, I hope?' She raised questioning brows as she came fully into the office and closed the door behind her, instantly shutting out the cold December wind blowing outside.

'Not yet.' Her sister looked up and smiled as she switched off the answering machine. 'So far he's just another person who seems to have forgotten that this is the season of peace and good will to all men.'

'I've always wondered what happened to ''and all women'' in that particular phrase,' Cally murmured as she slipped out of her thick outer coat, moving to hang it on the stand in the corner of the room. She appeared small and slim in the black business suit she wore, the thin green jumper beneath the jacket a perfect match for her eyes, long red hair loose about her shoulders.

Her sister, at twenty-eight the elder by three years, shrugged philosophically. 'Different century, darling,' she

189

said dryly. 'You mean we were even less equal then than we are now?' Cally snapped irritably, moving to sit down behind the second desk in this cosily welcoming room that constituted the sisters' base for their business.

Pam chuckled. 'What's upset you this morning? Or should I say, who?' she corrected knowingly. 'Playboy of the West been keeping you awake all night again, has he?'

Cally raised auburn brows. 'Would you care to rephrase that?'

Pam's grin widened. 'Not particularly. But I will if it makes you happy,' she added teasingly as Cally's scowl deepened. 'Let's see.' She paused for thought. 'Has your neighbour been keeping you awake all hours of the day and night again with his noisy arrivals and departures in that gorgeous red vehicle that is just too glamorous to be called a mere car?'

'It's a Ferrari,' Cally supplied disgustedly. 'And that was at midnight last night. This morning—at six-thirty, would you believe?—it was a helicopter!' And she could still clearly remember being startled awake by the noise of its engines as it flew over the gatehouse where she lived, before landing on the lawn of the main house— where the 'Playboy of the West' lived!

'A helicopter.' Pam nodded, suitably impressed.

'It landed on the front lawn of the main house, continued to run its engines for ten minutes or so, and then flew off again. I was not amused, I can tell you,' Cassie growled, not willing, at this moment, to tell her sister just how unamused she had been—she was still too angry about the whole affair!

'Did he wake Lissa, too?' Pam looked concerned.

'No,' Cally allowed grudgingly, sure that her young daughter would sleep through an earthquake.

'Have you managed to meet Noel Carlton yet?' her sister asked eagerly.

Pam had been fascinated by the comings and goings of Cally's neighbour since he had moved into the main house almost a year ago. Cally didn't share the interest; she wished he would just take his Ferrari, and his helicopter, in fact, his whole over-the-top lifestyle, and go back to wherever it was he had come from!

The fact that he had flirted with her when she'd gone up to the house to complain about the noise a couple of months ago hadn't exactly endeared him to her, either. Especially as he hadn't followed up on the flirtation but had suddenly become coolly aloof! a little voice taunted inside her.

'No,' she fibbed. She felt guilty not telling Pam the truth, but couldn't face the grilling Pam would insist on giving her if she knew Cally had met the man twice now.

'Still think it was a good idea to move out to the "peace and quiet" of the country?' Pam teased as she saw Cally's frowning look.

Until Noel Carlton had moved in next door it had been a brilliant idea. The gatehouse she rented from the Parker Estate was just perfect for her and her young daughter, Lissa. Added to that, Lissa loved her new school, and was also able to indulge her interest in horse-riding at weekends. Even the forty-minute drive into work for Cally had been worth it just to see the happy smiles on her young daughter's face.

But Noel Carlton had moved in almost a year ago and since then it had all become a bit of a nightmare. Even complaints to the agent for the estate that she had arranged to rent the gatehouse from initially had not elicited any satisfaction.

Which was why she had paid Noel Carlton a visit herself two months ago. At that visit she had found the man absolutely charming, a fact he'd obviously picked up on as he had suggested they go out to dinner together some time to discuss the problem further.

To say she had been stunned by the invitation would be putting it mildly.

She had been disappointed when he hadn't bothered to call her, but had seemed to look through her the next time he'd seen her. And had continued to do so ever since.

Although, she recalled with a grimace, she hadn't exactly given him the opportunity to ignore her this morning!

Cally set her shoulders. 'It was an excellent idea,' she stated firmly. 'I'm determined that he will tire of country life before I do!'

Her sister chuckled, shaking her head. 'I wish you luck. I—uh-oh.' Her hazel-coloured gaze moved to the huge window that looked out on the busy high street from where they ran their business.

'What—?' Cally's attention was also caught by the grim-faced man striding determinedly past the window, the colour draining from her face as she realized he was coming here. 'It's him!' she squeaked breathlessly, at the same time coming sharply to her feet.

Pam turned back with a frown. 'What—?'

'It's him!' Cally repeated frantically.

'I—where are you going?' Pam demanded as Cally made a quick exit in the direction of the back room where they made hot drinks and kept the stationery.

'To make some coffee. I—get rid of him!' she pleaded before disappearing behind the open door.

But she made no effort to go and make coffee, or indeed anything else, as she heard the outer door open before being closed with suppressed violence. Nothing had changed there, then!

'Can I help you?' she heard Pam offer politely.

'I certainly hope so,' the man rasped.

Noel Carlton!

There was no doubt about it, Cally accepted with a wince after taking a surreptitious peek from behind the slightly ajar door and easily recognizing her nearest neighbour.

She couldn't mistake that handsomely chiselled face, or the dark hair he wore much longer than was fashionable. His suit, even from that brief glance, looked expensively tailored, as did the handmade black leather shoes.

Not that any of that mattered just now. There could be only one reason for this man turning up here: her comments this morning had obviously elicited some sort of response, after all!

'A human being at last,' he continued scathingly. 'You are a human being, aren't you?'

'Indeed I am,' Pam answered in her most soothing voice, always the calmer one of the two sisters—a fact Cally had always blamed on her own vibrantly red hair as opposed to Pam's more muted auburn. 'Would you be the gentleman who rang earlier?' she queried.

'Five times!' he confirmed indignantly.

Noel Carlton was the angry man on the answering machine?

'We don't actually open until nine o'clock, I'm afraid, Mr…?'

'Carlton,' he snapped.

'Mr Carlton,' Pam acknowledged smoothly—giving no indication of having recognized the name at all. 'I'm sorry there was no one here to take your calls earlier, but, as I said, we don't actually open the office until nine o'clock. However, I'm obviously more than happy to offer you any assistance that I can now.'

No, don't say that! Cally mentally tried to communicate with her sister. Noel Carlton was the last person either of them even wanted to talk to. Until they had consulted a lawyer, at any rate. Not that Cally thought she was even slightly in the wrong with her complaints, but that didn't mean that her neighbour saw it that way, too.

Cally took another peek around the door, just in time to see the man lowering his long length into the chair opposite Pam's desk, his back towards Cally now as she frantically tried to attract her sister's attention over one of his broad shoulders.

Pam shot her a questioning glance, obviously still none the wiser as to why Cally had disappeared so swiftly.

Cally quietly opened the door a little wider, raising her hands to make a movement as if she were holding the steering wheel of a car.

If anything Pam just looked even more perplexed!

Cally gave her sister a frustrated frown, pointing at Noel Carlton's broad back, then at herself, before repeating the action of holding a car's steering wheel.

Nothing.

Her sister looked completely puzzled now, at the same time staring at Cally as if she had gone slightly insane.

And maybe she had, Cally conceded heavily. She might

have been extremely upset this morning, and told him
exactly what she thought of him—but having Noel
Carlton turn up at her place of work was the last response
she had expected!

'The thing is that I need— Do I have your full attention...Mrs Davies?' Noel Carlton prompted, having
paused briefly while he read the name on the front of the
desk.

Pam broke her gaze away from Cally, a blush in her
cheeks now. 'Of course you do, Mr—I'm sorry, what did
you say your name was?' she encouraged in a slightly
hushed voice, her eyes widening now with sudden recognition.

At last! Maybe there wouldn't be any need to hit her
sister over the head with a book later, after all!

'Carlton,' he supplied again through clenched teeth.
'The thing is that I need—Mrs Davies?' he bit out impatiently as he obviously sensed her attention wandering
again.

Not surprisingly really; Pam's gaze had returned to
Cally as she stood behind him. The look in Pam's eyes
was a mixture of recognition and excitement, tinged with
wariness as to what he was actually doing here.

Cally had a pretty good idea as to the answer to the
latter, although she hoped not to have to discuss that with
her sister in front of her neighbour.

'What the—?' Noel Carlton, having followed Pam's
gaze and glanced behind him, stood up abruptly as he saw
Cally standing there. 'You!' he accused.

Her.

And Noel Carlton looked no more pleased to see her
again than she was to see him!

CHAPTER TWO

THE two of them continued to stare at each other, Cally challengingly, Noel Carlton's expression now completely unreadable as he looked at her with those deep blue eyes.

In Cally's opinion, it wasn't fair that one man should be so good-looking. As well as that overlong hair being thick and darkly waving and his eyes being a beautiful deep cobalt-blue, his nose was straight and arrogant, his lips perfectly sculptured—the lower lip sensually fuller than the top—his jaw was square and determined, and his body tall and muscular, totally belying the thirty-five years or so that Cally guessed him to be. All that and rich too, Cally dismissed scathingly.

'Er—do you two know each other?' Pam was the one to break the chilly silence that had descended after Noel Carlton's initial outburst, her gaze accusing as she shot Cally a pointed glance.

Completely deserved, Cally accepted with an inner wince. But she simply hadn't had a chance yet to calm down enough to be able to rationally discuss the full events of this morning with her sister. Not that she thought Pam would be too impressed with that explanation, but it was the only one she had.

'No!'

'Yes.'

Noel Carlton and Cally spoke at the same time, Cally in the negative, Noel Carlton in the positive.

But if he thought having invited her out to dinner two

months ago, and then promptly forgetting he had ever made the invitation, along with the argument this morning, gave him any right to claim an acquaintance with her then he was sadly mistaken; in fact, it was the opposite!

Pam gave the two of them a gleeful smile. 'Come on, now, which one is it?' she taunted.

'We most certainly do *not* know each other,' Cally answered before he even had chance to do so.

'Oh, come on, Cally,' Noel Carlton drawled, those deep blue eyes mocking now as he looked at her challengingly. 'That's not the impression I had earlier this morning.'

Cally's eyes widened indignantly, a blush creeping into her freckle-covered cheeks as Pam repeated, 'Earlier this morning, hmm?'

'Don't take any notice of him, Pam.' Cally glared at her infuriating neighbour. 'He's just trying to be clever!'

'And succeeding,' Pam pointed out. 'Dare one ask how it is the two of you happened to be together earlier this morning?' The look she gave Cally clearly said, You certainly didn't tell me that!

Cally drew in a sharp breath at her sister's speculative expression. 'It's really quite simple—'

'Oh, very,' Noel Carlton agreed mildly. He folded his arms across the width of his chest now as he looked at the two women. 'Tell me, are the two of you related? I seem to see a certain resemblance in the colouring and bone structure...'

'Sisters,' Cally supplied economically, not seeing what possible interest that could be to this man; if he had come here to cause trouble, then why didn't he just get on with it instead of standing there looking so damned irresistibly attractive?

Because he most certainly was! Cally found her pulse

was beating rather faster than it should be, that blush having stayed in her cheeks as she became fully aware of his
mere physical presence—mere? There was nothing 'mere'
about this man!

Everything about him was overpowering, from the way
he looked, to the way his height and size just dominated
the room. And the people in it!

Well, they would see about that, Cally decided, giving
herself a mental shake. Okay, so the man was good-
looking and rich as Croesus, but that didn't mean that
every woman he met had to fall down worshipping at his
feet. Even if, that little voice taunted inside her again, her
real anger towards him was based on the fact that he had
never followed up on that dinner invitation…!

'Hmm, I should have guessed.' Noel Carlton gave Pam
a smile warm enough to melt the flesh from her bones.

Something her elder sister welcomed, Cally realized
disgustedly as she saw Pam return that smile and look at
him from beneath lowered lashes.

Really, her sister had been happily married to Brian for
the last eight years, had two little boys of school age, and
yet here Pam was blushing like a schoolgirl herself just
because Noel Carlton had smiled at her!

'I can't imagine why you should,' Cally dismissed.
'And while I appreciate that you went to some trouble to
find me, I really have no intention of continuing our earlier conversation here.'

'That's very good,' he mocked, turning to smile at Pam
once again. 'Your sister seems to be—the more emotional
one of the two of you, shall we say? Has she always been
that way?' he enquired.

'Always,' Pam confirmed, grinning at Cally's obvious

discomfort at being discussed in this way. Her sister had patently decided it was the least Cally deserved after not telling her that she had actually met this man earlier this morning.

But there was a perfectly good reason why she hadn't told Pam about that meeting. In fact, there were several reasons. Firstly, losing her temper was never something she was particularly proud of. Secondly, even as she had been losing her temper with Noel Carlton she had found herself once again attracted to him. Thirdly, she had been able to tell by the warmth in his gaze that he returned the attraction…

'Hmm,' Noel Carlton murmured now appreciatively, at the same time giving Cally a look that it was impossible to see as anything else but a totally male assessment, taking in the rich redness of her long hair, the wide green eyes, her heart-shaped face dominated by those freckles, her determinedly raised chin, her slenderness in the black business suit, the long length of her legs.

Really, Cally thought crossly, did this man ever switch off his playboy mode?

'Could you just say what you want to say, Mr Carlton, and then leave?' she encouraged impatiently.

'Of course. I'm sure we're all busy people.'

'Nice of you to realize that,' she drawled.

'Cally,' Pam began warningly.

'Oh, don't be concerned, Pam,' she assured her sister lightly. 'Mr Carlton is perfectly well aware of my opinion of him!'

'Now, let me see…' Noel Carlton paused for dramatic effect. '"A rich, overindulged, totally selfish, egotistical idiot" was the phrase you used earlier, I believe. Did I miss anything out?' he asked, eyes openly laughing at her now.

'You know that you didn't!' Her cheeks were burning with indignation at the realisation that she had obviously amused him. And something else. It was that 'something else' that caused her to look away from him in some confusion.

She simply couldn't still find this man attractive! Oh, of course he was good-looking, but as far as she was concerned, after inviting her out and then not even bothering to call her, he had nothing else to recommend him, and she had no intention of being taken in by looks alone. That had already happened in her life once, and look what a disaster that had turned out to be...!

'Actually—' he glanced at the name on the badge attached to the lapel of her jacket '—Mrs Turner—'

'Miss,' Cally corrected. 'Miss Turner,' she enlarged almost defensively as he looked at her enquiringly, at the same time waiting for some cutting comment from him. One of the things she had thrown at him this morning in their heated exchange—well, to be honest, hers had been heated, Noel Carlton had looked as if not too much made him exert himself at that time of the morning!—had been that he had woken not only her up with the arrival and departure of that helicopter but her young daughter too. It wasn't true, of course. Lissa had still been fast asleep, but it had sounded good at the time.

His brows rose slightly before he spoke again, 'Miss Turner,' he acknowledged with an inclination of his head. 'Well, I hate to disappoint you, Miss Turner, but I'm afraid my being here today has absolutely nothing to do with you, and everything to do with the unfortunate predicament I find myself in.'

Cally blinked, staring at him in disbelief. Was he seriously expecting her to believe his coming to her workplace was just a coincidence?

'What predicament would that be, Mr Carlton?' Pam was the one to ask. 'I did detect a certain element of desperation in the telephone messages you left earlier,' she added sympathetically.

'Desperation!' He gave a huff of grim laughter. 'I'm beginning to wish I could just scrap Christmas altogether.'

'Bah, humbug,' Cally murmured tauntingly.

'Just call me Ebenezer,' Noel Carlton conceded. 'Not that I have anything against the present giving, or the decorations, or the fact that we get in more food and drink than we will ever be able to consume in two days—'

'Then what do you object to?' Cally queried with a puzzled smile. 'You seem to have got Christmas more or less covered there!'

'That's the problem—I haven't.' He sighed heavily. 'I don't object to any of it—I just haven't done any of it!' His voice started to rise in agitation. 'My parents and my two siblings are due to arrive from the States in two days' time, and I haven't done a damned thing towards providing them with the English Christmas they're all so looking forward to!'

'Ah,' Cally breathed as understanding slowly began to dawn. 'And you thought Celebrations may be able to do it for you?'

After all, it was what she and Pam did; arranged parties and weddings, and even Christmas, for people who were too busy, or just too disorganized, to be able to manage it for themselves, organizing decorations, food, drink, staff if they were needed—in fact anything a client needed to make the celebration a success.

The two sisters had started out quite small five years ago, working from Pam's home, as a way of them both earning some money, with the added bonus that they could arrange their jobs around the demands of their young children. During that five years they had built up a solid reputation, but unfortunately only locally, with other parents from school, or recommendation from them by word of mouth. And so they had discussed it with Pam's husband, and decided that, although it would be a struggle financially for a while, the only way for them to make a real success of the business—to eventually make money!—was to enlarge the business by moving into premises in town.

Something they had done only six months ago...

Cally just hadn't thought that Noel Carlton would be one of those disorganized people they were called in to help.

She smiled. 'Well, I'm really sorry about this, Mr Carlton...' the brightness of her tone telling him that she wasn't sorry at all '...but I'm afraid that we're fully booked this week—'

'Actually, we're not,' Pam admitted softly.

Cally turned sharply to her sister. 'What do you mean, we're not?'

Her sister gave a shrug. 'I haven't had chance to tell you yet, but the Neilsons telephoned early this morning and left a message on the machine too.' She gave Noel a smile. 'Apparently they have had some sort of emergency in Sweden, have had to return home unexpectedly, and don't expect to return to England until after the New Year.'

'But I was due to go and put all the decorations up today! And what about all the food we have stored in the freezer?' Cally gasped her dismay, having been working exclusively on the Neilsons' Christmas for the last week. 'What are we supposed to do with all of that?' She groaned at the thought of all that work wasted.

And the fact that they weren't going to get paid!

'Excuse me,' Noel Carlton put in pointedly.

Cally shot him a narrow-eyed glare as she easily caught his meaning. 'Forget it,' she bit out, at the same time knowing that she and Pam couldn't afford to lose all the money they had expended on the Neilsons' Christmas; the deposit paid by the Neilsons wasn't refundable, but by the same token it in no way covered what had already been spent.

'But, Cally, it would seem to be the perfect solution to everyone's problems,' Pam reasoned, a worried frown furrowing her brow as she also thought of the money they were going to lose.

'This is my mother's first visit to England since she remarried and moved to America twenty years ago,' Noel Carlton argued persuasively. 'The last thing I want to do is disappoint her and my stepfather by not giving her the sort of Christmas she remembers.'

'Shouldn't you have thought of that earlier?' Cally frowned, not at all impressed by his attempt at emotional blackmail—even as she felt a faint stirring of concern for a woman she had never met.

The perfectly sculptured mouth firmed, his eyes narrowing to angry slits of dark blue. 'I did think of it. It's just—a series of—unexpected events have unfortunately made it impossible for me to complete my plans,' he explained.

'Oh, yes? And just what sort of "unexpected events" could a man like you—?'

'A man *like me*?' he interrupted in a softly, dangerous tone of voice.

'I think Mr Carlton has already told us as much of his predicament as we need to know, Cally,' her sister declared, standing up decisively. 'Mr Carlton has come here to ask for our help. Because of a last-minute cancellation, we are in a position to provide that help. I may be wrong, but I thought that was what we were in business for?' She gave Cally a pointed look.

They were. Of course they were. There was nothing more rewarding, after days, possibly weeks, of hard work, than to see the look of happiness on a client's face when their particular celebration passed off successfully because of Pam's and Cally's efforts. Cally just wasn't inclined to see that look on Noel Carlton's face. Unfortunately she could see by the stubborn set to Pam's mouth that her sister, quite rightly, was thinking of the overdraft on their bank account rather than whether or not Cally was comfortable with this commission.

'We still have the Neilsons' deposit,' she tried half-heartedly, knowing it wasn't enough. 'Besides, you're completely tied up at the moment with the arrangements for the Gregorys' wedding on Christmas Eve,' she reminded her sister hopefully.

'Yes, I am,' Pam confirmed, glancing down at her wrist-watch. 'In fact, I have an appointment at the florist's in fifteen minutes,' she realized. 'But you, Cally, on the other hand, are totally free for the next three days.'

'I'm more than willing to pay extra, petrol money, whatever, if you will just agree to help me out,' Noel Carlton enticed.

'Bribery and corruption usually work, do they?' Cally snapped.

He grinned. 'Every time.'

'I thought so.' Cally gave a disgusted shake of her head.

'Cally!' Pam gasped reprovingly.

'Sorry,' she muttered, feeling as if she were swimming upstream—and rapidly losing the battle. Besides, a part of her knew that Pam was quite right to grasp this replacement commission with both hands. If only it weren't Noel Carlton's hands they were grasping!

'There's the added benefit that you'll be working close to home,' Noel Carlton encouraged, his smile one of false brightness when Cally gave him another frown for reminding her that he was her neighbour from hell. As if she needed any reminding of that!

But, in actual fact, it would be a benefit, more so than this man probably realized, if she agreed to arrange Christmas for him and his family.

She would be able to pick Lissa up from her sister's house much earlier in the day. Brian was looking after the children, school having finished for the Christmas holidays. It didn't happen very often that either Pam or herself couldn't care for the children during the holidays, but Christmas was such a busy time that it invariably ended with Lissa staying with her uncle Brian, a self-employed accountant who worked from home, for part of the Christmas holidays. Not that Lissa didn't enjoy being with her cousins, because she did, but it was a lot to expect Brian to cope with three children instead of two for long hours.

'I really do have to go now, so I'll leave you two to discuss it,' Pam stated briskly, moving to collect her outer coat. 'But, whatever the outcome, I do sincerely wish you a Happy Christmas, Mr Carlton.' She gave him a warm smile.

In other words, Pam was leaving the decision completely up to Cally as to whether or not they took pity on the man and agreed to work for him.

More to the point, her sister was leaving her with the knowledge that if she didn't agree to do this because of present—and past!—resentments towards Noel Carlton, then they probably wouldn't even have enough money in their bank account to cover their monthly rental on the shop premises.

Great.

Just great!

CHAPTER THREE

'I WANT you to know that I really do appreciate—'

'Fine,' Cally cut Noel off rudely, busy unloading the boxes of decorations from the boot of her car, not in the least mollified by the fact that her newest client had been waiting outside Parker Hall when she'd arrived ten minutes ago, with the obvious intention of helping her carry the boxes inside.

She hadn't wanted to do this job at all, but at the same time she was well aware of what Pam's reaction would be if she returned to the office and found that Cally had refused to help him after all. That, she told herself firmly, was the only reason she was here at all. That, and the thought of his poor mother's disappointment when she arrived to spend Christmas in England and found her son had done nothing about arranging it. No, she certainly wasn't doing this for Noel Carlton.

He straightened, arms folded across his chest as he gave her a considering look. 'Tell me, is that heavy?'

She frowned, looking at the box in her arms. 'Not particularly, no.'

'I wasn't referring to the box,' he drawled.

Cally blinked; she really didn't have the time to play word games with this man. In fact, she didn't have a lot of time at all, and would have preferred it if he hadn't been here! 'Then what were you referring to?' she asked distractedly.

'The monumental chip you have on your shoulder,' he said dryly.

'Can I take a guess at that having something to do with the fact that it's *Miss* Turner instead of *Mrs*?'

Cally stiffened. 'I beg your pardon?'

Noel Carlton drew in a deep breath. 'I said, does that monumental chip on your shoulder—?'

'I heard what you said,' she snapped.

He nodded unconcernedly. 'I thought that you did.'

She scowled at him. 'I was just giving you the opportunity to retract the question!'

He shrugged. 'An opportunity I have no intention of taking. Look, I really am sorry you were woken up by the helicopter this morning—'

'I can assure you, your insulting remark just now certainly hasn't helped the situation!' she assured him.

'I can see that.' He grimaced. 'Look, Cally—may I call you Cally?'

'I believe you just did.'

'And I'm Noel,' he told her unnecessarily, giving an impatient sigh as she looked unimpressed. 'Cally, I want you to know that Celebrations comes highly recommended—you organized my secretary's wedding last week,' he enlarged as she looked at him questioningly. 'Debra Hayes,' he supplied as she still looked blank.

'Oh, yes.' She smiled as she remembered the glowingly lovely bride she had spent months consulting with to make absolutely sure the elaborate wedding plans worked out successfully, that smile fading as she also remembered that Debra and her husband, Giles, were supposed to be honeymooning in Barbados right now. 'Exactly when did Debra recommend us to you?'

'I telephoned her last night, if you must know,' Noel Carlton revealed reluctantly. 'I was desperate, okay?' he added irritably as Cally raised incredulous brows.

She bit her lip in an effort to stop herself from laughing, finally giving up as she realized she was fighting a losing battle. 'I'm sure she and her new husband really appreciated that!' She chuckled gleefully.

Noel gave a rueful smile. 'I don't think Giles was best pleased.'

'Would you have been, in the circumstances?' Cally shook her head in disbelief as she continued to walk inside the house, depositing the box with the others in the huge hall at the bottom of the wide staircase. 'They're on their honeymoon, for goodness' sake!' She turned to grin.

'Yes. Well. I was desperate,' he muttered.

'So you already said.'

In actual fact, Cally had been slightly thrown off her guard when she'd arrived at Parker Hall and found Noel Carlton waiting for her, no longer wearing his business suit, shirt and tie, but dressed in faded denims and a rugby top that looked as if it might be a relic of his university days ten years or so ago. If anything, he looked more lethally attractive in these casual clothes than he had in his suit!

He raised a hand to sweep back that overlong dark hair. 'Ordinarily I could have asked Debra to help me out with this little problem—'

'Oh, so now it's a *little* problem, is it?' Cally teased.

It was Noel's turn to grin. 'It is now that you're here to help!'

'Don't expect miracles,' she warned. 'I'll do my best, but this is rather a big house.' She looked pointedly at the huge hallway they stood in, half a dozen doors leading off it, and this was only the ground floor; there were two more of them up the wide staircase.

Parker Hall was the old manor house to the local village of Axton, and had once housed the rich and influential family of Parker. But as with many of these old families, death duties and lack of interest in succeeding generations had almost brought about its ruin, the hall now rented out to whoever could pay the exorbitant fee being asked. Which Noel Carlton obviously could…

'As long as the Neilsons weren't going to eat smorgasbord for Christmas, or something equally unsuitable, I really don't care!' he assured Cally now.

'You're in luck. The Neilsons intended having a traditional English Christmas as they were in this country—roast turkey and all the trimmings.'

'Great.' He smiled his satisfaction, that smile fading as another thought obviously occurred to him. 'Do you have any idea how to cook a turkey?' he asked tentatively.

Her eyes widened. 'Don't you? No, obviously not,' she accepted as he gave her a derisive look from those deep blue eyes. 'Well, I'm sure that your housekeeper will know— What?' she questioned sharply as he shook his head.

He grimaced. 'My housekeeper, Mrs McTavish, was the one who flew off to Scotland in the helicopter this morning; I'm not expecting her back until after the New Year.'

'Well, that wasn't very sensible of you, was it?'

'Sense had nothing to do with it.'

'You can say that again,' Cally muttered unsympathetically.

'Have you always been a know-it-all?'

She shrugged. 'Pretty much.'

'Well, it's very unbecoming in a beautiful woman—'

'Flattery will get you nowhere!' she told him, knowing even as she said it that her heart had given a little flutter at being called beautiful by this wildly attractive man.

Forget it, Cally, she instantly instructed herself. Remember, he was the one who asked a woman out to dinner and then forgot to follow up on the invitation by telephoning to make a definite date!

'I never for a moment thought that it would,' he assured her. 'But it isn't flattery when it happens to be the truth,' he added huskily.

Cally's breath was caught somewhere in her chest, even the air around them seeming to have become still as her gaze caught and held Noel's, blue clashing with green.

A pirate, that was what he reminded her of, Cally suddenly realized, with that dark flowing hair, eyes that smiled roguishly, his skin darkly tanned, his body lean but muscular, his smile sensual.

A pirate! she instantly scorned herself. Get a grip, Cally Turner.

'Fine.' She was deliberately dismissive, breaking their gaze as she turned away. 'As for the turkey, I'm sure your mother will know what to do with it when she arrives,' she said; after all, she was just putting up the decorations and providing the food. She had nothing to do with the how and why of what he chose to do with it after that!

His brow cleared. 'Of course she will. Why didn't I think of that?'

'Probably because you've been too busy disturbing Debra and Giles on their honeymoon, and sending your housekeeper away to Scotland in a helicopter,' Cally derided.

'For your information, young lady, I did not send Mrs

McTavish away.' He totally ignored the jibe about his secretary. 'She fell down the stairs a couple of weeks ago and broke her arm. In the circumstances, she may as well go to Scotland and spend Christmas with her married daughter; keeping her here was a complete waste of her time and mine.'

'How considerate of you!'

His eyes narrowed to dark blue slits. 'You're determined to see the worst in me and my actions, aren't you?'

She gave him a falsely bright smile. 'Got it in one!'

He gave a heavy sigh. 'Look, Cally, there were—reasons, why I didn't—why I didn't follow through on that dinner invitation a couple of months ago. You see—'

'Did I mention anything about a dinner invitation?' she cut in quickly, her cheeks fiery red just at the mention of it.

'No, you didn't, but—'

'But nothing,' she interrupted a second time—she really didn't want to talk about that embarrassing incident.

He gave her a frowning look. 'You aren't even going to give me chance to explain?'

'No, I'm not—because there's nothing to explain!' She deliberately stood her ground as he took a step closer to her. 'Mr Carlton—'

'Noel,' he prompted softly, definitely standing much closer than was necessary. 'We're going to be pretty much thrown together for the next three days, so you may as well—'

'What?' Cally asked sharply, a sinking feeling in the pit of her stomach. 'But why are you going to be here? Don't you have work, an office, to go to?' she suggested desperately; spending hours, days, in this man's company had not been part of her agreement!

'Of course I have an office to go to. It just happens to be closed for the holidays.'

'But—but this morning!' she pounced frantically. 'You were dressed in a suit, obviously on your way some-where—'

'I thought I might make more of an impression on the owners of Celebrations if I dressed in a suit and looked businesslike.'

'You had already made impression enough, I can assure you!' Cally snapped.

'So it would seem.' He shrugged. 'But in my defence, how was I to know that one of the owners was my own dear neighbour?'

Cally's eyes narrowed. 'I'm not your "own dear" any-thing.'

Once again he looked down at her with those dark, fathomless blue eyes. 'But you could be,' he murmured throatily.

She eyed him suspiciously. 'I thought I warned you about trying to flatter me?'

He arched dark brows. 'Was I flattering you?'

Too late Cally realized exactly how her last remark had sounded. Without thinking she retaliated. 'Correct me if I'm wrong, but I'm sure that Debra, during one of our many meetings to discuss her wedding, once mentioned the fact that her boss—presumably you—was out to lunch with his fiancée?' She smothered a gasp—having just made the connection between Debra and her boss, she now realized why Noel had not followed up on his dinner invitation two months ago—already having a fiancée was definitely reason enough!

The humour faded from his gaze, his expression hard-ening. 'Ex-fiancée,' he corrected her.

'Really?' Cally was not altogether sure she believed him. 'Look, are you going to help me unload the rest of the decorations, or just stand there looking ornamental yourself?'

He looked thoughtful. 'Do you talk to your other clients in the way that you do me?' he asked slowly.

'No,' she came back pertly. 'It just seems to come naturally where you're concerned.' She gave him another, meaningless smile before striding back outside to collect more boxes.

'Only because you have me at a disadvantage,' he guessed shrewdly, having followed her outside to stand on the driveway beside her car.

Cally's grin widened. 'Is that what it is?'

'I should be careful about just how superior you feel, Cally Turner,' he warned softly. 'It comes before a fall, you know.'

'I thought that was pride?' she challenged, eyes gleaming with humour.

'Same thing,' he assured her. 'You never know when you're going to need a friendly neighbour, you know.'

Cally gave a scornful snort. 'I haven't needed him so far—and I see absolutely no reason for that to change,' she added firmly as he would have spoken.

'Please yourself.' He shrugged.

'I usually do,' she answered him dryly. 'Here.' She placed a box of decorations into his arms. 'If you insist on hanging around, then you really will have to make yourself useful!' She turned her back on him as she sorted through the boot of her car, picking up some of the things that had fallen out of the boxes.

But she was nevertheless aware of him still standing

behind her, of his gaze still on her as she leaned into the boot of the car, could almost feel it burning the back of her legs.

Finally, when she could stand it no longer, she straightened abruptly and turned to give him another verbal dressing down. Only to find herself looking at his back, he whistling softly to himself as he walked back into the house with that easy grace that reminded her of a big cat. A jaguar, perhaps. Or a panther.

Her breath left her in a sigh, the tension easing out of her now that he was no longer standing beside her.

These, she was perfectly sure, were going to be the longest three days of her life!

But at the same time she couldn't help but feel curious about his fiancée—ex-fiancée, she corrected slowly. Who had broken the engagement? Noel? Or the woman? And if so, why…?

CHAPTER FOUR

'YOU know,' Cally said as she twisted herself round on the staircase to fix the bowers of holly around the bannister, 'I'm not sure your Mrs McTavish was too good at her job even before she fell over and broke her arm.' She rubbed her dust-covered fingers together as she straightened to look at her handiwork.

'She wasn't,' Noel conceded with a grimace. 'But she was better than nothing.'

'I suppose,' Cally acknowledged distractedly, straightening the holly as it looked slightly out of line with the next piece down.

The two of them had started work on the hall first. Cally knew it was going to be first impressions that mattered, and that after their initial reaction Noel's family probably wouldn't take too much notice of the décor. It would be the food and the log-burning fire, that would please them after that.

But she really wasn't joking about Mrs McTavish's housework, and was glad she had returned to the gatehouse earlier to change into some of her old clothes before starting work; everywhere looked as if it could do with a good dust and polish. The old denims and loose cream shirt were better for working in than a skirt anyway, especially with Noel following her every move...

Cally nodded. 'Probably as well you whisked her away to Scotland for the holidays.'

Noel's eyes widened indignantly. 'You can say that, after the names you called me this morning?'

'Well...you could have scheduled her helicopter departure for a more convenient time,' she allowed ruefully.

In truth, she was slightly ashamed now of her outburst early this morning, knowing it had been the result of a broken night's sleep, and that ordinarily she would never have spoken to anyone in the way she had spoken to Noel.

He gave her a derisive look as he handed her another piece of holly. 'I'll try and remember that next time.'

'Thanks.' She grinned, adding the final touch to the bannister, then standing back to admire the results.

The front hall and staircase were transformed, a huge tree up and decorated downstairs, its lights blinking invitingly, a festive display of red and gold flowers on the table in the middle of the hallway, and real holly from the grounds acting as garlands up the stairs.

'So, what do you think?' She turned to smile at Noel.

'I think you've worked wonders in the last five hours.' He nodded his approval. 'I also think you need to take a shower or a bath; you even have a smudge of dirt on your nose!'

Cally attempted to wipe away the smudge. 'I'll take a shower when I get home.' Once she had picked Lissa up and collected a few groceries from the village store on the way back.

'I was suggesting you take one now.'

She looked sharply at Noel, finding only guileless innocence in his expression. 'No, thanks,' she responded dryly. 'I can wait.'

A mocking smile curved his lips. 'I'm not about to leap on you unexpectedly if you take a bath, Cally.'

She hadn't for a moment thought that he would, and

the offer was tempting; she had seen the luxury of the Jacuzzi bath earlier when she'd gone to use the bathroom, couldn't imagine anything more decadent at this moment, covered in dust as she was. But she still had no intention of taking a bath in Noel Carlton's home.

'We'll never know, will we?' she teased.

'Spoilsport,' he taunted.

'My middle name.' She laughed. 'Well, I think that's enough for one day,' she added briskly. 'I'll be back bright and early in the morning to start on the sitting-room.'

'Exactly how bright and early?' Noel queried as he followed her down the stairs.

'Six-thirty do you?' Cally looked back at him, brows raised pointedly.

'Very funny.' He grinned his appreciation at her dig at him for this morning. 'I thought about nine o'clock?'

'Fine,' she agreed; it was the time she had in mind anyway, needing to take Lissa to Brian's first.

'You know, you can be quite accommodating—when you aren't calling me names!' Noel told her as he stood outside with her on the driveway.

'The remedy for that would appear to be—don't wake me up at six-thirty in the morning!' Cally came back lightly.

'Not a morning person, hmm?' he mused slowly. 'I'll have to remember that.'

Her eyes narrowed at the thought of the only sort of situation when that information would be of the least interest to him. 'I wouldn't bother,' she said. 'It's never likely to matter!'

He gave her a considering look, making Cally very conscious of that smudge of dirt she was sure was still on her nose, her hair tousled from their machinations earlier with the Christmas tree, and her shirt no longer being clean, either.

'Was he anything like me?' Noel finally asked softly.

She frowned her puzzlement. 'Was who anything like you?'

'Your daughter's father—hey, I didn't mean to startle you!' Noel reached out and took a firm hold of her arms as she would have recoiled from him and the question. 'Sorry,' he muttered repentantly. 'I shouldn't have asked.'

Cally could feel how the colour had drained from her cheeks, her mouth feeling very dry too as she answered him. 'No, you shouldn't.'

'I just wondered if it was because I reminded you of him that you're so defensive with me.'

She gave him a tight smile. 'Believe me, I don't treat you differently from any other man!' The whole lot of them, apart from Brian, were only out for what they could get, as far as she was concerned. And the fact that Noel must have had a fiancée when he had invited her out two months ago certainly didn't make him any different!

He gave a heavy sigh. 'That's what I was afraid of.'

Her smile became genuine. 'I doubt that scares you too much, Noel.'

Those dark blue eyes looked into hers, seeming to see into the very depths of her being. 'You might be surprised,' he murmured. 'For instance, I was a little bowled over at the force of attraction I felt towards you two months ago.'

She swallowed hard. 'Obviously enough to forget you already had a fiancée!'

He gave an impatient shake of his head. 'I didn't have a fiancée then.'

Cally's eyes widened. 'You didn't…?' It must have been the shortest engagement in history. The shortest she had ever heard of, anyway!

'No,' he rasped. 'Look, could we just forget about my ex-fiancée?'

She frowned. 'It seems you already have. '

Cally was very conscious of the warmth of his hands on her arms, of the closeness of their bodies, of the soft warmth of his breath as it stirred the fiery tendrils of hair at her temples as she tried to break her gaze away from his, and failed.

'Cally…?' he questioned huskily.

Move, she instructed herself. Kick him in the shin. Do something to break this moment of intense intimacy!

But she couldn't seem to move, could only stand stiffly immobile as Noel moved closer, his head bending, his lips claiming hers in a kiss of extreme tenderness.

If he had been rough, or in the least overpowering, Cally could have resisted him, but it was his tenderness that was her undoing, her arms moving up slowly to hold onto the width of his shoulders, her lips parting beneath his as his hands released her and his arms moved about the slenderness of her waist.

With the parting of her lips the kiss deepened, Cally groaning low in her throat as Noel moulded her body close to his, able to feel every hard contour, to know the sheer strength of him.

She knew that she had to stop this. Now!

She wrenched her mouth away from his. 'No!' she said in a strangled voice, her palms pushing against his chest until he released her. 'I'm here to decorate your house Mr Carlton,' she insisted once he had reluctantly let her go. 'I have no intention of warming your bed as well!'

She was breathing deeply in her agitation, at the same time aware that she was as much to blame as him for what had happened.

Because, despite what she might say to the contrary, she had been attracted to him for the last two months, too!

He had knocked her sideways at that first meeting. The strength of his body had been shown to such advantage in the faded denims and a loose tee shirt he'd seemed to have just pulled on over his nakedness to answer her knock on the door, and the tightness of his denims had certainly left nothing to the imagination. Although that certainly hadn't stopped Cally's imagination running riot just at the sight of him!

She had been surprised at her reaction to him; she hadn't felt attracted to any man since—since Michael. Which was, of course, the reason she had given Noel her telephone number so that he might call her and arrange a definite time for dinner.

Initially she had been disappointed when he hadn't telephoned. But as the days had passed without a call from him that disappointment had quickly been replaced by relief; she really did find him too attractive for her peace of mind.

He gave a wistful smile now. 'But we're nowhere near my bed, Cally.'

'And we aren't going to be, either,' she said as she pulled open her car door. 'It might be better if you don't help me tomorrow,' she added, determinedly avoiding the pull of that cobalt-blue gaze.

'Is that a request or an order?'

She raised her head to frown at him. 'I don't believe I'm in any sort of position to give you an order.' After all, she was working for him... 'But if you want me to

finish the decorating and stocking up the freezer in time
for your family's arrival, then I would suggest that you
let me get on with my work.' She looked at him challengingly.

'That sounds suspiciously like a threat to me,' he said,
his gaze narrowed now.

Cally tossed back the long length of her red hair. 'Not
in the least,' she denied. 'I have my work to do, and I'm
sure you must have yours.'

'Holidays, remember?' he taunted.

Her mouth twisted. 'I'm sure there must be a way you
could make another million or two instead of just sitting
around doing nothing for two weeks!'

He drew in a sharp breath, his jaw set and his gaze
glacial now. 'You know, one day that chip is just going
to get too heavy and it's going to crush you!'

She smiled without amusement. 'Then I would advise
you to be well out of the way when it does.'

Noel gave a frustrated shake of his head. 'He must have
been one hell of a louse!'

'Oh, he was,' she confirmed heavily, not even going to
the trouble of trying to pretend she didn't know exactly
whom he was talking about.

Cally was only too well aware that she treated men the
way she did because of what had happened seven years
ago, that it had been her disastrous relationship with
Michael that had coloured all her dealings with other men
since that time. Which was why it was so surprising that
Noel had managed to get under her guard two months
ago. It was also why she was so defensive with him
now...

'A first class louse, in fact,' she added moodily.

Noel gave her a searching look. 'But without knowing

him you wouldn't have your daughter,' he pointed out softly. 'And I'm sure, even from the little you've said about her, that you love her very much.'

'She's my life!' Cally admitted.

'Exactly.' He nodded.

Cally continued to look at him for several long seconds, surprised—and a little resentful too!—that he seemed to have latched onto the one thing that made thinking of her relationship with Michael bearable: Lissa.

She deliberately made her smile dismissive. 'Take my advice, Noel—forget the amateur psychology and stick to what you obviously do best!'

He raised an eyebrow. 'And what would that be?'

She gave a pointed look at their opulent surroundings before answering him. 'Making money?'

He gave a shake of his head. 'I don't own this place, Cally, I'm just renting it for a year.'

'With an option to buy at the end of that time,' she said knowingly. 'Oh, don't worry, Noel, I haven't been prying into your personal business,' she assured him as she saw the far from pleased expression on his face. 'The agent for the estate told me that little piece of information the first time I complained about the noise; as a way of trying to console me, I think.'

'Why didn't you just come and talk to me?' Noel demanded.

'I did,' she reminded him huskily.

He frowned. 'I really wish I could explain what happened two months ago—'

'There's really no need—' Cally began.

'Yes, there is,' he sighed. 'I just—'

'Could we please just forget about it?' Cally grimaced self-consciously.

'Can we?'

They would have to—if the next couple of days weren't going to turn out to be one long nightmare!

'Tell me about your family,' she changed the subject suddenly. 'They live in America, you said?'

He smiled wryly, seeming to accept for the moment that she really didn't want to talk about them. 'My sister and brother, Honey and Josh, at eighteen and twenty, are from my mother's second marriage. I suppose technically that makes them my half-brother and -sister.' He shrugged. 'But none of us have ever looked on the relationship that way. Honey certainly hates like a real sister!'

'We all do at eighteen.' Cally smiled, feeling a reluctant curiosity about his family now.

'You were probably pregnant with Lissa at eighteen,' he put in quietly.

Yes, she had been. Eighteen, pregnant, and scared. Scared most of all. There had never been any question in her mind as to whether or not she would keep the baby, only the worry as to whether or not she would be able to cope. But she had.

'Talking of Lissa...' she gave a pointed look at her wrist-watch '...I have to go and collect her from Pam's husband now.'

He nodded. 'I wondered how you organized that.'

'Did you?' Cally gave him a puzzled frown, wondering herself why he had given it a second thought.

Noel stepped back. 'I've kept you late enough.'

Cally blinked at this easy acquiescence to her departure after what had seemed like deliberate delaying tactics minutes ago, but she got slowly into the car before driving off with a brief wave of her hand.

It was only as she sped off down the driveway, the

image of Noel still in her driving mirror, that she realized the last few minutes' conversation had completely driven her earlier confusion, at being kissed by Noel, from her mind.

Deliberately so?

Probably, she acknowledged ruefully.

It had also prevented him making any reply to her request that he not be at the house tomorrow while she was working, she realized with a groan of frustration.

Again, deliberately so?

Definitely!

CHAPTER FIVE

PARKER HALL felt very big, eerily so, without Noel
Carlton's annoyingly provocative presence in it...

Cally had arrived promptly at the house at nine o'clock
that morning, only to meet Noel going out of it, his car
keys in his hand.

'Got to run,' he'd only had time to call out to her. 'See
you later,' he'd added before roaring off in the Ferrari.

Well, it was a lot later now, the morning having passed,
her packed lunch eaten, and most of the afternoon having
passed too. All without sight or sound of another human
being.

Was she complaining?

If she were honest?

Yes.

How on earth did Noel live alone in this huge house,
every creak and groan of the floorboards contracting as
the central heating system fired into life seeming to echo
through its emptiness?

Not that Cally hadn't kept herself busy, because she
had. The house had been polished and cleaned from top
to bottom before she'd put up the tasteful decorations in
the sitting-room, and another Christmas tree. She'd also
draped more freshly picked holly along the top of the
hearth, and put a match to the logs in the fireplace as a
final nicety, pleased with the result as the flames crackled
and burnt, filling the room with seasonal warmth and
cheer.

But now she felt dusty and grimy from her Herculean efforts to turn this big old barn of a house into a warmly welcoming Christmas paradise, and was seriously tempted by the offer she hadn't taken up yesterday: that of soaking in that gigantic Jacuzzi bath!

It really was the most opulently luxurious bathroom she had ever seen in her life. The deep cream bath, which could have accommodated four people at once, took up the whole of one corner of the room. There were brown and cream tiles on the floor and on three of the walls, with a huge ornate mirror covering the fourth one. As for the cream towels on the heated rail, they looked softer and thicker than anything she had at home.

There was absolutely no competition between this and the bathroom in the gatehouse, where the white bath was old and stained, and the supply of hot water was erratic to say the least.

The hot water reached right up to her neck as she lay back in its scented depth, the bubbles tickling her nose as the Jacuzzi frothed the foam right to the top of the bath.

Heaven.

Absolute, unadulterated luxury.

Cally rested her head back on the side, her eyes closed as she imagined what it must be like to indulge like this every day. Not that she ever would, but she was going to enjoy it while she could!

'Oops!' exclaimed a deeply amused male voice.

Cally sat up with a startled cry, only to lie back down again as she realized the deep pink tips of her breasts were visible amongst the thick bubbles, the blush in her cheeks rising to meet that colour as she found herself staring across the bathroom at a man she knew she had never seen before!

Not that he looked in the least perturbed at the encounter—on the contrary, he was completely relaxed as he leant against the doorframe, blond brows raised as he grinned across the room at her. 'Well, well, Mama, and who's been lying in my bath?' he teased.

Cally continued to stare at him, having absolutely no idea who he was or what he was doing here, only knowing that she didn't appreciate the totally assessing male look in his sky-blue eyes.

'Tell me, do you have Noel in there with you?' he asked curiously.

'Don't be ridiculous,' Cally snapped as she found her voice at last, frowning across at him now, the bubbles decorously draped across her nakedness. She was not in the least reassured by the fact that he knew the owner of the house was called Noel, and was cross with herself for not thinking of locking all the doors before going upstairs for a bath.

He shrugged broad shoulders. 'Just a thought; you had such a sublimely happy look on your face when I came in!'

The blush deepened in her cheeks at his implication. 'Who are you? And what are you doing in here?' she demanded, knowing she would have remembered this man if she had ever seen him before. His hair was straw-blond, his face youthfully handsome, and he was tall and slim in faded denims and a heavy blue jumper.

'Shouldn't I be asking you that?' he taunted, making no effort to move.

'Would you mind leaving the bathroom so that I can get dressed?' she told him agitatedly.

He gave another shrug. 'Be my guest.'

'Go away!' Cally demanded, eyes sparkling like the emeralds they so resembled.

'Oh, but—'

'Josh? Josh, where are you?' called a pleasant female voice. 'I can't seem to— Oh!' A woman had come to stand in the doorway too now, still beautiful, despite obviously being aged somewhere in her late forties or early fifties. 'Hello.' She smiled warmly across at Cally. 'You must be Carol. Since Noel told us about you I've so been looking forward to meeting you!'

Cally was starting to feel as if this bathroom were in the middle of King's Cross railway station, the amount of people that just seemed to walk into it!

But she had also registered that the young man's name was Josh, which she remembered was also the name of Noel's younger brother. Now that she thought about it he did have a distinctive American accent—she had been too disturbed initially to notice! But if he was Josh, that probably meant the beautiful woman standing beside him was his and Noel's mother…!

That much Cally had managed to work out despite feeling more uncomfortable than she ever had in her life before. What she didn't understand was why Noel had bothered to tell his mother about the woman who was decorating his home for him. Or why his mother called her Carol, when no one had called her by her full name in years.

Although none of that really mattered just now. What did matter was getting out of this bath and back into her clothes, so that she did at least have some personal dignity left.

'Er—I'm afraid you've caught me at a complete dis-

advantage, so if the two of you wouldn't mind...?'
she said.

'Oh, how silly of us,' Noel's mother realized self-disgustedly.

'Come along, Josh.' She grabbed hold of his arm as he
would have continued to linger. 'Let's give Carol some
privacy while she finishes her bath.'

Josh gave one last lingering glance in Cally's direction
before reluctantly complying.

'I'll go down and make us all some tea, shall I?' his
mother offered brightly.

'Thank you.' Cally nodded, just wanting the two of
them to leave, breathing a sigh of relief when Noel's
mother finally moved away, closing the door behind her.

Could it have been any worse? she groaned inwardly
as she sank back down into the rapidly cooling bubbles.
Yes, came the immediate answer; it could have been Noel
who came home and found her in the bath instead of just
his whole family!

Just his whole family...! Well, no, she had been spared
his sister and stepfather coming to gawk at her in the bath,
too!

The humour of the situation finally began to kick in,
and a wry smile curved her lips. What a thing to have
happened. Noel certainly hadn't mentioned, before he'd
left in a such a hurry this morning, that his family were
going to arrive earlier than expected.

Which posed the question: where was Noel? He had
been gone most of the day, and—

'Enjoying yourself?' he queried sarcastically.

Cally made a startled move to sit up, and then sank
back down into the bubbles as she remembered what had

happened the last time she'd done that, frowning across at Noel as he was the one now standing framed in the open doorway.

'Do none of your family ever knock before entering a bathroom?' She sighed.

He shrugged. 'Only when we expect someone else to be in there.' He straightened, moving further into the room, closing the bathroom door behind him. 'And none of us expected you to be in here,' he added dryly.

'What are you doing?' Cally eyed him suspiciously as he strolled over to sit on the side of the bath. 'Your family are downstairs—'

'I'm well aware of that.'

Her cheeks were burning with the embarrassment of having him so close to her when she was absolutely naked! 'Would you please go away?' she groaned awkwardly, feeling her hair starting to fall down from where she had loosely secured it on top of her head away from the dampness of the bubbles.

Noel looked down at her with deliberately guileless blue eyes. 'Is something bothering you, Cally?' he mocked even as he reached out a hand and scooped some of the bubbles up into his palm.

'Stop that!' Cally gasped, frantically splashing more bubbles up the bath towards her.

Not that there were as many as there had been when she'd started, the scented froth starting to disappear as the water cooled.

She closed her eyes. 'I can't believe this is happening to me!' she cried.

'Actually—' Noel grinned down at her wolfishly '—neither can I!'

Cally opened her eyes again to glare up at him. 'Opportunist!' she accused disgustedly.

He gave a shrug, scooping up another handful of bubbles. 'Come on, Cally, you have to admit, this is a pretty unusual situation!' he teased.

And of her own making, if she were honest. It should have occurred to her that Noel, at least, could walk back in at any moment and find her in the bath. Let alone almost every other member of his family!

She gave another embarrassed groan. 'Whatever must your mother think of me?'

'Actually,' Noel repeated, his expression now suddenly unreadable, 'I'm more disturbed by what my little brother thinks of you!'

Cally blinked, wincing slightly as Noel's mouth twisted humourlessly. 'And what was that?' she asked reluctantly.

'Do you want the full version or will the potted one do?'

'I believe the potted one will do!' she confirmed with a pained look, even the rapidly cooling water not bothering her too much now.

'Well, Josh thinks you're the most beautiful mermaid he's ever set eyes on!'

'Oh.' She grimaced.

'My mother, on the other hand—'

'Please!' she cried awkwardly. 'I feel badly enough about this as it is, without being told what your mother thinks of the hired help luxuriating in your bath!'

Noel gave her a considering look. 'It's worse than that, I'm afraid,' he told her softly.

Cally gave a shake of her head. 'It couldn't be!' She had no idea yet how she was going to get dressed, go downstairs, and face all of Noel's family after what had happened. Because she did have to face them, had to try and explain herself. Even if that explanation did sound a little lame!

'Oh, yes, it could.'

Cally gave him a suspicious look. 'What have you done?'

'Me?' His eyes widened incredulously. 'Cally, I'm not the one who was found cavorting about in the Jaccuzi—'

'I was not "cavorting",' she defended herself. 'I was just lying here minding my own business—'

'Paying court to half my family,' Noel interjected.

'Only because they walked into the bathroom unannounced!'

'I accept that, Cally.' He sighed. 'But, nevertheless, it's put us both in a very awkward position.'

Cally's heart sank, wondering whether his family wanted more than an apology from her for making free with their son's bathroom—like making a complaint against Celebrations!

It didn't matter that in the five years she and Pam had been running their company from home they hadn't received a single complaint; they had stepped out into the big time now, and something like this was enough to cause their pristine reputation considerable damage before they had even really begun.

'I'll explain—'

'It's too late for that, I'm afraid.' Noel stood up abruptly, starting to pace the bathroom, a dark frown furrowing his brow.

'Look, I'm sure that if I explain, and apologize, it isn't going to be as bad as you're making out it is,' Cally pleaded, watching him worriedly as he paced up and down the small confines of the room. 'Your mother looked very nice,' she added hopefully.

In actual fact, his mother had looked very much like Noel himself; thick dark hair down to her shoulders, with warm blue eyes, her face a softer, prettier version of Noel's strong features.

'Oh, she is,' Noel confirmed. 'Very nice. She's also looking forward to being a grandmother some time in the near future.'

'Really?' Cally smiled. 'That will be nice.'

'You think?' Noel paused beside the bath, mocking humour lighting his eyes. 'Cally, I think you'll agree that, at this particular moment, you're very much a captive audience?'

She shifted self-consciously, wishing he wouldn't stand so close to her—especially when she was sure the previously frothy water was almost transparent by now! 'I'll agree that I'm not about to leap up and jump out of the bath while you're still in the room,' she conceded slowly, not sure where his remark was going.

He nodded. 'A captive audience.'

'Possibly,' she accepted warily.

'Did you notice earlier that my mother called you Carol?' he asked.

'Well, yes, I did notice that.' She frowned. 'But as it actually is my name, I just thought—' She broke off suddenly, staring up at Noel now. 'But you didn't know that, did you?' she realized.

He gave a wry smile. 'Not until just now, no.'

Several things began to click into place, things that had puzzled her earlier, but which could make perfect sense if—'Noel, was your ex-fiancée named Carol, by any chance?' She gasped as a terrible realization started to take shape in her mind.

He gave her an admiring look. 'You really are a very astute young lady, aren't you?'

Astuteness had nothing to do with it. It was all so obvious when she thought of the lack of surprise on Josh's and his mother's faces when they'd found her taking a bath, and the way the older woman had said how much she had been looking forward to meeting her. She hadn't been referring to the woman decorating Noel's home at all, but to his fiancée!

Noel was right: this was so much worse than she had thought!

CHAPTER SIX

A KNOCK sounded on the bathroom door. 'I'm sorry to interrupt, you two,' Josh called out cheerfully in a totally unrepentant voice, 'but Carol's sister is downstairs.'

Pam!

Could this situation get any worse if it tried? Cally groaned inwardly.

Not much, came the resounding answer. So far she had been caught lazing in a client's bath by his family, that family had mistakenly thought she was the fiancée of the eldest son, and in the middle of all that her practical no-nonsense older sister had to arrive.

'With Carol's adorable daughter Lissa,' Josh added as if on cue.

This time Cally shot up in the bath regardless of the fact that Noel was still in the room with her, reaching out to quickly pull one of the huge cream towels towards her as his gaze widened appreciatively on her nakedness.

'You didn't tell us about that one, big bro,' Josh said gleefully. 'Mama is downstairs absolutely drooling over Lissa right now,' he added for good measure, the sound of his laughter floating back to them as he walked off down the hallway.

'Going somewhere?' Noel taunted as Cally still hesitated about actually getting out of the bath.

'Well, of course I'm—Noel, you heard your brother; even as we speak, your family is probably welcoming Pam and Lissa into their midst!'

'Probably.' He nodded unconcernedly.

She looked at him warningly. 'Noel—'

'Cally,' he cut in firmly, straightening. 'As you seem to have deduced, we have something of a dilemma—'

'*I* don't have a dilemma,' she said heatedly, eyes flashing deeply green. '*You* do!'

'No.' He shook his head. 'As I see it, you're in this with me up to your beautiful neck. If you hadn't been lazing in the Jacuzzi, of course, then probably this mistake in identity wouldn't have occurred, but as it is...' He gave a fatalistic shrug.

'Will you stop going on about my being in the Jacuzzi?' Cally sighed frustratedly. 'You were the one who invited me to make use of the facility—'

'That was yesterday,' Noel reasoned. 'I would never have repeated the offer today, knowing that my family were about to swoop on me *en masse*—'

'You knew your family were arriving early?' Cally frowned. 'But if that's so, why did you just disappear for the day like that?'

'A misunderstanding about arrival times,' Noel dismissed carelessly.

Her gaze narrowed on his deliberately bland expression. 'You mean you got the time wrong?'

He gave a rueful grimace. 'Not only that—I got the wrong airport, too! For some reason I wasn't too attentive when my mother telephoned last night and told me the time and place of their arrival.' He gave Cally a pointed look. 'And so I've been waiting to meet the wrong aeroplane at Gatwick for the last five hours, and the family arrived at Heathrow three hours ago!'

Cally stared at him; surely Noel wasn't implying that

she had anything to do with his inattentiveness to his mother last night...?

Noel shrugged again. 'It's easy to see why they thought you were Carol.'

It was perfectly obvious to Cally what had happened, and why—she just didn't know how they were going to get out of it without looking like absolute idiots.

'Why don't your family know of your broken engagement?' She pounced on the possible escape.

He looked pained. 'I hadn't got around to telling them yet—thought it was something I could just break to them gently over Christmas—'

'Oh, like "Here's your Christmas present, Mama, and by the way I'm not getting married any more"? Something like that, you mean?' Cally prompted disbelievingly.

'Well...maybe a little more subtle than that.' He smiled slightly.

She gave a disgusted shake of her head, very aware that she was still standing in the rapidly cooling bath water, and that goose-bumps were appearing on her flesh, despite the towel round her shoulders—she needed to get out of this bath right now!

'Of course,' Noel continued thoughtfully, 'now I would also have to tell her that the woman she found in my bath had never been my fiancée at all, that she was actually just the lady who came in to decorate the house for me.'

Cally drew in a deeply controlling breath. 'Could you just go out of the room for a few minutes while I get dressed?' she said evenly, exerting extreme control to stop herself from screaming hysterically, very aware of Pam and Lissa waiting for her down the stairs.

'Well, I could,' Noel answered conversationally. 'But as we haven't come anywhere near to reaching an agreement about this...misunderstanding, I think I had better just—'

'I think you had better just get out of here!' Her voice rose dangerously, her cheeks hot from anger now.

'Okay, okay.' He held up defensive hands. 'There's no need to get your—ah, but, of course, you aren't wearing any of those, are you? So they aren't likely to get into a twist, are they—?'

'Get *out*!' Her voice went another couple of octaves higher, at the same time as she threw the wet sponge across the room at him.

Noel moved sideways, easily avoiding having the sponge hit him. The waterlogged article hit the far wall with a splat before sliding slowly down onto the floor. 'I suggest you wipe that up before you leave the room.' He grinned, opening the door. 'Otherwise the next person to use the room might slip and hurt themselves.'

'At this moment, if it happened to be you, I don't think I would care!' Cally assured him forcefully.

He tutted teasingly. 'I think I'll just pop down and talk with Pam and Lissa while you get dressed.'

'Don't you da—' Too late. Noel had already left the room, closing the door softly behind him.

Leaving Cally in a high state of agitation as she quickly hopped out of the bath and thankfully towelled herself dry, taking a brief moment to revel in finally setting warm.

But only a brief moment; who knew what further harm Noel could have done by the time she got downstairs?

'She's adorable,' Noel's mother came to stand by Cally as she stood transfixed in the doorway watching Noel and Lissa romping about the floor.

Lissa was smaller version of herself. Cally had obviously always been biased when it came to her young daughter. Lissa's hair was more of a strawberry-blonde than the red of her own, but otherwise the freckles and tiny features were all Cally.

She had prayed for that before Lissa was born, had inwardly dreaded having a mini version of Michael to look at every day. But once she'd held the totally defenceless Lissa in her arms for the first time, and looked down at the delicacy of her tiny face, she had known it wouldn't matter who or what she looked like; Lissa was hers, and she loved her.

But what held her so transfixed now was seeing Lissa playing so naturally with Noel, the two of them rolling over and over together on the carpeted floor while Josh, his sister Honey, and the man Cally guessed had to be Noel's stepfather, looked on indulgently, Pam nowhere to be seen.

Lissa obviously spent quite a bit of time at Pam's, enjoyed being with her uncle Brian, and loved the company of her two male cousins, but this was the first time Cally had really seen her daughter relate to an adult male in quite this way.

For a moment she felt an ache in her chest, brief uncertainty, as to whether she had done the right thing seven years ago in keeping Lissa's father in ignorance of his daughter's existence. She hadn't doubted the decision at the time, had believed that it had been the right one for everyone concerned, but looking at Lissa now, squealing with delight as Noel tickled her, she couldn't help wondering if it had been the right one for her daughter in the long term…

'Noel always did have a way with young children.' The woman at her side spoke softly as she watched her eldest son. 'He was wonderful with Josh and Honey when they were small too.' She smiled down at him indulgently before shifting that deep blue gaze back to Cally. 'It's the reason I was so happy when he told me the two of you were going to be married; he's going to make such a wonderful father. Of course—' she laughed softly '—I had no idea this was what he had in mind when he told me I was soon to be a grandmother!'

Cally reluctantly dragged her gaze away from her happily occupied daughter. 'Look, Mrs Carlt—No, it isn't Carlton, is it?' She became flustered as she seemed to be making one gaffe after another where this woman was concerned.

'It's Markham, but please do call me Hester,' the other woman invited warmly. 'And I understand from Noel that you prefer to be called Cally?'

'Yes,' she confirmed huskily. 'But about Lissa—'

'My dear, please don't feel you have to explain anything to any of us.' Hester frowned her concern as she put a reassuring hand on Cally's arm. 'I don't know how much Noel has told you, but I was alone with him until he was ten years old and I met and fell in love with Andrew.' She smiled across at her husband where he stood laughing at the antics on the carpet. 'He gave me back my faith in love and the permanence of marriage.'

Cally glanced across at the smiling man who stood so relaxed beside the fireplace watching his stepson, liking his easy smile, the warm glow in his brown eyes, the blond hair that had been inherited by both his children. Honey, Cally also noted, was a female version of Josh:

tall and attractive, her blonde hair worn long down her back, dressed like a typical teenager in denims and tee shirt.

'He looks very nice.' Cally turned back to Hester. 'It's just that—'

'Lissa doesn't know yet about you and Noel getting married,' the other woman finished gently. 'Yes, he told me that, too. But I really don't think it's going to be a problem, do you?' she added as Lissa giggled happily at being tickled by Noel.

No, Cally didn't think it would be a problem—if she and Noel really were going to be married. Which they weren't!

But Noel had certainly been busy confiding things to his mother in the few minutes it had taken Cally to dry herself and get dressed, seeming to have covered most of the questions they would probably have been asked by one member of his family or another.

Which was great for Noel. But not so great for her. Because she wasn't engaged to Noel, and had no intention of marrying him.

Chance would be a fine thing, a little voice inside her mocked.

Where on earth had that come from? Cally wondered dazedly.

After the disaster of her relationship with Michael, she had concentrated all her love and care on Lissa, on giving her the best that she could, consistently refusing any dates that came her way. In fact, she had become so adept at showing her lack of interest that, apart from Noel's invitation two months ago, she hadn't even been asked out on a date for the last two years!

So why was she even thinking that chance would be a fine thing?

Just because Noel Carlton, with his obvious wealth and playboy lifestyle, was like no one she had ever met before. Or was ever likely to meet again!

'Your sister had to leave, I'm afraid,' Hester commented. 'Something about getting back to the boys…?'

Cally smiled. 'Pam's husband, Brian, and their two little boys.' Although, if she knew anything about her big sister at all, Pam was going to be on the telephone later today wanting to know exactly what was going on!

'That's nice.' The older woman smiled. 'Families are important, aren't they?'

'Very,' Cally confirmed with perhaps a little more firmness than she had intended. 'At least, I think so,' she added less forcefully.

'I'm so glad you feel that way.' Hester nodded, linking her arm with Cally's. 'But then I should have known that Noel wouldn't choose to be with a woman who doesn't have the same values and interests that he does.'

Cally watched the man in question as he stood up, Lissa held in his arms. Obviously, despite her previous accusations about his not having bothered to be prepared for his family's arrival, his family was important to him, and there was no doubting that he did have a natural way with Lissa, and didn't mind in the least that his designer-label clothes were now slightly creased and rumpled. Perhaps he wasn't such a playboy, after all…?

'Mummy!' Lissa cried happily as she spotted her mother, reaching out her arms towards her. 'I've been having such fun.' She glowed excitedly, her smile revealing that she had recently lost one of her front baby teeth. But, if anything, it just made her more endearing.

'I can see that,' Cally murmured indulgently as she held her daughter in her arms, smiling up at her.

'And Noel says we're all going out for a meal together tonight,' Lissa told her ecstatically before turning to bestow a heart-melting smile on Noel as the benefactor of this unexpected treat.

Cally's smile faded somewhat as she felt something begin to tighten around her, trapping her in a situation that was rapidly spiralling out of her control.

Much as she knew Lissa would love to go, she knew it wasn't a good idea for them to go out with Noel's family for a meal, tonight or any other time, that, the sooner Noel told his family the truth about his broken engagement, the better it would be for everyone.

'That sounds nice, darling,' she answered her daughter noncommittally. 'Noel, would you mind walking back to the gatehouse with us?' She turned to him, her gaze warning him against refusing. 'There are a couple of things we need to talk about,' she added determinedly as she saw Noel's younger brother give him a teasing grin at what must appear to be signs of domesticity.

'Of course,' Noel complied lightly as he moved to her side, at the same time shooting Josh a scathing glance. 'Don't say another word until we get outside,' he muttered for Cally's ears only.

'I have no intention of doing so,' she assured him with a pointed look at Lissa.

'I'm afraid it was my idea about going out this evening,' Hester put in concernedly, obviously wondering if she had committed a *faux pas* of some kind. 'I do hope the two of you didn't have other plans? It's just that Noel says you've been working very hard to make everything so nice for us, that I thought it was the least we could do for you in return…?'

Cally felt the trap tightening even further, knowing she could hardly refuse to go out with them this evening when it was their way of saying thank you for all the hard work she had done on the house the last couple of days.

They couldn't possibly know that a cheque from Noel would more than compensate for that!

CHAPTER SEVEN

'OKAY, so what do we do now?' Cally asked as she and Noel sat at her kitchen table a short time later drinking coffee, Lissa safely ensconced in front of the television for a few minutes with juice and biscuits.

Noel shrugged. 'Well, the general consensus seems to be that we're all going out for a meal later this evening—'

'That isn't what I meant, and you know it!' Cally cut in irritably. 'I like your family, Noel, they're nice—'

'Thank you.'

She sighed. 'I didn't say that included *you*!'

'No,' he accepted softly, bending towards her slightly. 'But you do like me, don't you?' he murmured huskily.

'No, I—yes,' she sighed in defeat as he raised sceptical dark brows at the vehemence of her denial. 'But I was actually referring to the fact that I don't like deceiving your family in this way—'

'Then let's not deceive them,' he suggested, getting up to go down on one knee in front of her on the tiled floor, taking one of her hands firmly in his. 'Cally Turner, will you marry me?'

Cally stared down at him in horror. 'Will you get up?' she instructed desperately, pulling her hand away from his, all the time casting worried glances in Lissa's direction as she sat only feet away from them in the sitting-room.

'Not until you give me an answer.' Noel remained on one knee.

Cally could feel the heat of confusion in her flushed cheeks. 'You look ridiculous,' she spluttered agitatedly.

'I know.' He grinned unconcernedly. 'But I intend staying this way until you give me an answer,' he assured her happily.

She looked at him speechlessly now, totally nonplussed by the unexpectedness of what he was doing.

But what if his proposal had been a real one…?

She would still have said no!

Wouldn't she…?

The problem was, she didn't know any more. Until yesterday she had thought her nearest neighbour to be an arrogant show-off, with his fast cars and helicopters arriving on the front lawn. An arrogant show-off who didn't make good on his invitations! But this last couple of days she had come to know what he was really like. And, if she were honest, she *did* like him!

Noel had shown her yesterday that he wasn't afraid of hard work. Had proved by his actions this last couple of days that he was a caring, considerate son. Had got down on the floor and played with Lissa as if he were six instead of in his mid-thirties. And as for the way he kissed…!

Cally shied away from remembering that, determined to think only of the fact that he wasn't really serious about this marriage proposal, that until recently he had actually been engaged to marry someone else.

She stood up abruptly, stepping round him to move to the far side of the small kitchen. 'My answer is no,' she said. 'And I think, the sooner you tell your family the truth, the better it will be for everyone.'

She could only feel relief as he got slowly to his feet, although she wasn't quite so sure about that emotion as he came to stand in front of her, so close she could feel the warmth emanating from his body.

She swallowed hard as she looked up at him. 'In the circumstances, I'm more than a little interested in knowing the truth myself,' she said huskily, pressing back into the work unit as far as she could go in an effort to put more distance between Noel's body and her own.

'What do you want to know?' He gave her a considering look, one hand moving up to cup the side of her face, his thumb moving lightly across her lips.

Cally's breath lodged somewhere in her throat as she desperately tried to resist the impulse to run her tongue across her lips where he had just touched, her gaze locked with his. 'Your fiancée,' she managed to speak gruffly.

His mouth tightened. 'Ex-fiancée,' he corrected, shaking his head. 'Have you ever thought that someone was something only to realize later on that you had made a terrible mistake and they weren't what you thought they were at all?'

She glanced across at Lissa as she sat enraptured in the cartoon showing on the television. 'Oh, yes,' she acknowledged ruefully.

Noel followed that glance. 'Lissa's father?'

Cally nodded. 'I—he—' She gave a deep sigh. 'I thought he was warm, caring, and single.'

'And?' Noel prompted softly, his gaze searching the paleness of her face.

'He was selfish, immature—and married!' She grimaced self-derisively, still able to remember her humiliation when Michael's wife had paid her a visit, hugely pregnant with their second child, to lay prior claim to him.

After that, as far as Cally had been concerned, Michael's wife had been welcome to him!

'Ah.' Noel nodded understandingly.

'And Carol?' she asked tentatively, amazed at how painful she still found it to talk of her own past disillusionment.

'Well, I thought she was warm, caring, and single, too,' Noel said dryly. 'It turned out that she was single, but it didn't take me too long to realize the warmth and caring were sadly lacking!' He gave a disgusted shake of his head.

'Long enough for you to become engaged to her,' Cally pointed out, relieved to have the conversation moved away from her own past misjudgement concerning someone's character.

'Hmm.' He frowned.

Cally gave him a considering look. 'Noel…?' She sensed there was something he wasn't saying.

He straightened, his hand falling away from her face. 'It's nothing,' he dismissed briskly.

That wasn't what Cally believed at all. She felt sure there was something he wasn't telling her about his engagement. Not that it was really any of her business— except that, as far as his family was concerned, she now seemed to be engaged to him herself!

'Is it really going to be that much of a problem for you and Lissa to come out to dinner with the family this evening?' Noel asked.

'Not a problem, no…' From what she had seen of his family, they were all very nice; she just didn't think it was a good idea to perpetuate this deception about her supposed engagement to Noel. 'But couldn't you just tell them the truth?' She sighed.

To her surprise, Noel grinned widely. 'Who knows,

maybe if I delay doing that long enough, it will no longer be the truth!'

Cally frowned as she tried to follow his train of thought, her eyes widening incredulously as she realized exactly what he meant. 'I told you not to be ridiculous,' she snapped, not finding anything in the least funny about his proposal of marriage.

He shrugged. 'It seems like a pretty good idea to me.'

'That's because you're bordering on the insane,' Cally told him unsympathetically, clasping his shoulders to turn him firmly in the direction of the back door. 'Okay, we'll come out to dinner with all of you this evening,' she told him once he was standing outside the house, knowing that to do anything else would be a great disappointment to Lissa. And she tried never to disappoint her beloved daughter. 'But only on the condition that you tell your family the truth in the very near future!' she added sternly.

Noel's grin went from ear to ear, his eyes dark with approval. 'You really are a beautiful woman, Cally Turner!' he told her appreciatively before taking a deter-mined step forward and kissing her forcefully on the lips.

She didn't know whether she was beautiful or not, Cally thought confusedly as the kiss continued and she melted into the hardness of his body, but she did know she was falling in love with this man. No—that she was already in love with him!

She pulled sharply back as this shocking realization hit her with the force of a physical blow, staring up at Noel as if she had never seen him before.

And maybe she hadn't. She had spent so long denying that she wanted any man in her life, that there could be a 'perfect' man for her out there, that she had almost missed seeing him at all!

Noel was everything she had ever wanted in a man, sure of himself, charming, caring, patient, funny. And the strange thing was, he seemed to find her equally fascinating.

'Cally?' he questioned huskily now.

She gave a shake of her head, pushing those thoughts very firmly from her mind. Because Noel was also very rich, very sophisticated—and, until recently, had been engaged to marry someone else!

'Nothing,' she dismissed quickly, stepping back into the house. 'What time do you expect to go out?'

Noel continued to look at her for long, timeless seconds, finally saying, 'I'll pick you and Lissa up in about an hour, if that's okay?'

'Fine,' Cally accepted shortly, moving back to firmly close the door in his face.

Which was when she realized just how much she was shaking, her legs feeling weak, her whole body trembling with—with what?

With the realization that she had fallen in love with a man who could never be hers!

CHAPTER EIGHT

'EVERTHING all right?' Noel queried softly an hour or so later as they drove to the pub where they had decided to eat, Lissa safely strapped into the back seat. The rest of the family were following behind in the estate car they had hired for the duration of their stay.

'Fine,' Cally replied tersely—if you could call being given the third degree by your older sister for the last half an hour 'all right'!

Pam had been absolutely fascinated by the Markham family, even more so by what Cally had been doing upstairs with Noel when she had arrived at the house with Lissa earlier. Not that Cally intended satisfying her sister's curiosity about that!

She had no idea how to explain to Pam that for the moment she was trapped in a false engagement in an effort to try to salvage something of their company's reputation. Never mind her own!

'No Ferrari this evening?' Cally mocked in an effort to change the subject, although the Range Rover he drove now was very luxurious too.

'No room for Lissa. Actually, I'm thinking of getting rid of the Ferrari.'

Cally tensed warily. 'Why?'

Noel gave a shrug. 'It isn't exactly a family car, now, is it?'

Cally felt slightly breathless for a moment, quickly

252

fighting down that feeling as she answered him mockingly. 'But then, you don't *exactly* have a family, do you?'

He gave her a sideways glance. 'That could easily change.'

'Not so easily as you might think,' she came back sharply —and then wondered if she weren't just making a fool of herself; Noel couldn't have been any more serious about that marriage proposal earlier than his remarks were now.

He smiled. 'I've never minded fighting for what I want.'

And his gaze said he wanted her! But he couldn't be serious. Not really. This all had to be just a game to him.

She gave a dismissive shrug, deliberately turning away from him to look out the window at the darkness beyond.

'Cally, just relax, hmm?' Noel reached out and briefly squeezed her hand. 'Even if I do say so myself, my family are all okay,' he added as she turned to look at him.

'I know that,' she answered brittlely.

He sighed. 'Then it must be me who's making you so nervous—'

'I'm not nervous!' she denied.

He touched her hand a second time, that light clasp remaining this time. 'Then why are you trembling?'

Was she? She hadn't been aware of it. But, yes, she was trembling now that she thought about it. Not with nervousness, she quickly realized, but with rising awareness of the man seated at her side, the blood seeming to thrum through her veins as her body responded to the closeness of his.

She had never wanted anyone, or anything, as much as she wanted Noel Carlton!

'Cally!' he groaned as he must have seen some of that desire in her face.

She snatched her hand out of his grasp. 'I think your earlier insanity must be catching!'

'I certainly hope so.' He grinned.

Cally didn't know what she hoped any more. Her thoughts were all chaotic, all the resolves she had made before leaving the house earlier this evening crumbling to ashes once she was with Noel. Keep your distance, she had decided. Don't respond to any of Noel's more intimate remarks, she had instructed. Most of all, don't take any of what Noel said seriously.

Hah!

She wanted to launch herself into Noel's arms and forget the past, present, and future. She longed to respond to his every word. As for taking him seriously—she wished that she could!

Which was why it was probably just as well that they had arrived at the pub, all of them piling out of the cars to go inside, Cally finding herself seated next to Honey Markham on one side and Hester on the other. Lissa had very neatly placed herself between Josh and Andrew, both men paying court to her innocent charm.

Noel stood beside the table for several seconds, frowning, finally telling his brother to move up once he realized there simply wasn't any room for him on the padded bench seat next to Cally, scowling his displeasure across the table at his mother and sister.

Honey giggled softly next to Cally. 'My big brother has it bad, doesn't he?'

Cally swallowed hard, not sure she could keep up this subterfuge. 'Does he?'

'Oh, yes,' the beautiful teenager assured her smilingly.

'I always wondered what Noel would look like when he fell in love; now I know!'

Cally turned to give her a quizzical glance. 'And how does he look?'

Honey's grin widened. 'Pretty good, actually.' She gave her eldest brother a playful wink as he glanced her way, receiving a stony glare for her trouble. 'Incredible,' Honey murmured with a rueful shake of her head. 'Noel has always been super cool, you know,' she explained to Cally. 'But he isn't very cool about you, is he?' She grinned again.

Cool wasn't a word Cally would have used to describe either herself or Noel when they were together! Things were usually pretty heated between them, she had found, whether from temper or from passion.

'So when are the two of you thinking of getting married?' Honey prompted in a hushed voice after giving Lissa a brief look and establishing that she was totally engrossed in telling Andrew Markham about her school. 'I'll be nineteen in six months' time, and I always fancied being a bridesmaid while I was still a teenager,' she added happily.

'I—we haven't decided yet,' she answered evasively.

'Not too long, if I know Noel,' his sister predicted knowingly. 'It's pretty obvious he can't wait for the two of you to be married!' she said with another teasing glance at her eldest brother.

In fact, Noel's whole family seemed to be happy with the idea of the two of them marrying each other and bringing Lissa into the family too—so in a way it was a pity it was never going to happen.

In a way!

Cally was fast coming to the conclusion that she would

be happy to be marrying Noel too, and couldn't seem to stop looking at him as he finally relaxed and engaged his mother in easy conversation. He really was the most gorgeous looking man she had ever seen, her fingers once more itching to touch the dark thickness of his hair, to experience again the feel of his lips on hers, to have his hands—

This had to stop!

How could she become aroused just from looking at him? Because she was aroused, her nipples hardening pertly beneath the jumper she wore, her thighs feeling warm.

'What would you like?'

She gave Noel a startled look as he leant across the table towards her, wondering if her longing could possibly have shown on her face. And if it had, what he was doing drawing attention to it in front of his family! 'What?'

'What would you like to eat?' he asked softly, the affectionate teasing in the deep blue of his eyes telling her that he had indeed seen that longing.

'Oh,' she gasped, picking up the menu that lay on the table in front of her. 'The chicken, please.' She chose the first thing she saw. 'Lissa will probably have the same. Er—if you'll excuse me, I need to go to the Ladies,' she added abruptly, knowing she needed to splash some cold water on her face. 'Lissa?' she prompted her daughter as she moved past Honey.

Lissa turned to give her a beaming smile. 'I'm fine, thank you, Mummy.'

'Would you like me to come with you?' Noel offered as she squeezed past his chair, the warmth of his gaze resting tantalizingly on her lips.

Almost like a caress, Cally acknowledged achingly, a

melting sensation somewhere deep inside her. 'No, thank you,' she refused, moving hurriedly away.

This was awful, she groaned inwardly as she moved as quickly as she could through the crowded lounge bar to the Ladies situated in the adjoining room. She couldn't go on with this, she simply couldn't, was going to make a complete idiot of herself if she didn't—

'Cally? Cally Turner?'

She turned in the direction of that guardedly enquiring voice, staring blankly at the woman who had spoken to her, sure she had never seen the woman before. Nothing about her shoulder-length blonde hair and attractively made-up face seemed in the least familiar.

And then a memory stirred, a deliberately long-buried memory, overlaying the gamine features in front of her with a slightly plumper face, short brown hair, and much fuller figure.

Jane Shaw…!

Michael's wife!

CHAPTER NINE

'IT IS Cally, isn't it?' the other woman pressed. 'I don't know if you remember me, but—'

'I remember you,' she breathed hollowly, having felt her face pale as she stared at Jane Shaw with complete recognition.

How could she ever forget this woman? She had been the shatterer of Cally's dreams, but ultimately her salvation at the same time. As for what Cally represented to Jane Shaw…!

'Hey, I didn't mean to upset you.' The other woman frowned at her with concern. 'I just—perhaps I shouldn't have spoken to you.' She sighed regretfully. 'I—you're looking very well,' she concluded lamely.

So did Jane Shaw; now a slim, elegant, beautifully confident woman. She had been anything but that when Cally had last seen her: slow, cumbersome, with all the accompanying aches and pains that went with being seven months pregnant.

With Michael's second child.

Michael!

Was he here too? But a frantic look round in the general vicinity didn't show his presence anywhere near. Just as well; that would be just too much!

Cally turned back to the other woman, feeling completely flustered by this unexpected encounter with a woman she hadn't seen for almost seven years—and had hoped never to see again! 'What are you doing here?' she asked bluntly, too shaken to be polite.

'I live near here,' the other woman told her gently.

With Michael... How ironic that Cally should have moved out of the city to the country, only to find that Michael and his family had moved here too!

Cally shook her head, desperate to get away from this woman, and the humiliating memories she evoked. 'I really don't think—will you excuse me?' she said abruptly. 'I—I'm with some people, and—they'll wonder where I've got to.' She turned to leave, only to walk straight into the hardness of a chest that was completely familiar to her.

'Cally?' Noel reached up to clasp the tops of her arms as he steadied her, his gaze narrowed on the paleness of her face before he looked past her to Jane Shaw. 'A friend of yours?' he asked lightly.

A friend of hers! How wrong could he be? Cally wondered slightly hysterically!

'Jane Shaw.' The other woman held her hand out to Noel, her smile guarded as she glanced at Cally's stricken face.

'Noel Carlton,' he supplied slowly, briefly shaking that hand.

Jane Shaw's eyes widened fractionally as she looked at him. 'Of the communications network of the same name?'

'Yes,' he confirmed.

'And the international investment empire?' the other woman murmured appreciatively.

'That too.' Noel nodded.

Cally blinked, having had no idea herself what it was Noel did, or where his considerable wealth came from.

But even she, someone who didn't keep up-to-date had heard of the empire.

'But I prefer to think of myself as Cally's fiancé,' Noel continued his arm moving possessively about the slenderness of Cally's waist as he came to stand beside her.

Cally could only gape up at him disbelievingly now; wasn't it taking this subterfuge a little far to introduce himself to a complete stranger in that manner? Not that she particularly minded where Jane Shaw was concerned; at least it showed the other woman that she hadn't simply curled up these last seven years and pined away for love of Michael.

Jane Shaw smiled at them both warmly. 'Congratulations! Well, I really must be getting back to my friends. It was nice seeing you again, Cally,' she added.

Cally didn't see how it could possibly be that, for either of them! But without increasing Noel's suspicions any more she could do little else but smile in agreement.

'Mummy, can I come with you, after all?' Lissa pranced up to them happily.

Cally looked at her daughter, then quickly back to Jane Shaw, swaying slightly as she saw the way the other woman was staring down at Lissa.

Was there something of Michael in Lissa, after all, a likeness that Cally couldn't see? Perhaps in the curve of her cheek? Or the set of her sometimes stubborn little chin?

Cally didn't think so, but then she was biased, thought her daughter the most beautiful child in the world—with not a single attribute of the man who had never known he had fathered her!

Jane Shaw's husband...

Not telling Michael of her own pregnancy hadn't been

an easy decision to make when she'd discovered her condition seven years ago, but, as Cally's own relationship
with him had been over anyway after the visit of his wife,
to have told him of her own pregnancy would have ruined
so many lives, not least Jane Shaw's own. There had also
been the lives of Jane's child and unborn baby to consider.

No, Cally had decided, better to leave things as they
were; after his deceit she had no longer loved or wanted
Michael anyway, whereas Jane had seemed to have forgiven him for his relationship with Cally.

Although none of her reasoning then would help her
now!

Would Jane tell Michael she had seen Cally when she
got home? Worse, would she mention that Cally had a
little girl of six or so with her—?

'Mummy?' Lissa looked up at her again.

Who called her Mummy!

Cally broke her gaze away from Jane Shaw's questioning one to look down at her daughter reassuringly. 'Sorry,
darling. Excuse us.' She smiled vaguely before taking
hold of Lissa's hand and hurrying into the adjoining room,
breathing a sigh of relief once she was away from Jane
Shaw and her enquiring looks. Only the trembling of her
legs told of the shock she had just received.

It was only as she stood outside the cubicle waiting for
Lissa to come out that she realized she had left Jane Shaw
and Noel alone together!

But surely Noel wouldn't— Even if he did, surely the
woman wouldn't—

She closed her eyes, groaning inwardly as she imagined
the conversation that could be taking place between Jane
and Noel right this moment.

She certainly wasn't prepared to find a grim-faced Noel

leaning on the wall outside waiting for her when she emerged into the noisy room with Lissa!

Cally looked at him searchingly as he straightened, but as he smiled down at Lissa it was impossible to tell anything from his expression. To know whether or not the other woman had told him that Cally had once had an affair with her husband and that he wasn't aware he had an illegitimate child!

'Ready for your dinner, young lady?' Noel teased Lissa as she slipped her hand into his.

'Yes, please.' Lissa beamed, walking along happily at his side.

Cally watched the two of them together with an ache in her heart. Why couldn't she have met someone like Noel seven years ago? Before Michael had broken her eighteen-year-old heart. Before she'd become disillusioned with men and love. Then perhaps Noel could have been Lissa's father, instead of a man Cally had grown to despise for his weakness and duplicity.

If only wishes were real.

Cally gave a rueful smile as she remembered her mother's teasing comment whenever she or Pam had wished for this or that when they were younger. She missed her mother. And her father. But they had both died in a car accident eight years ago.

Before Michael.

Before Lissa.

But how the two of them would have loved Lissa! Cally had absolutely no doubts about that. Never had. Had known that her parents would lament, for Cally's sake, the circumstances of Lissa's birth, but that they would have loved this grandchild as wholeheartedly as they would have loved Pam and Brian's children.

'Do you want to leave?'

Cally looked up dazedly at Noel's softly spoken question, suddenly aware of where they were, of Noel's family sitting at the table a short distance away, Lissa having already rejoined them. 'No,' she decided firmly. 'No, I'm fine,' she insisted, forcing a bright smile to her lips.

Noel looked down at her with narrowed blue eyes, the scepticism in that gaze telling her that he wasn't in the least convinced by that smile, that he knew something was seriously wrong. And that her meeting with Jane Shaw had something to do with it...

But unless the woman had told him about their history, Noel couldn't possibly guess the reason why, Cally acknowledged heavily. Who could...?

'Besides, the food's arriving,' she added lightly as two waitresses walked over to the table with four of the meals they had ordered. Although quite how Cally was going to eat after the shock she had just received...!

Noel continued to look down at her for long, timeless seconds, and then he gave a brief nod of his head. 'But the two of us are going to talk later,' he warned huskily.

She frowned her alarm. 'There's no need—'

'There's every need,' he rasped. 'Something is going on, and I want to know what it is!'

Cally raised auburn brows. 'And do you always get what you want?' she challenged dazedly, sure now that Jane Shaw hadn't told him the truth.

'Not always, no.' He gave her a look that was unmistakably pointed. 'But this time I don't intend taking no for an answer!' he added grimly.

'Really, Noel,' Cally taunted, her relief that Noel didn't know the truth making her feel almost light-hearted. Almost... 'There's no need to sound so serious!'

'Isn't there?' His expression remained grim.

'No,' she answered evenly.

Because whatever Jane Shaw chose to tell her husband, whatever Michael's reaction was to knowing he had another child, it would not affect Cally or Lissa.

She simply wouldn't allow it!

CHAPTER TEN

'THANK you, Noel, we had a really lovely evening,' Cally told him as he stopped the Range Rover outside the gatehouse a couple of hours later. 'Didn't we, Lissa?' she prompted her very tired daughter as she almost lay on the back seat.

'Lovely,' Lissa echoed in a very sleepy voice.

'I'll carry her inside for you,' Noel offered as he turned off the engine and swung out of the vehicle.

'There's no need!' Cally called after him, having hoped to escape into the house without Noel coming in with them, knowing, as he gave her a triumphant look as he lifted Lissa up into his arms, that she was going to be disappointed. 'Fine,' she accepted ruefully, getting out to unlock the door. 'First door on the right up the stairs,' she instructed as Noel stood in the hall with Lissa in his arms, following behind him as he walked up the stairs.

Lissa was so tired after her evening out that she was more than happy to just change into her nightgown, snuggling down under her duvet before turning over in bed and falling fast asleep.

Ordinarily Cally would have been pleased at her daughter's easy acquiescence in going to bed, but not tonight, not when Noel stood outside the bedroom waiting for her to go back downstairs...

No doubt Noel had decided it was time for them to 'talk later'!

Except that Cally still wasn't ready to do that. Wasn't sure that she ever would be!

Getting through the rest of the evening with his family had been strain enough, although it had been helped a little by the fact that Jane Shaw and her friends had left the pub about twenty minutes later, the other woman giving Cally a brief nod as she'd left.

But all in all it had been a dreadful evening, not even the continuing warmth and friendliness of Noel's family helping to alleviate that. How could it, when she was all too aware that it was because of the deceit of her fake engagement to Noel that they were behaving that way? Not that she thought the Markhams would have been unfriendly if the situation had been any different from what they thought, but the fact that they were treating her as a prospective daughter and sister-in-law made her feel very uncomfortable.

'Noel, tomorrow is Christmas Eve.' Cally turned to him decisively once they were in the privacy of her sitting-room. 'I won't keep up this deception to your family for any longer than that, so I would advise you to tell them the truth—'

'Whatever happened to, "Please, take a seat" or, "Can I get you a coffee?"' he cut in.

She gave him an irritated frown. 'Please, do take a seat,' she invited reluctantly, although he might be easier to talk to if he were no longer towering over her in this forceful way! 'But forget the coffee,' she told him heavily as he sat down in one of the armchairs. 'I have a very busy day tomorrow stocking up your freezer and refrigerator with food for over the Christmas period, so I would like to get to bed very shortly. Alone!' she added firmly as he raised questioning brows.

'Pity,' he murmured. 'So, who is Jane Shaw? And why did meeting her tonight upset you so much?' he asked shrewdly.

Cally stiffened. 'She's just—an old acquaintance,' she dismissed with deliberate unconcern, at the same time not quite able to meet Noel's searching gaze. 'But you're wrong, I wasn't in the least upset at meeting her—'

'Oh, yes, you were,' Noel said with certainty, blue gaze narrowed piercingly. 'Don't lie to me, Cally,' he warned softly. 'I may be easygoing for the main part, but never take me for a fool!'

She never would have done that. The fact that he was the power behind the Carlton Empire was evidence enough of his shrewd business acumen, even if she wasn't already aware of the intelligence behind those deep blue eyes.

'I wasn't doing that,' she assured him before turning away to look down at the unlit fireplace, her thoughts racing as she tried to decide what to do for the best. 'But Jane Shaw is my business,' she told him as she looked up again, having made her decision. 'Not yours.' She looked at him with unblinking challenge.

Although looking at him was almost her undoing! She loved this man, knew it as surely as she loved Lissa, and the urge to tell him about Jane Shaw, to confide in him the entire truth about the past, was very tempting indeed. Cally had already told Noel that Michael had been a married man, but she hadn't admitted to Noel that she had kept Lissa a secret from Michael all these years. Cally wasn't sorry she had done so, but would Noel be horrified with her, thinking that Michael had a right to know his own child?

Also, how would Noel react to being told that Jane

Shaw was the wife of the man Cally had been involved with seven years ago? Not only that, but she was the mother of Michael's legitimate children? Noel might say he understood that Cally, at eighteen, had just been young and stupid, but, having met Jane Shaw and seen how lovely she was, would his sympathies swing away from Cally and towards Jane Shaw?

Noel easily met the challenge in her gaze. 'And if I choose to make it *my* business?' he asked, giving every appearance of being relaxed as he sat in the armchair—while at the same time ready to pounce!

'Then of course I can't stop you.' She sighed. 'There's a possibility I shall be giving my notice in at the gate-house after Christmas, anyway, so it really doesn't matter to me what you do.'

Until the words actually left her mouth, it hadn't even occurred to her that was what she intended doing! But as she said them she knew it was what she would have to do with Michael and his family living somewhere close enough for his wife to be in a local pub. Otherwise she was going to spend all of her time here looking over her shoulder, wondering if a simple trip to the local supermarket would bring a surprise meeting with Michael himself. Worse, she could have Lissa with her at the time!

Lissa!

She didn't want to move, knew that Lissa was happy here, that it would mean changing schools and friends all over again. But what other choice did she have…?

Noel rose slowly to his feet, Cally backing away slightly as he took a step towards her. He came to an abrupt halt, his expression grim, his jaw set. 'When did you suddenly become frightened of me?' he growled.

When she realized she had fallen in love with him!

And it wasn't fear of Noel that had her backing away from him; it was fear of herself, of her feelings for him, of the way she simply melted in his arms every time he touched her. She had already made one disastrous mistake in her life, she didn't intend making another, even worse one, with Noel!

She straightened. 'I'm not frightened of you,' she declared.

'No?' He took another step towards her, his mouth twisting as she tensed even more.

Cally couldn't help that small tell-tale response, could feel her pulse rate quicken, her breathing shallow, her hands slowly clenching into fists at her sides—and knew there was nothing she could do to stop it.

'Noel, I've had a very busy day, have an even busier one coming up tomorrow, as I've already explained, and I'm really too tired to stand here and play power games with you.'

'I agree, you are.' He nodded, standing in front of her, one of his hands moving up to smooth the hair back from her cheek. 'I want to kiss you, Cally,' he told her huskily, his eyes darkly blue now.

'I know,' she whispered.

'I want to do more than kiss you,' Noel acknowledged hoarsely.

'I know that too!' Cally sighed weakly, unable to look away from his mesmerizing gaze. 'I just—Noel, I don't want to make any more mistakes in my life!' she told him achingly.

'And you think I would be a mistake?' he prompted gently.

'Yes! No! I simply don't know!' She shook her head, tears blurring her vision now.

His hands cradled both sides of her face as he forced her to look up at him. 'Do you trust me enough to believe me when I tell you I won't be a mistake?'

She blinked the tears away, feeling their dampness against her cheeks as she looked up at him searchingly. He looked so solidly sure, of himself, of her, of whatever feelings were between them, that Cally knew she wanted to believe him.

'Cally, I'm not going to hurt you. I would never hurt you!' One of his hands curved about her jaw as his thumb moved to caress her lips, his gaze fixed on their pouting invitation. 'I just want you so badly…!' He groaned before his head lowered and his mouth took fierce possession of hers.

Cally melted, her body melding perfectly with his, hard against soft as Noel crushed her to him, his arms tightening about her waist as his kiss deepened.

She clung to the broad width of his shoulders, giving a choked sob as she realized this might be the one and only time she would ever be in his arms like this.

She wanted him too. Wanted him so much she ached inside with the need of him.

She offered no resistance when he lifted her up in his arms and carried her over to the sofa, sitting down with her on his lap, all the time his lips sipping and tasting hers as he kissed her with ever-increasing hunger.

Cally moved slightly, lying on the sofa beside him now as he followed her down, her hands feverishly caressing his back, the heat between them rising to an almost unbearable degree.

Her back arched instinctively as his cupped her breast, the nipple already hard with arousal, and she gasped as she felt the caress of his thumb against that sensitive tip, heat like molten lava coursing through her body as she pressed herself closer against him.

Noel raised his head to look down into her flushed face, his eyes almost black with his own desire, holding her gaze as his fingers undid the buttons to her blouse before releasing the front fastening of her bra. Then he finally looked down at her nakedness, and a nerve pulsed rapidly in his tightly clenched jaw.

'Kiss me, Noel,' she moaned achingly, her fingers entwined in the dark thickness of his hair as she guided him down to her. 'Kiss me!'

His lips closed over one rosy tip, gently suckling as his tongue moved moistly against her, over and over again. Each gently pulling caress increased her pleasure, and the evidence of Noel's arousal throbbed hottly against her hips.

Cally's head rolled back on the cushion as she arched against him, feeling the increasing moistness between her thighs as Noel hotly pleasured her, wanting—oh, wanting!—so much more…! She simply couldn't—

'Mummy? Mummy, are you there?'

Cally jerked away from Noel as if a glass of cold water had suddenly been thrown over her, staring up dazedly into his grimly set face for several seconds as she tried to remember who she was—let alone where, and with whom!

'Mummy…?' Lissa voiced again, uncertainly this time.

Noel rolled away from Cally. 'You had better go to her,' he acknowledged gruffly, sitting on the carpeted floor now as he kept his profile turned firmly away from her.

'Yes.' Cally swung her legs to the floor, already

straightening her clothing even as she hurried up the stairs to see what had disturbed Lissa.

All the time knowing that her daughter couldn't be half as 'disturbed' as she was herself!

What had she been doing? How was letting Noel make love to her supposed to help the situation?

It didn't, she acknowledged with a choked sob, but she loved him so much, wanted him so much, that logic and caution had nothing to do with it when she was in his arms.

'Are you all right, Mummy?' Lissa queried sleepily as Cally entered her bedroom to sit on the side of the bed. 'You look upset.' She frowned.

Cally swallowed down the tears as her daughter's concern threatened to be her complete undoing. 'Never mind me,' she dismissed softly. 'Did you have a bad dream?'

'Not really. It's just that it's only one more day until Christmas!' she sheepishly explained her excitement.

Cally smiled emotionally, brought back down to earth as she looked at her beloved daughter. This was her reality, Lissa and the life they had together, and nothing— and no one—would ever be allowed to threaten that.

'I know, darling.' She smoothed Lissa's hair back from her brow. 'I wonder if Father Christmas will bring you everything that you asked for?' she thought of the bag of toys she had hidden away in the top of her wardrobe next door, the much-asked-for doll amongst their number.

Lissa's smile could hardly contain her excitement. 'I hope so.' She trembled.

'Right then, young lady, back to sleep,' Cally told her firmly as she stood up to straighten Lissa's duvet. 'Or Father Christmas will never come,' she warned teasingly.

Lissa looked up at her, entirely angelic in her sleepy,

tousled state. 'What have you asked Father Christmas for, Mummy?'

She drew in a sharp breath as she felt a shaft of pain through her chest, knowing that what she wanted for Christmas could never be hers. 'Some of that lovely foam bath I use,' she answered instead, knowing that Lissa had been out with Pam and bought her exactly that.

'Oh, goody!' Lissa grinned her pleasure. 'I'll go back to sleep now, Mummy,' she promised, snuggling back down with her much-loved teddy from baby days, closing her eyes to fall instantly back to sleep, it seemed.

The sleep of the young and innocent...

'Okay?' Noel prompted softly as Cally turned and found him standing in the doorway.

Cally had given a start of surprise as she'd turned and found him there, but hardened her resolve to leave here as she preceded him down the stairs; Lissa was just too precious to her to take any risks. Not that she thought Michael would particularly want his daughter, but he was bloody-minded enough to demand his paternal rights if he felt so inclined. And she had no intention of Lissa becoming an emotional pawn between herself and Michael—because the only loser in that would be Lissa herself!

Having Noel in her life could only complicate matters. Which meant that she had to leave him. Completely and for ever.

'You want me to leave now, don't you?' he guessed ruefully once the two of them were downstairs again.

Cally couldn't look at him—or the sofa where they had so nearly made love! 'I think that would be best.' She nodded.

'Cally—' Noel broke off, sighing his impatience. 'I'm not going to just disappear out of your life, you know.'

She did look up at him then, her expression one of scepticism. 'Aren't you?' she scorned, forcing herself to remember that it was only weeks ago this man had been engaged to marry someone else.

His mouth thinned. 'No,' he told her with certainty.

'We'll see.' She shrugged.

'Yes, we will, won't we?' He strode across the room, grasping her arm to turn her to face him, his eyes blazing deeply blue as he saw the challenge in her face. 'I'll see you tomorrow,' he finally bit out.

Cally nodded. 'I should be finished by lunchtime. The bill will be sent out to you—'

'Damn the bill!' he cut in harshly. 'Cally, I refuse to believe you're as cool towards me as you're pretending to be—damn it, I know you aren't!' he added, his smile grimly satisfied as he saw the colour that entered her cheeks at being reminded of the heated passion they had shared such a short time ago. 'Tomorrow,' he repeated, stepping back.

Tomorrow, or today, nothing would have changed; he would still be the rich 'Playboy of the West', and she would still be a single mother desperately trying to make ends meet.

And trying to keep Michael out of Lissa's life!

CHAPTER ELEVEN

'MICHAEL SHAW is dead,'

Cally nearly fell into the chest freezer she had been stocking with all the food for Christmas at Parker Hall as she heard those words, the blood in her veins certainly becoming as cold as ice as she took in the full import of Noel's bald statement.

Michael was *dead*...?

She slowly reached up and pulled down the lid to the freezer, her shoulders tensing as if for a blow as she breathed deeply before turning to face Noel.

He stood in the doorway of the utility room, his face pale against the darkness of his hair, the expression in his eyes guarded as he looked across at her.

'Did you hear what I—?'

'Yes, I heard what you said!' Cally cut in sharply, a trembling beginning at her feet and spreading quickly up her whole body. She was shaking so badly now that she had to put out a hand on the top of the freezer to stop herself from falling. 'Are you sure?' she asked in a hushed voice.

'Oh, yes, I'm sure.' Noel nodded.

'But—I—how—?' Cally shook her head disbelievingly, barely aware of the sudden tears that fell hotly down her cheeks. 'I can't believe it!' she choked emotionally, before burying her face in her hands.

She had wished for a way to stop Michael from coming back into her own and Lissa's lives, had prayed for a solution to his presence nearby, one that wouldn't involve her uprooting Lissa again. But she would *never* have wished for Michael's death.

'Come on.' Noel spoke gently as he lightly grasped her shoulders and turned her into the main house. 'We'll go to my study,' he said gruffly, his arm about the slender ness of her waist as he guided her through the kitchen and down the hallway.

Cally was numb. Totally stunned at the thought of Michael actually being dead. She had hated him with a vengeance when she'd discovered his duplicity seven years ago, had hoped never to see him again after what he had done, but this—this was something she had never even thought of!

'Here, drink this.' Noel held a glass out to her once he had seated her in the armchair in front of the fire in the privacy of his study. 'It's brandy,' he explained as she looked up at him dazedly. 'For the shock.'

Oh, it was definitely a shock. Especially coming so quickly on the heels of the realization that Michael's family actually lived in the area somewhere.

But not Michael. Because he was dead.

Cally swallowed a little of the brandy, its fieriness melting some of the icy shock she felt inside. 'How can you be so sure? How do you know—?' She broke off, swallowing down the nausea that suddenly threatened to engulf her.

'Jane Shaw,' Noel told her economically. 'I went to see her this morning,' he explained as Cally looked at him frowningly.

Noel had been conspicuous in his absence when Cally had arrived at the house this morning. Honey had informed her, before she and the rest of the family had gone out shopping, that Noel had gone out on business but would be back later. But Cally had assumed that his absence might have had something to do with the way they had parted last night, rather than a real need to go out on business. It seemed she'd been wrong!

She moistened dry lips with the tip of her tongue. 'How did you know where to find her?'

Noel gave a dismissive shrug. 'I just did, okay?'

'No, it is *not* okay!' she snapped, eyes flashing her anger at the efforts he must have gone to to trace Jane Shaw. 'For one thing, you had no right to interfere. For another—'

'Despite everything, do you still love him?' Noel interjected swiftly.

Cally stared at him. Still love who—Michael…? Noel was asking her if she was still in love with *Michael*?

She had been eighteen when she'd met him, a student to his lecturer, had been bowled over, flattered, when he'd singled her out for his attention. But she wasn't sure she had ever been in love with Michael, and his flippant response to her discovering he was a married man, with no intention of their relationship ever being a serious one, had killed any infatuated feelings she might have had for him.

She certainly didn't love him now!

'Damn it, I think I need one of those!' Noel rasped at her continued silence, moving to the drinks tray to pour himself a glass of brandy, and then drinking it down in one swallow.

Cally looked at him, still bewildered, not really sure what to say to him. But it appeared she needn't say anything yet; Noel hadn't finished what he wanted to say!

'Thirty-six years it's taken me to find the woman I love

and want to marry,' he ground out harshly. 'And she's in love with a man who has been dead for over a year!' He shook his head in self-derision. 'How stupid can I be?' he snarled. 'You—'

'Whoa,' Cally squeaked breathlessly. 'Could you go back a couple of sentences?'

'To where?' Noel rasped. 'To the fact that you're in love with—'

'No!' she cut in excitedly, getting slowly to her feet as she stared at him in disbelief. 'The bit about the woman you love and want to marry,' she prompted as he scowled at her.

'You.' He nodded impatiently. 'Cally, from what Jane Shaw told me of her ex-husband, the man was a womanizer and adulterer long before you even became involved with him. And he continued to be so until the day Jane Shaw left him three years later and took her children with her!' he added contemptuously.

'Jane left him…?' Cally repeated in shock.

'Three years after his relationship with you.' Noel nodded tersely. 'What is it, Cally? Thinking of all the time you could have been with him if you had known—?'

'Noel, shut up,' she gently interrupted him, crossing the room to stand in front of him, her gaze steady as she looked up at him. 'I don't love Michael, not now, not then,' she told him succinctly. 'I cried just now because— it was relief, Noel. Relief! I know it's selfish of me, but now I need never worry about him trying to take Lissa from me,' she said simply. 'I didn't know Michael was married when I met him, was flattered by his attention. I was only eighteen, Noel, I didn't even know what real love was at that age; I doubt that many people do. I do know that Michael could be vindictive, and that if he had learnt of Lissa's existence—!' She shook her head. 'I was worried you might think I should have told him about Lissa's birth.'

'You're saying he would have tried to make some sort of claim on her?' Noel guessed harshly. 'He would have had to come through me first!' he assured her grimly. 'And you made the decision you thought was best for you and Lissa. I would have supported you whatever had happened.'

Cally smiled. 'I didn't know what love was then—but I do now,' she said huskily, reaching up to tentatively touch the hardness of his jaw. 'Noel, you're the first, and only man I've ever loved,' she murmured, her breath catching in her throat as she waited for his response to her declaration.

He continued to look down at her unmovingly for several stunned moments, and then the frown cleared from his brow, his eyes blazing deeply blue as he reached out to grasp her arms. 'Do you really mean that?' he finally choked out.

Cally gave a radiant smile. 'Oh, yes.' She nodded with certainty.

'And you'll marry me?' he pushed forcefully.

Cally swallowed hard, not sure she could quite believe this was really happening. 'Lissa—'

'Already has me, and every other member of my family, firmly wrapped about her adorable little finger,' Noel assured her warmly. 'Any other reservations?'

Maybe one or two! But none of them really seemed to matter if Noel loved her and wanted to marry her! Except, perhaps one...

'What is it?' Noel asked concernedly as he saw her frown.

She drew in a deep breath before answering. 'Carol.'

'Hmm.' The frown settled back on his own brow at the mention of his ex-fiancée. 'That could be a little harder to explain…'

Cally blinked. 'Because you still love her?'

'No—because I never did.' He sighed. 'Cally, don't look at me like that!' he groaned as her eyes widened incredulously. 'The reason this is hard is because—even though I didn't love her, I don't want to be ungentle-manly.'

Cally thought back over the last few days, of Noel saying his mother was looking forward to being a grand-mother soon, of Hester's own comments on the same sub-ject—and everything became suddenly clear.

She looked up at Noel with shadowed eyes. 'You were going to marry her because you thought she was preg-nant,' she said hollowly.

'Yes! No!' He gave a pained grimace. 'Yes…' he ac-knowledged heavily as she continued to look at him. 'That day two months ago, when I asked if you would have dinner with me, I knew then how attracted I was to you, but—by sheer coincidence Carol came to see me later that afternoon,' he recalled bleakly. 'She said she was preg-nant. That the baby was mine. We had been involved, briefly, a few weeks earlier, so I had no reason to doubt her. I wasn't in love with her, but if the baby was mine… That's the reason I didn't call you as I had said I would.'

'Oh, Noel!' Cally sighed, moving forward to rest her cheek against the hardness of his chest, loving him more than ever; Noel had been going to do the honourable thing Michael would never have dreamt of doing in the same circumstances.

'She's the sister of an old school acquaintance.' He

began to talk. 'We met quite accidentally, at a party, and once we both realized that I knew her brother Sean, we spent the rest of the evening together. He and I weren't close friends, you have to understand, but we knew each other enough for Carol and I to exchange anecdotes about schooldays.' He gave a humourless smile. 'We went out together for a couple of weeks, nothing serious—or so I thought!—just having fun. I'm not an angel, Cally—' he looked down at her openly '—but in my defence, I really thought that we both looked on our friendship in the same way.'

'Until she told you she was pregnant,' Cally stated evenly.

'Yes.'

'And was she?'

'No,' he bit out abruptly. 'She wanted a quick wedding, I wanted to wait until my family were over here for Christmas. I couldn't see what difference it made whether she was six weeks pregnant or ten.' He gave a shake of his head. 'Obviously it mattered to Carol—because she wasn't pregnant at all, had just decided, for some reason, that being my wife was what she wanted.'

Cally shook her head at his naïvety; Noel was rich, handsome and charming—but most of all rich. It was the oldest trick in the book, of course; Noel was just too sincere and up front himself to have seen it that way. But Cally certainly didn't think less of him for what had happened; in fact, she just loved him more!

'What happened next?' she enquired gently.

He drew in a harsh breath. 'I invited my family over for Christmas so that they could meet Carol. We would get a licence and be married at New Year. But Mrs

McTavish fell over and broke her arm. For which I will be eternally grateful!' he added forcefully.

'I beg your pardon?' Cally gave a choked laugh as she raised her head to look up at him. 'What does Mrs McTavish have to do with anything?'

'Sounds incredible, doesn't it?' Noel allowed ruefully. 'But with Mrs McTavish out of action, and my family due to arrive anyway—'

'It was left to Carol to arrange Christmas!' Cally realized knowingly. 'She didn't want to do it,' she guessed.

Noel's brows rose. ''Didn't want to do it. Had no intention of doing it. Didn't see why a man in my position couldn't get himself a new housekeeper. In fact, Carol didn't want to spend Christmas here at all, and fancied going to Canada skiing instead. Something that I didn't think was a good idea when she was pregnant. Her exact words when I insisted we stay here were, ''If this is what being your wife is going to be like, being nothing more than a skivvy'',' he mimicked, '''then I would rather not bother, thank you very much!''' He paused, his face pale now. 'For good measure, she admitted that there was no baby. There had never been a baby. And if she had her way, there never would be a baby!'

Cally closed her eyes as she could easily visualize his pain at being told these things. One thing she now knew about Noel—and which Carol had obviously realized too!—was that, despite what Cally had accused him of two days ago, he was very family oriented. He was also very aware of his responsibilities, and would have seen Carol's baby—his child—as his prime responsibility. Even if that had entailed marrying a woman he wasn't actually in love with.

Which made him so much more a better person than Michael could ever have been.

As if she had needed any convincing of that!

She smiled up at him indulgently. 'I can see, my love, that you need someone to look after you—possibly two someones,' she teased.

'You and Lissa?' he said hopefully.

'Me and Lissa.' She nodded.

'How do you think Lissa will react to that?' he voiced his concern. 'There's only been the two of you for so long.'

Cally smiled confidently. 'I think having you as her daddy is going to make the dolly she's been wanting for Christmas for so long fade into insignificance.'

Noel gave a relieved smile. 'And how about you?'

Her smile became mischievous. 'Well I don't want you as my daddy—'

'Idiot!' His arms closed about her possessively. 'How will you like having a husband?'

A husband. Something she had never, ever dreamt of having. Until Noel.

Her eyes glowed confidently as she looked up at him. 'As long as it's you, I'm going to love it!' she assured him.

'Oh, it's going to be me,' he said with certainty, holding her tightly against him. 'I love you, Cally Turner.'

'I love you too, Noel Carlton,' she responded emotionally.

What a wonderful, wonderful Christmas this was going to be, after all.

What a wonderful life they were going to have. Together...

MILLS & BOON®

Live the emotion

A Christmas Engagement

A time for giving...and receiving – a ring

In December 2004 By Request brings back three festive favourites by our bestselling Mills & Boon authors:

Claiming His Child *by Margaret Way*
A Nanny for Christmas *by Sara Craven*
Lisa's Christmas Assignment
by Jessica Matthews

A perfect Christmas...the perfect gift...

Make sure you pick up your **'perfect Christmas gift'** which will be on sale from **Friday 3rd December 2004**